Death Under Sail

Death Under Sail

C. P. SNOW

CHARLES SCRIBNER'S SONS   NEW YORK

1 3 5 7 9 11 13 15 17 19   F/P   20 18 16 14 12 10 8 6 4 2

*Library of Congress Catalog Card Number: 81-50155
ISBN 0-684-16735-2 (cloth)
ISBN 0-684-17431-6 (paper)*

Printed in the United States of America

Contents

v

Death Under Sail

CHAPTER ONE

Six Pleasant People

I kept turning down lanes, every one of which was exactly the same as the one before it. I began to lose my temper after the third mile.

It had seemed pleasant when Roger had written, asking me to join a party of our friends for a fortnight on the Broads. Every year I found it more of an effort to tear myself from my pleasant chambers, where I could indulge my bachelor habits, enjoy good food and sleep in comfort; but at sixty-three I was still prepared to submit to a little mild discomfort for the sake of friendly company. And I knew that at any of Roger's parties one was certain to meet some amusing young men and women.

Besides, I have always liked flat country, and lazy motion through slow water, and the sunsets one can only see when there are no hills within a hundred miles. Even the fatuity of following another lane, still muddier than the one before it, did not destroy a sort of irritated pleasure provoked by the livid skyline broken by a solitary ridiculous windmill.

Nevertheless, I was annoyed with Roger. The party had already been sailing for a week before I could get away from London. He had told me to go by train to Wroxham and find my way on foot to a staithe near Salhouse. In his letter he had said: . . . "it is easy to find and not very far." I told myself that I ought to have remembered that, since he began to deal with well-to-do women patients, Roger's misplaced optimism had been considerably strengthened. So here I was at eight o'clock on a September night, amid a light rain carried by the fresh wind. I was getting damp—and I was beginning strenuously to resent the weight of my suitcase. I felt I was too old for this sort of thing.

Then I saw the glint of water over the reeds as the river turned towards the Salhouse marshes; a few hundred yards away the bare mast of a yacht stood black against the sky. The yacht was moored for the night, and there were patches of light through the port-holes and a green shine under the canvas of the awning. As I hurried to it, I heard a booming voice which could only belong to one man in the world.

I never have heard anyone who made a noise like Roger. It was a welcome sound now, for I had a prospect of a comfortable seat in the cabin and a pretty girl to hand me a drink. With that in mind, I was prepared to forgive Roger his fog-horn of a voice and even his causing me to tramp miles through a moist night.

I almost recovered my temper as I walked along the side of the staithe and called for Roger. There was a rumble of movement inside the yacht, and Roger's head appeared between the flaps of the awning.

"That you, Ian? Where have you been?" he said heartily.

"Taking part in the oddest obstacle race you ever saw," I said coldly. "The conditions are set by an idiot. It's like this: One walks an interminable number of miles on a cold, wet night carrying a heavy object to an indeterminate part of the earth. If one doesn't reach it, one loses and dies; if one *does* reach it, one wins and kills the idiot."

Roger guffawed.

"Come along in and have a drink. You'll feel better soon!"

I climbed on to the yacht.

"Better!" I said. "I only hope for death."

Roger laughed again, and I followed him down the hatch

into the cabin. I noticed, as I walked behind him, that he was getting fatter than ever.

The cabin was full of light and noise and the clink of glasses.

"Here's Ian!" someone shouted, and I was pushed on to a bunk and Avice poured a golden-looking cocktail into a long-stemmed glass.

Whenever I saw Avice I always felt that, had I been twenty years younger, I should have looked at her with even greater appreciation and much less ease of mind than I actually did. As it was, at my age, I was grateful for the pleasures of contemplation.

It seemed almost a shame for anyone to be as pretty as she was to-night. Only Avice could pour out drinks as though it were a task of great importance and charm, to be done with an air of melancholy gaiety, which made me admire all the more her discontented mouth and her thin white hands.

She was lovely, from the brown hair smoothed from her high forehead to her long and slender legs; but I felt, as I took the cocktail from her and saw her smile, that, with every-thing taken away except her eyes, she would still be a charm-ing creature.

"Your eyes are attractively sad, my dear," I said. After all, I was forty years older than she was, and age gives one the liberty to pay compliments—even if it takes away the reward for which compliments are paid.

"You *do* say nice things, Ian," she replied, and lit a cigar-ette for me.

"Long practice: when I was young I wasn't anything like so good at it," I murmured, sinking back into my corner.

"Her eyes really are attractively sad," said Christopher, who was sitting in the opposite corner. "As sad as anyone's can possibly be who's never had anything unpleasant happen to her in her life." His brown face came out of the darkness of the corner for a moment, and there was a smile round his firm mouth.

Avice blushed quickly and laughed happily at him. I remembered that there was a rumour that at last they were likely to be married. For two years he had been in love with her and, like many of her friends, he had often been driven to despair.

At least so I imagined from what I had seen, and I decided that he deserved her if he had captured her at last. I liked him; he was a young man with a vigorous mind and a strong personality.

Even his many merits, however, did not altogether allay a twinge of jealousy which I ought to have out-grown at my age. I looked at Avice as she laughed at him, and I wished that I too, as well as Christopher, were young and sunburnt and twenty-six.

However, they were a pleasant pair, and I told myself it was far better that Avice should marry him than Roger—and I knew that Roger not long ago had pursued her with the same rough, optimistic energy that he brought to every occupation of his life. She had refused him, and he had been bitter at the time. He was not used to being refused anything.

I was glad, though; as I was thinking of that affair, I studied Roger as he sat by the cabin door. He was becoming red-faced and noisy, and there would have seemed something sacrilegious about a marriage between him and Avice. I knew of his growing fame. He had planted a foot successfully in Harley Street, and was spoken of among doctors as the best man in his own line of his generation. But that was not enough. He was too—what shall I say—'robust' for Avice. They were utterly different in every way; curiously enough, they were cousins, a fact I found it almost impossible to believe. In any case, all that business about their marriage

4

was fortunately over; Avice, so far as I could judge, was fond of Christopher, and Roger had recovered and was his old jovial self. I had a suspicion that this yachting party had been arranged as a signal that everything was well again.

The voice of Roger himself broke upon my thoughts. It was very different from my idea of the voice of a man suffering from a broken heart. It said:

"Ian, you're looking like a stuffed fish."

"I was thinking," I said.

"What of?" said Roger.

"Of the increasing expansion of my host," I said.

Roger laughed his loudest laugh.

"I suppose I am getting fatter," he said. "It comes of having a contented mind. But there's someone here you haven't seen. Have you ever met a girl called Tonia?"

"Not yet," I said. "But I hope to."

"Here she is." Roger pointed with a fat hand. "Philip brought her—she's Tonia Gilmour."

I had been so busy watching Avice that I had scarcely noticed the exact constitution of the rest of the party. Philip had grinned cheerfully at me as I came in, but I had not paid much attention to the girl reclining on the bunk by his side.

"Let me introduce you," Roger said. "Tonia, this is Ian Capel. He's very, very old—at least sixty. I invited him as a sort of concession to Edwardian gentility."

"I think I should have liked the Edwardians," said Tonia in a low husky voice, and I blessed her for it. She was a girl who immediately held one's glance, not with the delicate appeal of Avice, but with a striking quality all her own. Very high eyebrows under masses of hair, which shone red as it caught the lamp-light, made a setting for long narrow eyes, one of which, I observed with almost a start, was brown and the other grey; her mouth was painted deep red on a darkish skin. Her slim body was covered by a dress of bright

5

green, and a black belt wound round a narrow waist. Bare sunburned legs were drawn up on the bunk and Philip was playing with her ankles.

"Philip's taste is better than we had any right to expect," I replied; and everyone rapped their glasses on the table, for Philip was popular with us all. He had never done anything in his life but be charming to his friends; he had idled his way through Oxford, writing a little poetry, acting a little, talking a great deal; and now, at twenty-five, he sauntered over Europe, still doing nothing but be charming. His father could afford to let him, and it was difficult not to forgive Philip whatever he did or wanted to do.

As he lay now, his hands caressing Tonia's ankles and a mass of hair falling over his mobile eager face, I for my part was prepared to laugh at any of his escapades, for his own sake and for the sake of this enticing vital Tonia whom he had brought amongst us.

He echoed my remark.

"Taste? Taste, Ian, you old scoundrel! If you say any more, I'll tell everybody about the flat-faced woman with the twisted nose."

This was utterly new to me. I looked lost. There was a general chuckle. Philip went on:

"Ian met her on a bus. She was reading a book. Ian, the old dog, went and sat down by her and said: 'Wouldn't you like to read another book?' and she said; 'What book?' And he said: 'The railway time-table.' She said: 'What for?' Ian said: 'So that we can go away together!' She had an absolutely flat face and a twisted nose."

Roger led a chorus of laughter in which I joined, after a protest which was drowned in the merriment. Then William's hard, clear voice broke in:

"Ian is a man of taste, so *that* adventure can't have happened to him. And Philip hasn't any imagination, so he

6

can't have invented it. I can only conclude it must have happened to Philip himself."

Philip grinned unashamedly, and Tonia gently pulled his ear. I raised my glass to William, and said:

"William, my boy, you've saved me. Greetings and thanks!"

It was characteristic of William to have said nothing until he considered it necessary for him to make a direct remark.

He was sitting as we had so often seen him sit, with the trace of a smile on his pale face and one hand fondling his square chin. Four years ago Roger had introduced him to me, and had said he was a young doctor with a future; and lately I had heard that he was likely to usurp some of Roger's own reputation. I confess I was not surprised; though William was not yet thirty, there was a confidence and directness about his thinking, and a fixed ambition under his impassive manner, that marked him as destined for whatever heights he chose.

There he sat beyond Roger, his pale clever face contrasting oddly with Roger's round red one, and I know that if ever I had to choose a cancer specialist—and I prayed that it would not be necessary, for I had and have all the fear of doctors of a man who has been healthy all his life—I should go to William without a second's hesitation.

The seven of us almost filled the cabin. I drained my glass and, with the warm well-being that comes at the end of a good cocktail, I surveyed the party.

In order to appreciate them more, I described them to myself as though I were taking an inventory for the use of an acquaintance.

It was pleasant to be among youth—and among friends. There was Avice Loring on my left, with a cigarette between her lips, looking at me in her grave charming way. Sitting next to Avice, between her and the door, was her cousin,

Roger Mills, our host, the exuberantly successful doctor who, as I glanced at him, raised a tumbler of whisky to his mouth. William Garnett occupied the whole of the end seat farthest from us, but, like the unrestful young man he was, he sat on the edge of it with his face supported in his hands; I told myself that soon he would be the most distinguished of them all. On the side bunk away from the door Tonia Gilmour was stretched languorously, her fingers twisted in Philip Wade's hair. Philip was basking with his eyes closed, every inch the pleasant idler. And, my glance returning to my end of the cabin, there was Christopher Tarrant in the other corner, with his thin brown face half in shadow and his deep-set eyes fixedly watching Avice's hands.

They were six pleasant people, I thought, and life seemed good as I watched them. Except for Tonia, who was a stranger, so far as I knew, to everyone but Philip, we all knew each other well. Three years ago, the other six of us had formed part of a large house-party in a villa in Southern Italy, and there had sprang up an intimacy between us all that was a very dear thing in my life and, I hoped and believed, in the lives of the others. I looked at them all, and smiled with content.

Avice leaned against me, and said:

"Beginning to be smug already, are you, Ian?"

I was pleased to be mocked by Avice.

"My dear," I said, "being smug is one of the compensations of getting old. We all of us enjoy being here, and being with people we like. But you young people have to conceal it from yourselves that you enjoy it. I just feel pleased and admit it."

"It must be wonderful to be old," she said, and I think that she sighed.

"It has its drawbacks," I replied, as I looked at her parted lips.

Roger produced another bottle of whisky from the cupboard, and filled our glasses in turn. There had been a time when I should have been surprised to see girls like Avice and Tonia drink spirits, but I had come to accept it as another of the things which are inevitable in these troubled days of ours—and I could not see any possible reason why they should not drink whisky if they liked it. William tasted his glass, then looked across at me, and said:

"Ian hasn't heard the news yet. He doesn't know we're celebrating to-night."

"What are we celebrating?" I asked, and added: "Except our being here together."

"Christopher has just been given the job of supervising all the rubber growing in Malaya," William said.

"Splendid! I'm so glad, Christopher." I turned to him, and said: "I hope it's profitable, as well as essential."

Avice broke in quickly:

"Oh, they're going to give him such a lot of money!"

"This is the best news I've heard for a long time," I said. I was aware that Christopher depended entirely on what he earned, and I was excited to hear that success had come to him like this.

"All of you—I give you Christopher!" I lifted my tumbler, and we drank.

"It's terribly good of you," said Christopher, and his face, often hard, looked affectionate and young. "It isn't quite settled yet"—and he smiled as he said it—"I've got to be looked at by various heads of the company: so that they'll be sure I shan't go ga-ga as soon as I get out there."

We laughed and shouted: "Christopher!" again. Then Philip inquired plaintively:

"Isn't anyone going to celebrate me getting a job, too?"

Avice said sweetly:

"My dear Philip, we should all be horribly annoyed if you

9

did. The fact that you're doing nothing at all is the one certain thing we know."

Philip drew himself up with a comic pretence of dignity:

"Avice, you're a child, and know no better. As a matter of fact, Tonia is seriously thinking of employing me as her secretary."

Tonia put a hand on his shoulder, and said huskily:

"His only duty would be to open my letters."

I was surprised, and asked her:

"Why ever do you want him to do that?"

"To make him jealous, of course." She arched her high eyebrows. "He's far too English to read them without being paid to. He'll have to plough solemnly through them, and I hope it'll rouse him. Even if I have to write love-letters to myself." She let her eyes dwell on Philip for a moment, and I fancy that only Roger prevented them kissing in front of us all. But Roger could be relied on to interrupt any tense situation, and in his most boisterous voice he said:

"Now then, you children, it's time for bed. I want to sail up to Horning before breakfast to-morrow."

"We shall have breakfast at Horning, I suppose," Philip murmured. "That means getting up indecently early."

"Why in the name of our good friend Mr. Willett *do* you always sail before breakfast?" Christopher asked, yawning.

"As I always get up at eight and sail her myself, I don't see that it matters. You slackers manage to get another hour in bed," Roger replied, smiling at Christopher.

I noticed that they were on friendly terms, which, I thought, after their rivalry for Avice, did credit to them both.

"And it's good for everyone to be made thoroughly uncomfortable for a fortnight in their lives," he chuckled.

"Where am I sleeping, Roger?" I put in gently. "On the

roof of the cabin—I should be quite reasonably uncomfortable there?"

Roger got up and stretched his bulk, his face shining red and moist.

"No, you and I sleep in these two double berths in here. We're the oldest and the fattest and we need the room. All last week the girls here have had the other two double berths in the aft cabin. Why, I don't know. We just pamper them. These other parasites have the three single berths in the middle of the boat. That's how we've been sleeping all the week."*

"You don't really believe in your Spartan theories at all, or you'd hang head downwards from the mast and sleep like that," Avice said to Roger, as she gathered up the glasses from the table.

"My dear Avice," Roger burst out very loudly, "none of you have ever got it clear what this sort of holiday depends on. It's really 'roughing it in comfort'. That is, we live in a thing we have to sail ourselves: a motor-boat would be a lot more convenient, but nothing like such fun. On the other hand, we have decent food: we might live on lard and black bread, but that wouldn't be such fun. Like all games, we make the rules for ourselves. Getting up early in the morning is part of the game!"

"Very lucidly put, Roger," I said. "I'm going to think over your wisdom outside, while you enjoy another part of the game—which is getting this cabin ready for me to sleep in. Good night, everyone."

They were all going to their berths as I left Roger clearing up cigarette-ends and bottles. I went up the fore-hatchway, which was just outside the cabin, and felt the air cool on my face as I stood on the narrow deck.

* For a plan of the wherry which explains the sleeping arrangements, see p. 13.

For a few minutes I thought about the people inside the yacht, what they meant to me and what they would do. I am an oldish man; there have been times in my life when I have doubted whether there is the slightest justice in this world of ours, which is arranged so casually and so haphazardly that one man can divide his year between languid days in a yacht and still more languid days by the side of the Mediterranean, while another spends fifty weeks in a year in Oldham and the other two in Blackpool.

But as I grow older those doubts get less and less. I am certain that in the end there is no arrangement which will be better than this uneven balance. If this world of comfort and leisure were swept away, there would be too much lost! I said this to myself as I stood on the yacht that night before the real beginning of the story I am going to tell.

There would be too much lost! Often I have heard the fierce indignation with which some of my acquaintances say that any change must be for the better. Often I have sat uneasily, my slow mind unable to explain my attitude. Yet, alone on deck on this tranquil night, I felt that if I had them here I could perhaps make them understand.

From below there came Avice's low and rippling laugh. To think of her charm lost irretrievably in a drab work-a-day routine! More strongly than ever, I felt that a state of affairs which could produce her is justified by its results. I thought of the others on the wherry. Why should not gay and pleasant idlers like Philip and this Tonia of his be allowed to go their own diverting way? They make their contribution to the colour of life, and if they and their kind go, then it will mean the destruction of a world. A world which, whatever its faults, gives more of the good things of life to more people than any other which has been devised. Through that world there move, Heaven knows, more fools and vulgarians than I care to count; but it contains also the

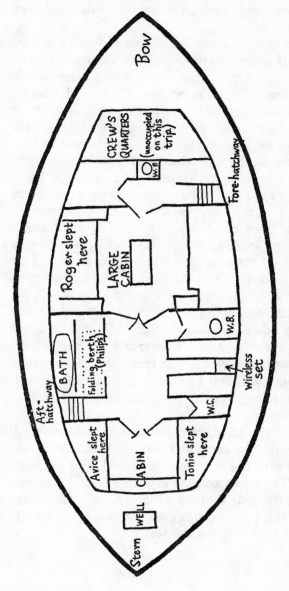

FINBOW'S PLAN OF *THE SIREN*

most pleasant people whom it has been my good fortune to meet.

I thought of my friends in the party. Some had been born with comfort round them. Avice, for example, had lived all her life among a circle where the use of leisure was the only serious concern. William, on the other hand, had carved a niche for himself armed with nothing but his wits; ten years before he had been working fiercely, intensively, in a Birmingham secondary school. Philip had always had everything that he might want, but Christopher was the son of a schoolmaster and, as he himself used to say in his bitterly humorous way—"I've always been too poor even to learn how to get into debt properly."

Wherever they came from, here they were together in Roger's party, some of the pleasantest people whom I had ever known. If their world ever comes to an end, I thought, then the gracefulness and the light will have gone out of life!

It was an absurdly solemn reflection for a fattish man well on in middle age, standing late at night on the deck of a wherry, but I do not excuse myself. I *did* think like that, and I record it as showing how I regarded my friends before the incidents which affected all of them and me so profoundly. I confess, however, that I felt a little ashamed, when I found myself pondering over the problems which one should have settled for oneself at twenty.

I lit a cigarette, and watched the red end mirrored in the water: I caught the damp marsh smell, which made me shiver slightly; I heard the thin hoot of an owl, and the soft beat of its wings. The reeds and the sky were dark, for there was no moon, and the only light was that which streamed from our port-holes and lay in shining bars across the river. It was a quiet night, very still on the water.

CHAPTER TWO

Roger Sails Alone

I went down into the cabin, and found Roger sitting at the table with a thick ledger-like book open in front of him. He was writing with his head bent over the paper, for the lamp had burnt low and the walls of the cabin were deep in the shadow. When I had sat down on my bunk and was beginning to take off my collar, he looked up.

"The others have gone to bed," he said. "I'm just writing up the log-book. I'll read it to you when I've finished."

"Good," I replied, trying to keep a note of resignation out of my voice. Reading aloud what one has written seems to me almost the least amiable of the practices of humanity; but it is a common passion and very dangerous to thwart. I have suffered a good deal from it in my time. But I have always tried to listen with a good grace. If one is going to be martyred, one may as well do it in style. As I enjoy seeing other people pleased, I not only listen to the novels, poems, and letters of my friends, but—sometimes I actually beg to hear them. In my disillusioned moments I think that my reputation as a man of discriminating taste may not be unconnected with this habit.

And so, although I had no particular wish to hear Roger's account of a day's sail, I tried to assume an eager interest when he promised to read it to me.

"I know you'll enjoy it," he boomed, his head bending over the book again after he heard my "Good." "Everyone always enjoys listening to the log-book," and he went on writing in his jerky scratching hand.

"Yes," I answered, and searched the wall over my bunk in order to find a resting-place for my collar. I discovered a shelf, and arranged my watch, studs and tie on it in the methodical way which has become engrained into me: I doubt whether I could sleep if I did not perform my simple ritual of putting my watch on the left-hand side of my studs.

Roger coughed in order to attract my attention, and began to read loudly:

" 'Sep. 1. Starting from Acle. *The Siren* got under weigh about eight o'clock according to the usual custom of the skipper.'

"That's me," Roger explained.

"It would be," I said.

" 'Who,' " Roger read on, " 'in the self-sacrificing spirit he has shown during the voyage, sailed her single-handed until breakfast-time. Breakfast was delayed till half-past ten on account of the slackness of the female members of the crew, who were too busy with their different methods of self-adornment to pay any attention to the physical needs of their lords and masters.' "

He looked at me. "That's rather good, don't you think?" he said, and laughed heartily. Despite my long experience of listening to recitals of my friends' works, I am still sometimes amazed at the parts of them which they single out for applause. I suppose there *are* reasons why words which meant less than nothing to me should strike Roger as being extremely funny. He was shouting with laughter at the ideas his last sentence had produced; while I had difficulty in mustering a feeble smile.

Still laughing, Roger continued to read:

" 'After breakfast, Christopher and Philip took turns at sailing her down the Bure. The wind was light, and the

16

skipper felt justified in entrusting the party to the skill of the novices. He was pleased to see that Christopher showed signs of making strides in the science of sailing, which is more than can be said for Philip, who is the most incompetent sailor in the party. With a few days' practice Christopher would prove as good a sailor as William. During the morning Tonia sun-bathed in the bows, to the great interest of all the young men on the river.'

"That's a good one," Roger chuckled, looking red-faced and fat. I noticed that his forehead was moist in the warmth of the cabin.

He went on reading:

" 'Philip, in fact, became so anxious that he considered it necessary to sit with her in order to act as a screen. As this was the first sign of Philip breaking through his laziness, the party cheered when they saw him taking action. It amused some of them to see how Philip considers Tonia so much his personal property that he won't let other people look at her.'

" 'We had a running lunch, as the skipper decided that he could not give the time to moor the yacht if he was to get to Salhouse that night. We had arranged to meet the veteran of the party near-by, and the skipper didn't want to let him down. This was the first running lunch since we came on board a week ago, but nevertheless William was mutinous.'

"William's not an easy man in a party," Roger looked up and said. "Do him good to show him that I don't approve."

" 'Thinking that Christopher probably wanted to talk to Avice, the skipper himself sailed the yacht all the afternoon, William not being allowed to as a penalty for disaffection at lunch. Christopher and Avice tactfully separated themselves from Philip and Tonia, but the two pairs sat forward all the afternoon. In fact the skipper was the only member of the party to enjoy the delight of watching the country on a dull

17

windy afternoon; the others were engrossed in each other or in themselves.' "

Roger smiled broadly. "I liked writing that," he said, and read on:

" 'Just after five *The Siren* had reached the appointed place for meeting Ian, and there was a debate as to what should be done about dinner. Everyone was hungry after the makeshift lunch, and it was decided to sail into Wroxham, have an early dinner at a pub, and get back in time to see the veteran arrive. This was done We had an adequate dinner in Wroxham, returned and moored the yacht half an hour before Ian got to Salhouse. He, of course, was late; but then he always *was* inefficient. The skipper forgave him.' "

"Confound your impudence, Roger," I protested, laughing.

" 'The skipper forgave him, and we all settled down to an evening of cocktails and talk. Christopher's health was drunk (it ought to have been mentioned that on arriving at Wroxham for dinner Christopher had found a letter waiting, which said that the Malay job was going to be given to him), and, after Philip and Tonia had, as usual, behaved as though they had been and were attached to each other for ever, the party went to bed.' "

"There!" he said triumphantly.

"Excellent," I replied, and I meant it, for I did not expect the account to come to an end so soon.

"It's great fun writing up the log-book," boomed Roger. "Great fun. I always enjoy it."

"I'm sure you do," I said.

"Now I'll go and put it away. I like keeping everything in its place," said Roger, slipping off his rubber shoes. "Then we'll turn in."

"Splendid," I answered. "Where are you going to put it, though?"

"In its proper place—at the top of the aft-hatch. There's

a little shelf there." He began to move softly out of the cabin.

I took my clothes off rapidly, and was wriggling myself awkwardly into the blankets before he came back.

"Hallo," he said, with a loud laugh. "You're soon in bed. You won't sleep much to-night, you know. A bunk's a bit hard until you've got used to it."

I turned my face to the wall and murmured: "Good night." For a few minutes Roger rustled about, and then I heard a deep grunt as he settled himself in his bunk and put the lamp out. I became aware that a bunk is a very uncomfortable thing. My hip-bone began to ache; I tried to ease my position, but it only made it worse, and the cabin seemed to get hotter the more I moved. So I settled myself to discomfort, gave up hope of sleep coming easily, and let my thoughts wander.

Roger's heavy breathing came regularly to my ears, with a low rhythm that made my wakefulness more unpleasant. I remembered resentfully how he had insisted on reading the log-book when I was anxious to lie down; and now he was asleep and I was painfully awake. I thought how typical the log-book was of him. It was just like Roger to call himself 'the skipper', and to make sly digs at Tonia and the others, and to resent William's having a mind of his own. Yet, as a rule, I enjoyed his boisterousness and his vanities; memories of Roger in Italy and elsewhere flitted through my mind.

When I woke the next morning, it was some seconds before I drowsily noticed that the red blur on the other side of the room was Roger in pyjamas. He was just beginning to dress. When he saw that I was turning in my bunk, he said unnecessarily: "You awake?"

I made a noise which might have meant anything.

"You needn't get up yet," said Roger. His voice, always loud, seemed like the crack of doom as I struggled into wakefulness. "It's only eight o'clock."

I groaned. Roger went on:

"I'm going to sail her to Horning by myself. I told you last night. We'll have breakfast there. You and the others get up soon."

He had put on a cricket-shirt and grey flannels, and pattered out of the cabin in bare feet. For some time I heard the straining of ropes as he hoisted the sail, and the pad of feet along the deck and the clatter of rond-hooks as he cast her off fore and aft, and then the gentle patter of water against her sides as the wherry began to move. I lay still, and was lulled into drowsiness again by the lapping which I could faintly hear.

At half-past eight I roused myself, got out of my bunk, and went up the fore-hatch. The morning was brightly peaceful. There was a touch of cold in the air, although the sky was cloudless. A light breeze from the west filled the wherry's great sail. On both banks the reeds were tall and green, but there came a gleam, now and then, when the sunlight caught the water which lay hidden beneath them.

I felt an ease of mind which, I think, is the special gift of flat country. I shouted to Roger, whom I could not see, for the cabin top was between me and the well:*

"Wonderful day, Roger!"

He was sailing round a bend near Salhouse Broad, and for a second I heard nothing. Then, as he took us into a straight stretch, I caught some sort of jovial reply. I sat a little while longer, then suddenly realised that an elderly gentleman ought not to disport himself in pyjamas on a cool September morning: so I ran down to my cabin, fetched a towel, and went to the wash-basin at the bottom of the hatchway. While I washed I heard voices from the other cabins; the only coherent remark that came to me was a husky: "Good morn-

---

* See plan of wherry on p. 13. The well is the hollowed-out part of the deck from which the tiller is controlled.

ing, darling!" which, I was certain, must have been said by
Tonia.

Then, quite loud, came the strains of the 'Erlkönig',
When the music stopped, a brisk voice said something in
German which was followed by the opening bars of 'Die
Forelle'. I remembered that Teutonic broadcasting authorities are firmly of the opinion that housewives ought to listen
to good music while they wash up the breakfast things. I
went to my bunk, threw on an old suit, and opened the inside door of the cabin in order to listen.

The first thing I saw was Tonia, leaning against the door
of the middle cabin.* She obviously dressed as carefully for
the night as for the day; white silk pyjamas with a black belt
emphasised her queer attraction as strongly as the green dress
had done the day before. I noticed with amusement that her
lips were already painted—before breakfast.

"Hullo, Ian," she said. "I'm going to call you Ian, of
course."

"I should be insulted if you didn't," I replied.

"Come and listen to the wireless." She pointed inside the
middle cabin. "We have it on every morning so that people
can hear it while they wash."

"A curious custom," I said.

"Not a bit. Getting up slowly is the chief aim of a perfect
life. And, anyway, we can't all wash at once—there are only
three places, you know." She drawled in her throaty
way, and her eyes in the dim light of the passage looked
strangely different in colour, one hazel and the other bluish
grey.

I waved to Avice, whose dark head looked out of her door
for a moment, and Tonia and I entered the middle cabin,
which was shared for sleeping purposes by William and
Christopher; apparently at nine o'clock it became a sort of

* See plan of wherry on p. 13.

musical common room. Inside the cabin, the noise from the loud-speaker was deafening. Christopher was alone in the room. He was lying on his bunk writing a letter, dressed in luxurious pyjamas of the same colour as his sun-browned skin; when we came in he smiled at us cheerfully.

"Hullo, you people. If you want to appreciate music you had better go away," he said.

"Meeting here is really a social event. The music's only an excuse. We all come to inspect your wonderful pyjamas, Christopher," said Tonia, with a sidelong glance.

"Where are the rest?" I asked.

"William's washing," said Christopher.

"Avice never appears until she's utterly exquisite. I leave her in our cabin. She takes hours." Tonia had a trace of malice in her voice, I thought. She went on: "As for Philip, lazy pig, he's always in bed. I go and say 'Good morning' to him every day—he just rolls off to sleep again."

"Do I, you little devil?" Philip whispered, as he came quickly into the room. He slid an arm round Tonia's shoulders. Do I, indeed?" He was in pyjamas, but his hair was as smoothly in place as though he were just going to a dance.

I sat down at the end of Christopher's bunk in order to be as far as possible from the wireless set, which stood on a small table near William's pillow. Philip sat down opposite to me, on William's bunk, and, on the pretext that the room would soon be full, drew Tonia on to his knee. She writhed a long thin arm round his neck and said huskily:

"Lizard-wizard," which is the most curious love-name that I have ever heard. Christopher watched them for a moment with an amused twisted smile, and went on writing his letter.

A minute or two later William came in, wearing his dressing-gown; he muttered a curt "Good morning," and took his place at the pillow end of his own bunk. He lit a pipe and sat silently, completely ignoring Philip and Tonia's embraces, which were going on within a foot of him.

Christopher sealed his letter into an envelope, and went out with: "I'm just going to wash." William smoked quietly; Tonia kissed Philip lightly on the cheek, and looked across at me:

"You look bored, Ian. Wouldn't you like someone to make love to *you*?"

"Not before breakfast," I replied. "When I was young and these things happened to me, I had one golden rule: Never make love before breakfast."

"You were never in love," Tonia said scornfully.

"Little you know," I answered—and I had a picture of an evening twenty years before. But Christopher returned in time to prevent me from pursuing my sentimental journey, and I asked him: "Do you think I was ever in love, Christopher? When I was your age?"

He smiled, a little bitterly, I thought.

"I hope not, for your sake," he said, and then, as though considering, "I don't know: it may be worth it."

"Of course it's worth it," came Philip's voice, half smothered by Tonia's arms. Christopher laughed, and then asked me to move up a little. "I must get away from that infernal machine for a few minutes," he said, pointing to the wireless.

As he was sitting down, Avice strolled in, elegant and charming, the only member of the party besides myself to be fully dressed. She greeted us all in her quiet way, said "Good morning, my dear," softly to Christopher, and sat down opposite to William on my side of the cabin.

"Why do we have the wireless on at all?" Philip inquired plaintively. "It's far too loud—but we always come in here and listen to it."

"Tradition, my boy," William broke in sharply. "Like the

M.C.C. and the Public Schools. Doing a thing twice is good enough reason for doing it for ever."

"Now then, William, you're just getting bitter," Tonia remarked. "You'll mellow when you get older." She put a cigarette in her mouth, and then said:

"Anyone got a match to light my cigarette? Philip never has. William? Christopher?"

Christopher brought out a box from the pocket of his pyjamas, and tossed it across to her. The box fell on the floor.

"No manners before breakfast," Tonia grumbled, as she struggled off Philip's knee and picked up the matches. "You might have lit one for me."

"He's always like that till ten o'clock" Avice said.

"Poor creatures, men," Tonia commented. "But I think I'll go and make myself look nice for them: though they don't deserve it."

She walked slowly out and Philip leaned back in his corner with a long sigh.

"She is an extraordinarily attractive young woman," I said.

"Glad you think so. You're a nice old creature, Ian," Philip replied.

For a moment or two we sat without talking, and listened to 'Verborgenheit'. Then Philip got up:

"I suppose I'd better go and clean myself, too," he said. "It's an awful bore; one of these days I shall stop washing altogether and grow a honey-coloured beard."

"I doubt if you *could* grow a beard," Christopher chaffed him, but Philip had gone. William stretched his legs:

"Christopher and I ought to get some clothes on. We can't stay in pyjamas all day," he said.

Avice gave a faint smile, and suggested to me that we should go on deck and leave Christopher and William to dress. I agreed willingly; I was tired of the stuffy cabin, and the beat of the music was going through my ears. Avice, with me following, climbed up the aft-hatchway—and I, God forgive me, admired her lovely long legs—and we stood for a moment on the deck, with the wherry gliding so smoothly through the water between the silent marshes that time itself seemed to have stood still.

Then we turned down into the well to talk to Roger. Suddenly Avice gripped my arm, and ran forward a few steps towards the tiller. I followed, with a sudden fear. When I caught her up, she hid her head against my sleeve and pointed with a trembling finger into the well. I looked, and saw a thin stream of dark blood, and then Roger, and shivered.

For we were being sailed by a dead man.

CHAPTER THREE

I Propose Another Crime

It was a sickening sight. Like most men of my generation, I have seen violent death in all its forms, and some of the memories will remain vivid before my eyes as long as I live. I walked over the battlefield at Ypres a few days after the first gas attack. Worse still, I was in Dublin in the Easter of 1916, and saw a street in which the corpses seemed to have been arranged by a malevolent buffoon—a boy propped up against a wall, his mouth open, surprised-looking, and a few yards away a fat, red-cheeked old woman lying across an overturned perambulator, from which whisky was flowing in streams along the pavement.

But Roger dead in front of me was the most hideous thing I have ever seen. He was sitting against the side of the well, with the tiller jammed between his body and the crook of his arm; my eyes were fascinated by the blackened hole in his shirt, and the thin stream that ran down his body. For a time I stared at the wound. When at last I brought myself to look at his face, I felt a sensation of black and utter horror; on his face there was still the jovial, happy smile with which he would always greet a friend.

Avice trembled against my arm. Suddenly she laughed shrilly, and the sound seemed to fit Roger's dead smile.

"Ian," she said, forcing out her words, "Ian, this is absurd. It just can't have happened."

For an instant her strained voice echoed in my ears, and I,

too, had a sense of unreality, of some ghastly joke. Then I tried to steady myself.

"It's real all right, my dear," I said. "We'd better call the others. William!" I called. "Come up here, will you? Something rather unpleasant has happened." I did not smile at myself then for the ridiculous understatement.

William came running up the aft-hatchway. He was naked to the waist. He dropped down into the well and took a glance at Roger.

"Dead," he said, and though I had known it already, the short word sounded like a knell.

"Can't you do anything?" I asked futilely.

William grunted.

"He's shot through the heart," he said, with a cold, professional certainty. "Fetch the others, Avice. We must get the wherry moored."

Calmly, he took control. When I called for William, I had unconsciously known that he was the one man amongst us to whom action was as natural as breathing. He disengaged the tiller from Roger's dead hand, unlashed the main-sheet from its cleat,* and began to sail the wherry with the precise confidence that he brought to any practical matter.

Christopher and Philip came on deck together.

"Roger's dead," said William simply. "We've got to moor her at once. You two go forward and get ready."

"Dead?" said Christopher. Philip was white-lipped, and stood silent for a moment. Then he seemed to grip hold of himself.

"Are you serious, or——?" he asked, in a voice that quavered a little.

"Get forward and don't talk," William cut in sternly, and there was no argument.

While William was looking for a place to moor the wherry,

* A cleat is a projection round which a rope is wound.

Tonia came along the deck to the stern, where I was standing with a rond-hook.

"Roger's been killed," I said in an undertone.

"I can see that," she replied. Her voice was very husky, and there was a curious twist to her reddened lips.

Soon William found a ridge of hard bank* among the interminable reeds, and decided that we should bring up against it: working in a strained silence, we moored the wherry and furled the sail.

Then William said in a business-like way:

"We'd better leave it there"—he pointed to the body—"and we'll put up the awning. Because if we don't, people may go by on the river—and wonder what we're doing with an odd corpse on deck."

I saw Avice wince from his cold words, and I resented the tone myself, but putting up the awning was more important than paying attention to the niceties of behaviour. When it was done and the wherry presented to the passing eye merely the sight, common enough on the river, of a boat trimmed for the night, William commented:

"Good. Now we've got a bit of time. We'll go into the big cabin and talk things over."

On the way William said:

"I must go into my cabin and put a shirt on. I won't be a minute. The rest of you go in and sit down."

We arranged ourselves in the main cabin. By an unspoken agreement we left the end place for William; I sat on the right of it, and Christopher on the left. Philip and Tonia sat beside Christopher, and Avice was next to me, with one elbow on the bunk and her chin resting on her hand. She looked somewhere near collapse, too far gone to see the anxious glances that Christopher threw at her. We were all

* See map of river on p. 73.

very quiet. While we waited for William, the sight of the empty place seemed to batter at my heart.

Then William came in and sat down. He lit a cigarette, and I noticed that his fingers were steady. He began:

"You all know what's happened. Roger has been murdered within the last half-hour."

"Is it certain that he was murdered?" Christopher asked.

"There's no sign of a revolver. It must have been thrown overboard," said William. "It's not easy to throw a revolver overboard after you've shot yourself through the heart."

Christopher assented. William went on:

"It's quite clear that Roger's been murdered, and within the last half-hour."

"How can you fix the time?" I was impressed by his confidence. "Rigor mortis?"

"There's not time for it to have started. And, anyway, no one but a fool or a knave puts much trust in rigor. A body stiffens according to all sorts of different factors—how much exercise had been taken before death, for instance." William was contemptuous. "No, I should fix half an hour as the absolute limit, just because a dead man can't steer round corners. I don't know this river, but I don't mind betting there's a bend within ten minutes' sail."

"We can check that easily enough," I said. "It's nine-forty now. It was about nine-twenty-five when Avice and I went on deck."

"That means we can fix the murder at nine-fifteen at the earliest," William said quickly. "That's all right, then. Roger was murdered between nine-fifteen and nine-twenty-five." He stopped for a second and continued in his cold, impassive way. "By one of the six people at present in this cabin."

My heart bumped; I heard Avice at my side utter an "Oh!" that was almost a sob. Philip began to protest, but William silenced him.

"Don't be a child, Philip," William said. "Do you think that someone swam to the wherry, took a casual pot-shot at Roger and swam back again—just as a sort of morning exercise? How would he know that there was no one else about?"

I felt a chill, and I think that all of us had an oppressive fear as we eyed each other. For my part, I was thinking who could it be? For, despite all my emotions, I knew that what William said was true.

William's quiet voice went on mercilessly.

"Roger was shot from close quarters. You can see the powder blackening on his shirt. Do you really think that a stranger would have climbed on board, and prodded him with his revolver, and then shot him?"

It was all too true. I said—and I am not ashamed to say that my throat was tight:

"You're right, William."

After a little hesitation, Christopher nodded. Philip had a dazed expression in his blue eyes. Tonia brought out a small mirror, lengthened an eyebrow with elaborate care, and spoke from the bottom of her throat:

"Well, who was the one of us who did it?"

William laughed dryly:

"I suppose whoever it was, he—or she—won't tell us."

Then I made a suggestion which, though it was illogical, unethical, and useless, I still think to be the most sensible way out of the abominable position in which we found our-selves.

"Look here," I said, "I'm thirty years older than any of you, and if you'll let me I want to tell you what I think of this. We're all friends: and I take it we want to arrange everything so that the least possible harm is done. Roger's dead, and killing someone else won't help him or any of us. Whoever murdered him did an unforgivable thing, a thing

I can never forgive. But even if I can't forgive, it doesn't mean that I want to see him"—and I had to add "or her"— "going to an unpleasant death. I don't believe in self-righteous revenge. It seems to me too much like the crime itself. So I suggest that we take a vow that if whoever did it confesses to us, we will first of all make the whole thing look like a suicide, and after that never disclose anything of it to a living soul. On the single condition that whoever did it gets out of our company and our life, and does not come back."

There was silence for a moment. William broke it by saying, with an unaccustomed warmth:

"You've said what I should never have had the courage to say, Ian."

"Will you all take the vow?" I asked them. The cabin was deathly still. Who will confess? Who will confess? My heart hammered. I felt my forehead get coldly wet. I spoke with difficulty:

"I'll ask everyone to promise silence upon whatever is disclosed." No one uttered a word. I said:

"So be it then. First I'll promise myself—that whatever is confessed, or whoever confesses, I will say nothing of it while I live. If anyone won't promise, they must say so now."

There was no word. "You agree to that then," I said. "Now I'll go round the cabin and ask you all to repeat your promise —or else confess."

With a finger that I saw was quivering, I pointed across the cabin.

"I'll begin with Tonia," I said. "Tonia, will you promise silence?"

Tonia's stare met mine, and her eyes glinted brown and grey. Suddenly I realised how strong her face was.

She said indifferently:

"Of course I will. What do you expect?"

There was the slightest breath of a sigh from someone. So Tonia was out of it—feverishly I passed on.

"Philip?" I asked. He seemed to have gone limp, and I saw Tonia's face turn towards his. Then he shrugged his shoulders, with a half-smile:

"I will," he answered.

Tonia caught at his arm, but I scarcely noticed them, now. Christopher or William or Avice?

"You, Christopher. You'll promise silence?"

"I will," said Christopher quietly. His thin brown face was stern. Three had promised silence: it left only William or Avice to confess. Not William surely? I tried to take hold of my excitement, I looked at William's clever face; one hand was rubbing his square chin, and his eyes searched mine as I asked:

"You'll promise, William?"

"I will promise," he said. There was a fraction of a second in which his voice sounded very hard. Then, the meaning followed the three words, and I dug my nails into my palms. There was a rustle in the cabin.

With dread I turned to Avice on my left. Her sobbing had ceased, but still she lay with her face in her hands. Avice? Avice alone was left to confess. My knees trembled. A fierce pulse beat in my neck.

"Avice?" I whispered.

I saw everyone lean forward as she raised a tear-wet face.

"I'll promise silence," she said. And then, with a woeful smile: "But it doesn't seem much good, does it?"

The tension was broken. With a relief that was beyond emotion, I closed my eyes and heard, as in the far distance, the husky laugh with which Tonia broke the strain. We had all watched with fear and hope and suspicion in order to see which of our friends was a murderer; all had seriously promised that they would be silent for ever: and there was nothing to be silent for. After a moment, all of us laughed, partly owing to the ordeal of the last few minutes, and partly because of the anti-climax; I do not condone it, but I think it can be forgiven.

William controlled himself first.

"Anyway, one of us did it," he said sharply. "We've got to settle what we're going to do."

Christopher tapped his foot on the floor.

"We'd better let someone know, I suppose," he said.

Philip slowly agreed.

"If the damned fool won't confess, there's nothing for it. At least I suppose not," he said undecidedly.

William broke in:

"—But to let the police know."

I made one last effort. "It seems a pity," I said, "to drag all of us through a murder case. Do you all realise the questioning and the tortures that it means?"

"It'll be hell," said Tonia bitterly. "For everyone."

"There's nothing for it." William's voice was hard. "We must let the police get on to it at once. And one of us sooner or later will be found out, and sent to his—or her"—and the "or her", at which I had always smiled in legal documents, sounded forbidding as I felt Avice shrink—"rather dirty death."

There was another silence, and the low cabin seemed hot and oppressive with all the fears that beset one in the dark. Avice began to whimper. After a moment William's voice came again:

"That's all. We can't talk any more. I'll get the police."

"Wouldn't it be better to phone to Norwich, and get a man of some sort of intelligence?" Christopher suggested. "If you get a policeman from one of these little villages, it'll take us hours and hours to explain that there is anything wrong."

"Good," said William. "Christopher and Ian and I will

take the dinghy into Horning and get Norwich. Christopher and Ian will be useful to row the dinghy—and also to see that no one runs away. Because, remember, we're all under suspicion."

"Of course," I said.

"That means," said Christopher thoughtfully, "that the police will want to keep us under supervision. Where are we going to stay the night? We can't sleep on the wherry."

"That's a problem," William said.

"We'd better go to a hotel somewhere," Tonia suggested to William.

"It would be a bit awkward. People staring at us and knowing that one of us killed——" William answered.

"I know," Christopher broke in. "A friend of mine owns one of those big bungalows the other side of Potter Heigham. He'd lend it to us for as long as we want; and we can all live there with a squeeze."

Tonia laughed.

"With a policeman on the premises, if necessary. I rather dote on policemen, you know, Philip darling."

"Splendid," William said. "If you can get it, that would be a lot more comfortable. We could keep to ourselves until the police have done all they want to."

"We'll sleep there to-night then," I agreed.

"There's one thing more," William said, rubbing his chin. "We're all going to live at very close quarters; and there'll be all sorts of suspicions flying about. We're going to get on each others' nerves. The question is—What attitude are we going to adopt?"

"As though nothing had happened," said Tonia.

"How can we, when something *has* happened?" Christopher interposed. "I suggest we try and keep on precisely as we were, but the sooner the whole business is cleared up the better."

William went on impatiently: "What I meant was, are we all going to spy on each other in order to find out who did it?"

"Oh, we can't," Philip protested. "We're not policemen."

"On the other hand," said William firmly, "this murder habit may get infectious. And I rather deplore the prospect of letting myself be shot like a rabbit."

"The only reasonable thing is to be as normal as we can possibly manage," I suggested. The words sounded very feeble even to me. I hurried on: "We can't make any hard and fast rules of what we shall or shall not do."

"I suppose that's so," William concurred, and then with an air of finality he said: "That's everything settled. We'll go and see about the police and the bungalow."

Quickly William and Christopher went out of the cabin up the fore-hatchway. That way led to the shining deck and the sunlit river; the aft-hatchway led too near to a green awning. Tonia and Philip followed them, hand in hand. I was going out of the door when I heard a stifled voice from Avice:

"Ian, please!"

"My dear," I said, and looked at her. Her face was piteous, and her delicate beauty drowned in tears. "Whatever is the matter?"

"They'll think I did it. I know they will!"

I put my hands on her shoulders.

"Now then, don't be a little fool!" I was a stern as I could make myself. "Why ever should they think that?"

"They're bound to. They're bound to. Don't you know that I'm the next heir after Roger to all his uncle's money? Ian, they're bound to think I did it. And they'll hang me——"

"Of course they won't. It's utterly impossible," I tried to soothe her.

35

"They'll hang me," she quavered. "Ian, you've got to prove that I didn't do it. That somebody else did. Ian, you've got to *prove* it."

I had a sense of helplessness. In some ways, I think, I am not more inefficient than most men: I am fairly competent at observing people, and I have a good memory for detail; but I simply do not possess the puzzle-solving mind. It was obvious that the unravelling of this problem was beyond me. Yet I could not bring myself to explain this to the girl who was looking up at me, trying to keep back her sobs.

"I'll do my best," I muttered, but suddenly I thought of the man who, of all people, was most suited to find out the truth of Roger's death—and most to be trusted with the truth when he had found it. For I could not suppress a fear of the consequences that the truth might bring.

"I know the very man we want," I said triumphantly. "You've heard me talk of Finbow?"

"Yes," she said.

"I'll get him to clear everything up. You needn't worry. I must go—William will be waiting."

I left her standing in the cabin, looking desolately sad.

I got into the dinghy, and found William and Christopher sitting in it, staring bad-temperedly at one another.

"You must row, I tell you," William was snapping.

"My dear William," Christopher replied. "We've let you run everything up to now; but really you must learn that your word isn't exactly law."

William tightened his lips, and then said:

"It doesn't matter about that. The point is, you pull a better oar than I do—and we've got to get to Horning as soon as we can."

Christopher shrugged his shoulders:

"Oh well, if you put it like that it's rather more reasonable. It would be better if you explained first and commanded afterwards, though," and he began to row us rapidly towards Horning.

I saw with a twinge of dismay that already the strain was beginning to tell, and that little differences of temperament were becoming magnified into causes of quarrels. Soothed, however, by the rhythm of Christopher's oars, I forgot William's sullen face and blessed myself for my inspiration in thinking of Finbow. I had met him just after the war in Hong Kong. I was there on business (I had, of course, not yet retired)—and Finbow was, and still is, in the Civil Service. At the time he was Third Assistant Colonial Secretary, or something of the kind. He was quite a young man then, but before long I had learned to estimate him as wiser on human affairs than anyone whom I had ever known.

Why he buried himself in the East, and why he stayed there, I never completely knew; but, at any rate, he had built a life for himself with which he seemed content. He enjoyed the graces of living, good food, good wine, good talk; he read Chinese poetry and played cricket; but chiefly he gratified what was apparently his only passion—the watching of men and women as they performed their silly antics for his amusement. He watched in a curious, detailed, scientific way; I remember the astonishment I felt when he told me more than I knew myself about an absurd romance I had whilst I was in China.

The chief impression which he made on me was of an amused and rather frightening detachment. When I knew him better, I liked him more, and found that there was a kindlier side to him than he was willing to admit. About a month before the wherry party I had seen him, home for a year's leave, and I ventured to point out that he was not so inhuman as he liked to pretend. He smiled, and told me he was infinitely more unemotional than I could possibly believe.

Whatever he was, though, there would be no one better

37

able to help Avice and myself, and no one quicker to see light through whatever play of forces ended in the killing of Roger among his friends. I thanked my good luck that Finbow was in England just as I most needed him.

Christopher was pulling quickly to Horning, and William's eyes were fixed on the red cottages round the bend in the river.

I announced, casually:

"If you don't mind, you two, I think I'll ask a friend of mine to come and stay with us in the bungalow."

William frowned:

"Curious time to indulge in hospitality," he said. "Who is he?"

"A man called Finbow," I answered.

Christopher chuckled.

"One of the silliest names I've ever heard," he said. "Who is this Finbow?"

"He's a man from Hong Kong. I don't think he'll get in the way; and he may be useful. It might be a good thing to have someone who's not mixed up in this, and whom we can rely on. He's certain to know all the legal ropes."

I tried to be as casual as I could, for I thought it wise not to let anyone suspect my real purpose in inviting him.

"We're competent enough to look after ourselves," William said.

"I'm sure Finbow would be a help," I persisted.

"Have him if you want," William said ungraciously. "Though I must say it's a little queer. Still, perhaps he'll make up a four at bridge, when Philip wants to go and kiss that girl of his."

Christopher smilingly agreed:

"I don't mind a bit, Ian. Have the entire race of Finbows, for all I care."

We telephoned from the Swan at Horning. William took

38

on the task of getting into touch with the Norwich police, and his clear, hard voice got more and more impatient as the conversation went on. Christopher and I were puzzled, hearing only William's side, and it was not until later that we learned it went like this:

"Norwich Police Station?" asked William.

"Yes; who's there?"

"Listen. Doctor Roger Mills has been killed on his private wherry, *The Siren*, within the last hour."

"Who?"

"Doctor Roger Mills."

"What about him?"

"He's been killed."

"Who's been killed?"

"Doctor Roger Mills."

"Has he?"

William became irascible.

"Be quiet, and get this clear," he said coldly. "A wherry, *The Siren*, is now moored half a mile on the Wroxham side of Horning. On it, its owner is lying with a bullet——"

"What?"

William compressed his lips.

"A bullet—a bullet through his heart. He is, not unnaturally, dead. Will you send someone at once?"

There was a pause, and then he turned to us.

"It's all right. Someone called Birrell—Detective-Sergeant Birrell—is coming over to take the case in hand."

We received the name of Birrell in perfect calm; a few hours later we felt other emotions when it was mentioned.

Christopher got his call through quickly, and borrowed the bungalow with an easy assurance that I admired. I had to wait some time before I was able to speak to Finbow at his flat in Portland Place; first the line was busy, and then I had to stand by whilst he got out of bed. The others got im-

patient and walked back to the dinghy. When at last I heard
his voice, oddly distorted over the telephone, I explained the
affair to him as briefly as I could.

There was a long "So"—a favourite monosyllable of his—
and then:

"Of course I'll come," came distinctly to my ear, and I have
not often heard anything more welcome. He spoke again:

"I'll be on the yacht in two hours. Good-bye."

I joined the others in the dinghy with a sensation of relief.
A black and twisted shadow still hung between me and the
bright morning; there were still the images of Roger, dead
with a smile on his lips, and of Avice crying in my arms; but
I knew that I had done the best that I could. In an hour or
two I should be able to tell everything to Finbow, and leave
the whole dark story to him.

As I sat down in the dinghy, Christopher asked:

"Your friend coming?"

"Yes," I said. "He was rather glad to. He had nothing
to do."

William grunted, and moved towards the oars. Christopher
stopped him.

"I'm going to row," said Christopher.

"You rowed here," William replied. "I'll row back."

"I must teach you that you can't always have your own
way," said Christopher. "I rowed here because you gave me
a decent reason why I should: I'm going to row back because
I want to."

William grunted, and Christopher rowed us towards the
wherry skilfully and in silence. I was thinking—and I was
sure that the others must be, too—of the scene to which we
were returning: of a green awning over a well, where, a little
time before, a cheerful, red-faced man had sat and swung the
tiller. I looked at the dark even shadow of the high reeds on
the water. It was all peaceful and undisturbed. Yet I felt

that death also was peaceful and undisturbed. What were we going back to?

As I thought, there was a chill at my heart. By some queer chance, Christopher had the same uneasiness.

"I hope," he said, as he brought the oars out of the water, "that nothing else has happened on the yacht. I hope Avice——"

William said curtly:

"She'll be safe enough."

But I wished she was with us.

Suddenly, down the river from Horning, came a hum that swelled into a tumult, and I saw an outboard motor-boat bearing down on us at a great speed. There was a wash as it passed, and one of our oars was jerked from the rowlocks. Christopher cursed, and the dinghy twisted broadside to the waves. A second later, I found myself swimming, with Christopher, William and the overturned boat a few yards away.

The motor-boat came back to us rather more slowly. A black-haired man with a round, red-cheeked face was driving it. He called to us in a loud, unapologetic voice:

"That was a silly thing to do. I suppose you can manage."

"I suppose we can, you damned fool," said William fiercely. He had swum to the dinghy and was trying to right it. Christopher was retrieving the oar. "I suppose we can. But what in the devil's name do you mean by rushing about at that speed?"

"I'm on important business. Most important business," said the round-faced man. "I'm Detective-Sergeant Aloysius Birrell of the Norwich Police, and I'm investigating a crime that's happened just along here. I can't waste any more time. You'll be all right."

The motor-boat charged up the river. That was our first sight of Aloysius Birrell.

CHAPTER FOUR

Aloysius Birrell and Finbow

We got into the dinghy after some struggling, and William took the oars and rowed with bad-tempered sweeps. The upset put all forebodings out of my mind, and I was conscious only of clinging clothes.

But when at last we rounded a corner and I saw the wherry with the trim green awning over its stern, fear attacked me again, fear of what we might find when we got aboard. Then Avice appeared and leaned against the mast, and watched us approach; with one hand, she made a little fluttering movement that was almost a wave.

My anxiety disappeared in a flash. Soon she was saying:

"There's a queer sergeant-lad on board. He's asking all sorts of questions."

William snorted.

"That's the madman who swamped us, damn his eyes!"

As we climbed on board the wherry, Avice gave a soft and mournful laugh.

"You'd better go and get changed," she said.

"We're going to, my darling," Christopher replied, putting a wet hand lightly on her face. "I've a good mind to make you wet as well."

She smiled at him; and I was glad to see that she had recovered enough to take some pleasure in the banter of her lover. She murmured:

"Do go and get changed, Christopher. I'd rather like to try nursing, but I wouldn't be tremendously good at it."

"I wouldn't trust myself to you," he said. "I'd rather get changed—but I suppose we ought to report to this Birrell person first."

She frowned, and her eyes clouded.

"He's been asking me all about everybody on board," she protested. "And I think that now he's prowling round—Roger."

William broke in sharply:

"I'm going to get changed, and he'll have to wait if he wants to talk to me." He called harshly: "Sergeant Birrell!"

"I'm busy," a noise came from somewhere near the well.

"I'm wet!" William raised his voice impatiently.

After a moment, Birrell came on deck from the fore-hatch and walked towards us.

I had formed a confused impression of him from my glimpse of a round face in a motor-boat; now I saw that he was a short plump man, very brisk and cheerful and energetic.

"Oh," he said. "You're the people who fell in the water."

"We are," William answered, looking at him coldly.

"That makes the whole party of six persons," Birrell went on. "The couple down below, this young lady and you three. I must ask each of you some questions by himself: I'll fetch my papers."

"You may have noticed," said William, "that we're all extremely wet. And we're going to dry ourselves and put on some clothes. After that we'll tell you what we can."

I expected to see annoyance in Birrell's round red face. Instead, it clouded, like a child who has had a toy taken away. He seemed merely disappointed in us.

"I should have thought," he told William, "that you'd have enough enthusiasm to forget about your clothes for a few minutes."

"Enthusiasm for what?" I asked curiously.

"The investigation of crime," he answered in a rich resonant voice. "Don't you see that the investigation of crime is one of the greatest romances in the world? Don't you see how wonderful it is? It is the harnessing to good purposes of all our wilder selves! Years ago they used to write ballads about war and brute force and lust." I cannot reproduce the horror with which he intoned the last word. "Now they write detective stories in which all of men's energies are concentrated on seeking out the wrong. Don't you see what a change it is? If you look at it properly, detective stories are a sign of civilisation. And the investigation of crime is a sign of all the good in our modern world!"

I was completely taken aback by this speech. There was the light of genuine belief in Birrell's eye. Apparently he saw nothing abnormal in this statement of his faith; in fact, it ran so smoothly that I suspected it had been declaimed before. However, I was too worried to concentrate upon the eccentric behaviour of a detective-sergeant. I saw the others were equally at a loss. Christopher smiled slightly, and said:

"We'll do what we can, Sergeant, but we must get dry first. We shan't be long."

"Splendid," replied Birrell, mollified. "There are lots of measurements I want to take, concerning the—unfortunate gentleman."

Avice turned white and looked away, William and Christopher went down the fore-hatchway, and Birrell, with a glance at Avice and myself, ran with quick little steps to the well. I whispered to Avice:

"He won't worry you much."

Her mouth was drawn. "He's mad enough to do anything," she answered.

"Finbow is coming in an hour or so," I said.

"Oh, Ian, you are a dear!" She smiled at me, but there was still a line of distress etched on her forehead between the appealing eyes.

44

I changed my clothes as rapidly as I could and, with an
elderly man's concern for his health, took a stiff nip of brandy.
Then I joined Birrell and Christopher in the middle cabin.
William had dried himself and gone on deck. Birrell was
writing in an enormous square exercise-book. As he wrote,
he moved the tip of his tongue in sympathy with the words.
He looked up as I came in, saying:

"This is a very extraordinary case, Mr. Capel. I was just
taking my holiday and I happened to go to the station to pick
up a pen-knife I'd forgotten—and so I got the job of being
sent here. It shows you how little things can have big results."

I was rather puzzled, but assented.

He went on:

"If I hadn't gone to the station, I should have missed the
most interesting case I've ever handled. It's a very interesting case indeed. Just because it calls for some imagination.
I expect you think detective-sergeants don't ever have any
imagination."

"After seeing you, I am sure I could never think that," I
said. And I half meant it. Like a sensible man, I detest
generalisations about types and sexes and races and everything else. But when presented with a detective-sergeant I
did not expect—before I met Aloysius Birrell—to see a
youngish fresh-faced extremely loquacious man with a
flaming enthusiasm for anything that was connected with
crime.

He checked his discussion on imagination in sergeants and
asked me a great number of questions, writing down my
answers in a large round hand, moving the tip of his tongue
as he shaped the letters. He was uncommonly talkative; he
asked for a lot of superfluous information; but I discovered
that he was competent enough, in an absurd way, to extract
the essentials of the story as I have told in the second chapter.

He was very interested in my movements between the time

45

I got up and the time I went back to my cabin to dress.

"You say you called to Dr. Mills?" he asked.

"Yes," I said.

"And he replied?"

"Yes."

"That means," said Birrell, "he was alive at about nine— if you weren't mistaken."

He looked at me interestedly. Surely, I thought, the fool cannot suspect me?

"I was not mistaken," I said curtly.

"Perhaps you weren't," he admitted doubtfully. "When I've got everything collected I shall be able to say more about that. The tempo is the most exciting feature of this case."

I was left wondering what he could mean by 'tempo', and decided that I must have got the word wrong. Birrell went briskly on:

"Have you seen a revolver?"

"No," I said.

"I don't mean this morning: I mean since you've been on board?"

"I only came on board last night."

"That's true," said Birrell approvingly.

"Of course it's true," I said. "And I've not had much time to see revolvers, even if there were any."

"Humph," said Birrell. "There *was* one of course. Still.
. . . How did you discover the body?"

"I went on deck," I replied, "with Miss Loring. And we saw Dr. Mills had been shot."

"That's what Miss Loring said," he admitted. "Who suggested going on deck?"

"I think she did—but I should have gone up myself in a minute or two."

"Humph," said Birrell. "What did Dr. Mills look like when you saw him? How was he lying?"

"Very much as he is now—sitting up in the well. But when we saw him first, the tiller was tucked between his body and his arm as though he was still sailing," I replied.

"Who disturbed that?" said Birrell sharply.

"Dr. Garnett, when he moored the yacht."

"Oh," Birrell commented, his mouth slightly open, rapping his pencil against his teeth. "That will do for you for the present, Mr. Capel. I must see Dr. Garnett at once."

Christopher, who had been listening with an occasional amused tremor of the lip, fetched William.

"Oh, Dr. Garnett," Birrell began, when William had come through the door, "why did you disturb the body by moving the tiller?"

William sat down slowly on his bunk, and looked contemptuously at Birrell.

"How do you think I was going to moor a wherry without moving the tiller?" he answered.

"You needn't have moored the wherry," Birrell said. "You should have realised that the body oughtn't to be touched. It makes it more difficult when we don't know exactly how the body was."

"Do you think I ought to have let the boat just run straight into the bank as soon as there was a bend in the river? Just for the convenience of policemen?" William asked, thrusting out his jaw.

"I do," said Birrell, undisturbed. "It might have shaken the wherry up, but it would have been better."

"I happen not to be insane," said William.

"It may interest you to know," Birrell opened his eyes wide and spoke impressively, "that the only finger-prints anywhere near the body were found on the tiller."

William's temper, always a little uncertain, was getting frayed.

"It does not interest me in the least," he said.

"I took a special course in the use of finger-prints in the investigation of crime not long ago," Birrell told us. "And I've dusted every conceivable thing all round the body. The only finger-prints are on the tiller. I've made a drawing of them."

He showed us three small pencil sketches. Then he said, brusquely:

"I want your finger-prints, Dr. Garnett."

"You can have them," said William.

Birrell brought out a small black pad.

"Rest your fingers on here, and then press them on this piece of paper."

Christopher and I watched William's square capable hand as he obeyed. Birrell examined the impressions carefully:

"Dr. Garnett," he said with immense excitement, "the finger-prints on the tiller were made by you."

"That," said William, "is scarcely surprising, seeing that I took hold of it in order to moor the boat. In fact it would have been a great deal more interesting if my finger-prints hadn't appeared."

"Humph," Birrell seemed dubious. "I suppose that's reasonable. Miss Loring and Mr. Capel both agree that you *did* steer the boat."

"Of course I steered the boat," William broke in impatiently.

"Well, we'll leave that for a bit," Birrell conceded. "Now I want to know if you have any idea whether there was a revolver on board."

"I know that there was something of the sort on board," William answered.

"What? What kind? Whose?" Birrell was overcome with eagerness.

48

"Dr. Mills's own automatic," William replied, rubbing his chin. "It was given him after he had been an expert witness in the Cooper case."

"What bore was it?" Birrell was speaking before William had finished answering.

"A small automatic, I don't know what make," William said.

"Where did he keep it?"

"I don't know: he just mentioned that he'd got it with him, and said he might have a shot at some birds."

"Where is it now?" Birrell pressed on.

"How should I know?" William said.

"I shall search the boat," Birrell answered.

"Excellent," said William.

"Where was he likely to keep a pistol?" asked Christopher.

"The sort of place one would expect is on that little shelf at the top of the aft-hatch, where he used to put the log-book. But he might have found a hiding-place for it somewhere else," William answered.

"I'll try that shelf first," said Birrell. He asked William a number of questions, mainly about his movements during the time he was out of the cabin between 9 and 9.10. He surveyed us with an air of triumph.

"I've now questioned you three as well as the three others. I've asked you all where you were this morning between 9 and 9.30. You might like to hear my results," he said.

He read out:

" '1. The murder must have happened between 8.55 and 9.25.

" '2. No one heard a shot.

" '3. No one has a complete alibi.

" '4. There is no sign of an automatic in the vicinity of the body.'

49

"What does that suggest?"

Christopher and William and I glanced at each other with a trace of amusement.

"Nothing whatever," said William.

"It means," said Birrell unperturbed, "that you're all under suspicion. All six of you. I tell you quite frankly, you're all under suspicion."

"This is rather ridiculous," I protested.

"You will all have to be kept under observation," he went on.

"We thought you might have to do that," said Christopher. "So I've borrowed a bungalow near Potter Heigham where all six of us can live. You can have the place watched if necessary."

"That's a very good arrangement," Birrell agreed warmly. "A very good arrangement indeed. I'll go and tell the man with me to fetch a large motor-boat to take you there. I'll see that the bungalow is properly supervised."

"Yes," said Christopher. "You'll also see, I hope, that the Press don't get to know that we're living there."

"You can rely on me, Mr. Tarrant," Birrell answered him, and left the cabin. We heard him shouting instructions to the constable who had accompanied him in the small motor-boat; in a very short time he reappeared.

"That's all right," he said. "I've sent him for a boat to take you all to your bungalow. The next thing is to look for the automatic. I'd like to see the shelf you mentioned, Dr. Garnett."

William led us up the aft-hatchway, and pointed to a deep shelf near the top rung.

"The log-book's always kept there. As well as the silk pennant that Dr. Mills used for special occasions," he said. "And the automatic might easily be there too."

Birrell inspected the shelf carefully:

"But there's nothing here at all," he said irritably. "Not even the book."

"That's queer," William said, looking puzzled. Christopher agreed:

"It's more or less high treason not to put the log-book in its proper place. Roger was furious if it was moved."

"Perhaps he left it in the cabin: he was writing it up when we went to bed last night," William suggested.

I was able to contradict this.

"No," I told them. "He went out to put it away."

"I give it up," William said.

Birrell was impatient:

"It may be important. But what I want first of all is the automatic. It's either been thrown overboard or it's in the boat now. I'm going to make a thorough search."

"Still, it's curious," Christopher commented. "You'll look for the log-book as well, Sergeant?"

"Yes," Birrell agreed, "it may be a clue."

"There's another curious thing," said William, as we descended the hatch. "Where's the pennant?"

"The pennant?" echoed Birrell.

"The thing you fly at the top of the mast," William said scornfully.

"Oh, you mean the burgee," Birrell explained.

William suppressed a biting remark. He went on, sharply:

"Whatever you call it, it's a silk flag which Dr. Mills only used occasionally. Usually he flew an ordinary cotton pennant. It was always stored on that shelf. And it isn't there now. It's vanished."

"The log-book and the burgee may have an important bearing on the case," Birrell said. "But we must have the automatic first," and he opened his eyes suspiciously at William. I, myself, could see no possible connection between the absence of a log-book and a pennant and Roger's death.

A log-book, perhaps, might contain something which a murderer would wish destroyed, I thought vaguely; but a pennant, what use could that be to anyone? What could one do with a silk rag and a few inches of string? I dismissed the loss as a coincidence and followed the others round the wherry.

By Philip's berth we thought we had made a find. I saw a writing-pad, and under it a few inches of a brown paper cover which reminded me of the book I had seen Roger writing in. I touched the cover:

"This might be the log-book," I said.

"Nothing like big enough," William remarked, but Birrell had already pulled the book out and examined it. It was nothing more incriminating than a copy of *Claudine in Paris*, which Philip had apparently brought for light reading. Christopher chuckled sardonically as it was revealed; but, to my amazement, Aloysius Birrell blushed and very hurriedly put the book down.

For a moment I wondered what had happened. A detective-sergeant wildly enthusiastic over criminal investigation was strange enough, but a detective-sergeant with the suscepti-bilities of a Victorian heroine was incredible. I had noticed the intensity with which he had enunciated the word 'lust' a few minutes previously. Suddenly the significance of his name broke upon me. He was Irish, which explained it all. Several times I had encountered the extraordinary prudery of the Irish Catholic—a prudery responsible equally for the censorship in Boston (Mass.), gang warfare in America, Mr. James Joyce, and at the present moment the curious discom-fiture of Detective-Sergeant Aloysius Birrell.

His blush had scarcely subsided before he was shocked again. We led him to the cabin which Avice and Tonia had shared, as the last possible place in the wherry where an auto-matic might be hidden. He knocked at the door and went in. I had a glimpse of Tonia sitting on Philip's knee with her arms around his neck, and then the door was shut very quickly, and Aloysius Birrell went redder and redder in the face.

He pointed to the closed door.

"It's disgusting," he said. "Young men and women going about in parties like this and canoodling each other." And as an afterthought: "Particularly when somebody's just been murdered."

A pleasant voice broke in:

"As a matter of interest, people are far more likely to want to canoodle each other—as this gentleman brightly puts it— when a murder's just been done, than at almost any other time. Grief is far more effective than jazz bands as a method of excitement, you know."

I turned and caught a smile in Finbow's eyes.

He had just come down the aft-hatch and stood at the bottom, tall, well-dressed, unruffled. A girl had once described him to me as looking "like a foreigner's idea of a really handsome Englishman", but as she liked him more than he liked her, the phrase was perhaps an unfair one.

In some ways, however, she was near the truth. He was handsome in the way that all Continentals and most Americans envy, in the way which contrives at the same time to be unemphatic and distinguished. His face was long and rather thin, his hair greying, his nose pronounced; his worst enemy might accuse him of looking rather like a horse, but his best friend could claim with more justice that he was an extremely good-looking man.

I introduced them all to Finbow. Philip and Tonia came out of the cabin and met him, and I noticed that Tonia was very anxious to impress. Finbow, however, was busy talking to Birrell.

"Sergeant, you see it would be very much more convenient

for you, if there were someone in the bungalow who wasn't directly mixed up in this affair," said Finbow.

"That's true," Birrell admitted grudgingly.

"Also," Finbow went on suavely, "I've always had an ambition to *see* a murder case actually investigated. I've always wanted to see someone like you, Sergeant, cutting his way through the complications of a mystery like this. It must be a fascinating thing to do."

Under the influence of Finbow's smooth tongue Birrell's fresh face assumed a look of almost infantile delight.

Birrell replied exuberantly:

"You ought to follow the case from the beginning, Mr. Finbow, if you're going to get any benefit from it. The essential thing is the logical structure of investigation; and if you don't see the first steps you miss all the logic."

"Of course," said Finbow.

"It's a very curious case. I've made a thorough search of the entire yacht," Birrell said. "And I haven't found the automatic or the log-book or the burgee. They're all missing. But I collected a lot of data. So you'd better come into the large cabin, and see all the data I've got together in the last half-hour."

"This is extraordinarily good of you," said Finbow, and they went away together.

William had been following the conversation with a sullen face. After they had gone he said to me, suspiciously:

"So this friend of yours is keen on crime, is he?"

"He's interested," I replied. "He's interested in almost everything. It'll be useful to have someone capable around, if we are going to be inspected by any more Aloysius Birrells."

William and Christopher both gave short laughs at the name. Tonia said huskily:

"The poor man went a vivid beetroot when he looked into the cabin and saw Philip kissing me. I must educate him."

We all went on deck and found Avice still gazing listlessly over the marshes. She was, however, able to muster a smile when we told her of Aloysius Birrell's delicate sensibilities, and she told me in an undertone that she had been impressed by her first sight of Finbow. He had talked to her for a few minutes before he had come below to us.

We waited and talked on the deck of the wherry for nearly half an hour. We tried to be our normal selves, but it was not easy when, along the deck, we could see an awning which seemed at times more horrible than the horror it concealed. Actually for a good deal of the time we were bright and laughing; and then someone would have a second's recollection of the thing that had happened to us, and would plunge into a gloomy silence.

I would stress the fact that emotions are never continuous. I am not a callous man—I am, in fact, rather more soft-hearted than I ought to be—and Roger had been a friend of mine for years. Nevertheless, in the two hours since his death I had been amused by Birrell, concerned for Avice, glad to feel dry clothes instead of wet against my body—and all of these emotions and sensations drove any thought of Roger completely from my mind.

After the half-hour I went down into the large cabin, and found Aloysius Birrell declaiming excitedly to Finbow, who was smiling in encouragement.

"It's the tempo of this crime which is the feature of it!" Birrell exclaimed. "Murder's just like any other art. And what characterises a work of art is its tempo. And the tempo of one artist is always different from the tempo of another. Find who thinks and works in the tempo of this murder, and you've got the man!" Then he saw me and stopped. Finbow said:

"Hullo, Ian! We've just finished a very instructive chat. Sergeant Birrell's been explaining his theories of crime."

"Mr. Finbow is a most sympathetic listener," said Birrell fervently. "But you people had better get off to your bungalow. I'm very glad you're going to stay together. It makes it easier."

"What about the wherry?" I asked.

"I'm having it taken back to Wroxham. The motor-boat will soon be here to take you to the bungalow. I'll call on you there when I've got some more to ask. Remember the tempo, Mr. Finbow!"

There was a whirring noise outside.

"That's the motor-boat for you people."

When we got on deck the others were already in the boat. Before we left Birrell, I asked Finbow if he had seen the body. He said smoothly:

"Thanks to Sergeant Birrell, I've seen everything that I could possibly want. Thank you very much, Sergeant."

"I've enjoyed it," said Aloysius Birrell.

We were soon out of sight of the wherry. My last glimpse of it showed Birrell standing in the bows, pensively. I saw also a patch of green awning that I hoped I had looked at for the last time.

I breathed more freely as we went up the bright river.

In the fields to the right, we could see the sails of yachts which seemed to be moving placidly through the grass, like an unreal but pretty Dutch painting. Finbow spoke to me in a quiet tone:

"This is very interesting."

"What do you think of it?" I said.

"A very pretty problem," he remarked thoughtfully. "Seven people completely detached from the outside world —and one of the party killed. I wonder. . . . Still it's absurd to guess until you've given me all the facts."

"I suppose so," I said.

Then he smiled:

"Ian, you said you had a mystery for me. You never told me you had Aloysius Birrell as well."

I smiled:

"I didn't know him then."

Finbow murmured:

"He's not such an ass as he seems, of course. He'll collect his information perfectly efficiently. Unfortunately he'll also find it necessary to express his soul, which means that we shall have to side-track him. He represents roughly all the virtues and all the vices of an age of words. He knows all his books: he's read every detective story that's ever been written; he reads all the trials; he's read all the books on criminology, including the voluminous Gross. That's good. If he stopped there, he'd be a useful man at his job. Unfortunetly an age of words also means that everyone imbibes an immense amount of nonsense. More intelligent people than Aloysius Birrell show the same tendency. You heard him talk about 'tempo'. A word like that makes a comforting noise. When you've said it often enough, you forget that it's quite meaningless. You forget you only invented it to conceal your ignorance. We're all word-hypnotised. Philosophers and art-critics and parsons and psychologists— they're all of them Aloysius Birrells thinking that when they've said 'tempo' they've explained the universe."

"Yes," I said, which was the only reply to any long speech that Finbow felt called upon to make.

"I must explain the vice of words some day, but Birrell's more important just now," Finbow went on. "He's got hold of lots of phrases about murder and crime, by the way. The favourite besides 'tempo' is 'murder by the most unlikely person'! He waves that about proudly."

"Oh," I said.

Finbow lit a cigarette, and asked casually:

"I suppose you didn't do this murder, Ian?"

I was used to Finbow's sense of humour.

"No," I said simply.

"I fancied not," he replied, with a smile. "But Birrell thinks you did."

Five Questions by Finbow

I tried to laugh, but I imagine that anyone would feel worried at being officially suspected of murder, even if the official were Aloysius Birrell. I had an unreasonable anxiety . . .

"But this is ridiculous," I protested.

"Of course it is," said Finbow gently. "That's why he believes it; you see, acting on the principle of 'murder by the most unlikely person', he's arrived at you. You're the most unlikely person: so you've probably done the murder."

"I hope you've persuaded him that I've not," I replied.

"On the contrary, I've done my best to show that I think he's right," Finbow remarked, looking abstractedly at the flat country behind St. Benet's Abbey, which we had passed the minute before.

"What——" I was incoherent. The world seemed to have gone mad. Finbow had agreed with Birrell that I had killed Roger!

"It's all right," said Finbow. "I'm quite sane. I know perfectly well that you've not killed this man any more than I have. But it's very useful for Birrell to think that you have!"

I began to grasp the situation.

"You see," Finbow went on, "if he's bumbling round all the time, he would be an infernal nuisance. What I've tried to do is to let him think he's being rather subtle. So that he won't do anything more annoying than to watch you, and collect some information I rather want."

"Will he find anything useful?" I said.

"He may." Finbow smiled. "Fortunately, he can't do much harm. The main thing is to keep him quiet and make him feel that all's going well."

"He'll sleep under my bed, will he?" I was becoming amused.

"No, he'll just move tactfully about. He's also going to get a diving-suit and look for the automatic. It must be in the river, of course. If he finds it, which he won't, I should be rather pleased. And he's going to watch those two youngsters who're so fond of each other."

"Philip and Tonia," I said.

"He's just like all the moralists—he thinks that if people spend most of their time kissing, they're likely to commit even worse sins in their off moments." Finbow had a glint in his light-blue eyes and I knew that he was absorbed in the problem which I had set him.

"He can't suspect them as well as me?" I asked.

"They're his second string. If the 'most unlikely person' didn't do it, then probably 'persons of suitable psychological disposition' did. I think he must have got that from Miss Dorothy Sayers."

"Oh, well," I said, "so long as he's happy."

"And so long as he doesn't get Scotland Yard on to this," Finbow put in. "I want a clear field for a day or two: and while Birrell can assure everyone that there's no difficulty in the case, I shall get it."

"Would Scotland Yard worry you?" I asked, surprised. I was so used to seeing Finbow dealing tranquilly with any difficulties in his path.

"Naturally. They'd find out every conceivable scrap of knowledge about everyone who'd ever been near Roger. And if they amass enough facts, they can't help being right in the end. Scientific detection isn't scientific and isn't detection; it's just the dull and merciless accumulation of an extraordinary number of uninteresting details. But it must get there in the end. Well, I want to find out what happened first: because"—and his voice hardened from the smooth tone in which he normally carried on his commentary on people and things—"because there may be a side to this affair that will turn out darker and more bitter for you than you have any idea." He stood silently for a minute as the motor-boat rushed past the first straggling bungalows of Potter Heigham. Then he said in a low voice, which shook me by its unaccustomed seriousness: "I didn't think I had many illusions left about human beings. But I rather think there are one or two people in your wherry party who may make me feel that I'm still an innocent child."

We went quickly through the moored yachts and the river-side cottages at Potter, and, a few minutes past the bridge, saw the square grey tower of Martham Church away to star-board.

Christopher pointed to an isolated brown bungalow on the other side of the river, near where Kendal Dyke enters the Thurne.

"That's our place," he said.

"Oh," said Avice in a whisper, and I think that we all felt a sinking melancholy at the sight of it. For it was quite alone, led up to on land by a narrow footpath through the swampy fields; and in front of it there was an unkempt garden which ran down to the water. Set out there amid the deserted marshes, it seemed to my dejected eyes to represent the solitariness from which hope has fled—the solitariness into which a callous crime had thrown my friends, and from which one of them at least would not come back. As we entered it and saw through the back windows the reedy wastes of Heigham Sound, the atmosphere of gloom deepened amongst us all. We did not count William an impressionable man, but he said sombrely:

"A damned good place to live in after a murder. We might round it off suitably by all committing suicide or going mad."

Avice turned to me with a weary despair.

Under her eyes I thought I could see the traces of dark circles. Even Philip and Tonia were subdued. Finbow, however, who had been chatting to Christopher about Malaya, went to the piano in the sitting-room and gave an imitation of Maurice Chevalier. It would have shocked Aloysius Birrell; but it had the effect that he wanted, and in ten minutes we were arranging with considerable liveliness where we should sleep and when we should eat.

It was good to see Avice become quite animated in a discussion with Tonia on the possibility of their cooking us a meal—although I had a private hope that the possibility would never be realised.

In the middle of this argument, a small fat woman entered the sitting-room from a door which led to the kitchen. She surveyed us disapprovingly.

"Who's Mr. Tarrant?" she asked, in a Norfolk accent and a determined manner. Christopher admitted that he was.

"Huh," she replied. Then she said grudgingly: "Mr. Williamson told me to expect you. I'm the housekeeper— Mrs. Tufts." She eyed us all with a peculiarly unwelcoming expression.

"Splendid!" Christopher ventured. Mrs. Tufts remained unmoved. Avice gave her a long and melting glance.

"Oh, Mrs. Tufts, I wonder if Miss Gilmour and I could do some cooking. We'd love to. We're not much good——"

"I shall do the cooking," said Mrs. Tufts.

"We'd like to get some breakfast. We've not had anything to eat this morning," Tonia said.

Mrs. Tufts glared at her and even Tonia betrayed a trace of nervousness.

"Why didn't you have anything to eat this morning?"

asked Mrs. Tufts. Tonia looked away and stammered an incoherent response.

"There's something wrong," Mrs. Tufts answered, folding her hands on her stomach. "People don't come here at an hour's notice without their breakfast unless there's something wrong. You can't have breakfast now; it's gone eleven and I won't do it."

The fierce little woman dominated the room. No one reopened the question of breakfast. William made an attempt to subdue her.

"We've been settling which rooms we're going to have," William announced in his briskest voice, as though he were giving orders to a hospital nurse.

Mrs. Tufts came into the centre of the room.

"I'll tell you the rooms you're going to have," she said firmly. "You young ladies aren't married?" Avice and Tonia shook their heads. "Then you'll both sleep in that room there"—she pointed to a room leading out of the sitting-room, and looked round at us as though willing to withstand opposition. Philip suddenly burst out into a giggle which he had been trying vainly to suppress. Mrs. Tufts glared at him.

"I know what you young people are," she told us. And then, looking at me, Heaven knows how unjustly, "and some old enough to know better."

Finbow interrupted courteously.

"I'm sure everything you arrange will be perfect, Mrs. Tufts. May this gentleman"—he pointed to me—"and I share that room there?" This was the one opposite to the room which the girl were to have. "We're the oldest people in the party, and sometimes we like to talk to each other."

I have rarely seen Finbow rebuffed, but Mrs. Tufts was equal to it.

"I suppose you can sleep there if you like, but you ought

63

to have something better to do at your age than to want to talk to each other," she answered curtly. "And you three will have the other double room and the single one between you."

She dismissed Christopher, William and Philip from her notice. She went out of the room, throwing behind her as she went:

"Lunch will be at one. I never wait for anybody."

Finbow remarked thoughtfully:

"It's curious how completely powerless almost all Englishmen are, if they're brought up against genuinely thorough rudeness. And in our absurd muddle-headed way we always estimate it as a sign of character. Dr. Johnson and the Duke of Wellington and Queen Victoria and Mr. Shaw and Mr. Snowden—we find other reasons for approving of them, but actually we're just impressed by their sheer boorishness. Mrs. Tufts is very much like them. No one in England can be a great man if they have any manners. I am not a great man."

Avice gave him the shadow of a smile.

"Nice of you to try and cheer us up," she said.

"I'm afraid it wasn't done too well," said Finbow, "or else you wouldn't have noticed. Ian, I'm not a success as an entertainer; we'd better go to our room and unpack."

After a few minutes in our bedroom, Finbow and I took out deck-chairs on to the terrace, which ran down to the river. On the other bank, reeds were waving in the wind; and over them was nothing but the unbroken sky. Finbow stretched his long legs and said:

"It would be easy to be contented in a place like this, I think some day I shall get married, and live here and listen to the seagulls."

I knew from past experience that, when Finbow talked of content, his mind was flitting from point to point. I lay still, smoking my pipe and feeling the sun and wind on my face. Finbow got up, went into the house, and came back with a kettle of hot water, a teapot and two glasses. He put the hot water into the pot, took a tiny canister from his pocket and then threw a few leaves in the hot water. He watched the pot solemnly for a few moments, and then poured a thin straw-coloured liquid into the glasses.

"Best tea in the world," he said, sipping. In China he had cultivated a taste for the more expensive ways of drinking tea, and for the last few years he had usually carried a canister with him. The best tea always seemed to me to taste rather like hay, but I suffered it.

"If it weren't for you, Ian," he went on, sipping between words, "to-day I should be seeing Beds plays Bucks. Second-class county cricket is the only sort of cricket a man of taste can see nowadays. Since first-class cricket became brighter, it ceased to be cricket."

I gulped a little of my tea. It was always best to let Finbow talk as much as he wanted. In the same tone as he had used to mention Beds and Bucks, he said:

"I've got all sorts of thoughts about this murder of yours. Birrell told me a good deal. I had to get it sifted out before I heard your version. Now I want to know everything you can remember about all these people. Give me everything. I always envy your memory. Then tell me all about this morning."

Slowly and carefully I told Finbow what I knew. In effect, I gave him the material out of which I have now written the first chapters. I gave him no more facts than I have set down, simply because those were all the facts I had. In writing I have put the sequence of events more carefully and more logically than I did in conversation with Finbow, but essentially there is no difference between the two accounts.

Twice he uttered a long-drawn "So," an exclamation

which he made a habit of using in so many different circumstances that it was impossible to attach a meaning to it—but
the observations which evoked it as I told my story were,
first, the report that Avice had refused to marry Roger and,
second, the entry of Philip into the cabin when we were
listening to the wireless.

After I had described the way in which Avice and I had
found the body, Finbow lay back in his chair with his eyes
closed. Then he asked:

"What happened afterwards?"

I sketched out the manner in which William took control,
and the meeting in the cabin. When I came to the deductions
William had drawn about the time and the nature of the
death, Finbow pronounced a particularly emphatic "So."
Then I touched on my invitation to the murderer to confess.
I expected Finbow to be amused, but actually he seemed
deeply interested, though he did not repress a faint chuckle
when I mentioned how everyone in turn promised to keep
the faith.

Finally I told him of our going to Horning to inform the
Norwich police, and of our return to the wherry.

"Thank you, Ian," he said at the end, drinking tea which
had long since gone cold. "You're invaluable. I never could
have learned half the things you've told me. I've got a lot
more information from you than I did from Birrell's notes.
I'll just have another look at them, by the way, to refresh
my memory."

From a pocket in his waistcoat he produced a number of
pieces of paper covered with notes in a very small hand-
writing.

"These are my copies of the stuff our friend Birrell put
down," he said. "I missed out most of his superfluities, but
they're quite near the original. Perhaps you'd like to read
them."

He handed the notes to me in turn, after he had glanced at them.

They read:

BODY.

Shot through heart from close quarters and in front: rigor had not set in at beginning of police examination. Found in well of wherry, and all witnesses affirm it was not moved, except to detach tiller in order to move yacht. No finger-prints except on tiller.

MISS A. LORING.

Says she was in her cabin dressing until about 9.20, when she went into middle cabin. Saw nothing; heard nothing; about 9.30 went on deck with Mr. C.* and saw body. Affirms that tiller was between elbow and body. Offered no suggestions. Dr. M. was her cousin. She had known him well since she was a child. He had no particular troubles or enemies so far as she knew. Thought that she had heard him mention having an automatic, but was not certain. She had come on board The Siren *in Aug. with the rest of the party. The last week had been very pleasant, and there was no suspicion of any quarrelling.*

MISS T. GILMOUR.

Got up about 8.55; called Mr. W.; went into middle cabin with Mr. C., and stayed there until Miss L. had finished dressing. Listened to wireless. Saw nothing, heard nothing. Went to own cabin and dressed, and heard nothing until body was discovered. Knew nothing of automatic. No suggestions. Met Mr. W. in Paris three months ago, and was engaged to him just before going on wherry. Knew no one

* In Birrell's notes: Miss L. is Avice Loring; Miss G., Tonia Gilmour; Mr. W., Philip Wade; Mr. T., Christopher Tarrant; Dr. G., William Garnett; Dr. M., Roger Mills; and Mr. C., Ian Capel.

else in party. Very much liked all the others as soon as she met them. Very sorry for Dr. M.

MR. P. WADE.

Wakened by Miss G., and got up because Dr. G. wanted bath which was behind Mr. W.'s berth. Thought Dr. G. wanted bath to bathe bruises on knee due to fall on day before. After getting up, went to middle cabin and listened to wireless. Saw nothing. Heard nothing. Went to room to dress and came on deck after hearing Miss L. call. Was putting on wrist-watch and noted time: 9.27. Had known Dr. M. for five years. Knew nothing which could explain murder. Dr. M. a very cheerful happy man. Dr. M. very hospitable. The week on The Siren had been most enpoyable. Knew nothing of automatic.

MR. C. TARRANT.

Stayed in middle cabin until after Miss G., Mr. C. and Mr. W. had come in. Remembered Dr. G. entering, and then went out to wash. Returned in short time without seeing or hearing anything. Stayed in cabin until Miss L.'s call. Heard Mr. C. call Dr. G., but paid little attention. Went on deck as soon as Miss L. called. Dr. G. sailing and Dr. M. dead.

Had known Dr. M. for three years. Always found him most cheerful and likeable of companions. Could think of no reason for death. Was going to Malaya shortly, after marriage with Miss L. This was farewell holiday. Had found the week on board very pleasant. Had heard automatic mentioned, but hadn't seen it and didn't know whose it was.

MR. I. CAPEL.

Went on deck before 9 and shouted to Dr. M. Heard reply. Went below and stayed in middle cabin until Miss L. asked him to go on deck with her. Saw nothing. Heard nothing until he went on deck and found body. Tiller wedged in crook of Dr. M.'s arm. Estimates time as 9.25.

Questioned, confirmed accounts of Miss L., Mr. W., Miss G. and Mr. T. on their movements between 9 and finding of the body.

Had joined Siren the night before. Knew nothing of automatic.

Had known Dr. M. for ten years. Had never learnt anything which could suggest enemies. Had always liked him.

DR. W. GARNETT.

Went out of cabin to wash and bathe bruise about 9. Washed, and tried to get bath. Mr. W. still in bed. Went back to washing place, and several times called to Mr. W. asking if bath was available. Heard Mr. W.'s voice. After two or three minutes called again. Mr. W. had left and Dr. G. went in, put a little water in bath, bathed bruise, and re-entered middle cabin.

Confirmed accounts of others as given by themselves between this time and discovery of the body. On being called by Mr. C. went on deck, saw Dr. M. was dead, took tiller and moored yacht in first convenient place.

Knew Dr. M. had small automatic on board. Given him as memento of Cooper case. Had been helped by Dr. M. in early days of own medical career. Had come on board with rest of party.

Dr. G.'s finger-prints correspond to those on tiller.

INSPECTION AND SEARCH OF WHERRY.

Wherry was carefully searched. No evidence found. No sign of automatic, which must have been thrown overboard (propose to dive in order to find automatic). Log-book and burgee missing. These also not found during search.

"Those," said Finbow, "are the unaided work of our energetic sergeant. They're not so bad as they might be. Except, of course, that he solemnly asked all of them if they liked Roger—and they all solemnly said 'Yes.' I wonder what he expected them to say."

I had learned very little from Birrell's notes that I had not already known; but I had not realised that Avice and Christopher, as well as William, were aware of the existence of the revolver. I began to wonder why Philip and Tonia had not heard of it. It seemed queer that they alone should be in ignorance.

"Now let me think for five minutes," Finbow said. "I want to join your story to Birrell's notes, and make sense out of the mixture."

I smoked quietly, listening to the rustling of the reeds and watching the tiny reflections of the sun dancing in the wind-flecked water. I was more than anxious to pester Finbow with questions, but I forced myself to wait whilst he was grinding out the problem.

In a few minutes he smiled and spoke:

"Well, Ian, I've come to one conclusion."

"What's that?" I asked excitedly.

"That you didn't murder Roger."

"Tchah," I said.

"I can't prove it yet, but I can soon, if someone gives me a large-scale map of the Broads," he said.

"You needn't bother!" I was annoyed.

He chuckled.

"Oh, it may be useful to convince Aloysius Birrell when he wants to drag you off. Incidentally, proving that you *can't* have done it may help to show how someone else *can*."

"Good," I said. This was more promising.

"There are two fatal objections to being a Civil Servant," Finbow said, settling himself for a demonstration. "The first is that one acquires the habit of putting things down on paper. The second is that one always has the paper to put the things down on." He brought out some folded sheets of paper from an inside pocket. "I propose to put a great many things on paper at once."

I moved my chair close to his, in order that I could see what he wrote. In a small neat hand he wrote down a list of the party, and said: "It will be convenient if I call them by their Christian names:—

"1. Dr. Roger Mills.   Harley Street specialist.
    Aged 35.
"2. Dr. William Garnett.   Doing medical research on
    Aged 26   Roger's special branch.
"3. Christopher Tarrant.   About to take up administra-
    Aged 29.   tive job in Malaya.
"4. Philip Wade.   Adorns the world.
    Aged 25.
"5. Avice Loring.   Engaged to Christopher;
    Aged 23.   Roger's cousin.
"6. Tonia Gilmour.   Engaged to Philip. Stranger
    Aged 24 (?).   to party.
"7. Ian Capel.   Retired.
    Aged 63.

"That will help me to memorise everything," Finbow said. "Now I'm going to put down some facts." He wrote:

"(a) Roger was killed on September 8, 1931. He was unquestionably murdered by one of his own yachting party."

"William was absolutely right about that, of course," said Finbow, looking up.

71

"(*b*) The body was found at the tiller at 9.25 a.m. approximately."

"The other evidence all supports you on that," Finbow commented. "Philip was putting his watch on when Avice called him, according to Birrell's notes. It was 9.27 then, he remembers."

"(*c*) Roger had been sailing the boat alone. The boat therefore cannot have gone round corners whilst he was dead. That is, the earliest time for his death is the time when the wherry passed the last corner upon the stretch where the discovery of the murder was made."

"This is cribbed from William," said Finbow, "though I should have thought of it myself, I think."

Then he looked steadily at the words he had written, and remarked:

"And it happens not to be true. Because whoever killed him could have stayed at the tiller, and sailed the yacht round a bend or two after Roger had been killed. It wouldn't be much good, because the time of the murder isn't very important. What *is* important, is the exact time when the tiller was tucked between Roger's arm and his body and the boat was left to steer itself."

"That must have been down a straight stretch," I said.

"Of course. The last corner before that stretch ought to give us the earliest time that the body can have been left to sail the boat. That is our irreducible fact; William was a bit careless," Finbow said. "It's a rather pedantic point, anyway. Our job is to look for that straight stretch. Let's get a map of the Broads."

In the bookshelf at the bungalow I found a map, and quickly we studied the portion of the Bure which Finbow rapidly copied on to a sheet of paper.

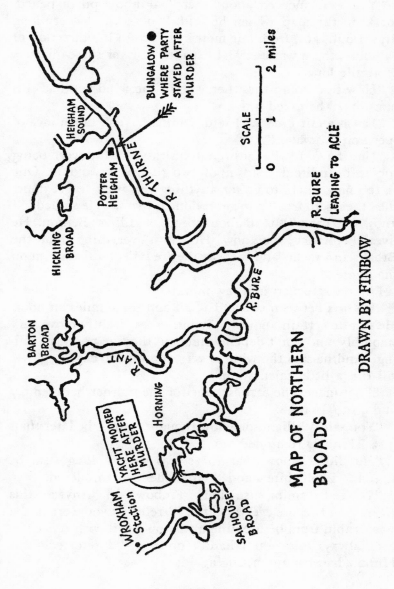

BUNGALOW WHERE PARTY STAYED AFTER MURDER

HEIGHAM SOUND

POTTER HEIGHAM

R. THURNE

HICKLING BROAD

R. BURE LEADING TO ACLE

R. BURE

BARTON BROAD

R. ANT

HORNING

YACHT MOORED HERE AFTER MURDER

WROXHAM Station

SALHOUSE BROAD

MAP OF NORTHERN BROADS

DRAWN BY FINBOW

SCALE

0   1   2 miles

"You were moored about there"—Finbow put a pencil-
mark on the map. Then he said: "So-o-o . . ."—very long
drawn out. For, from our mooring-place in the direction of
Salhouse, there was a straight stretch of river three-quarters
of a mile long.

"How fast would the wherry go in the wind you had this
morning?" he asked quickly.

"It was a fair breeze," I said. "But I haven't much idea of
speed on the water."

"Nor have I," he answered quickly. "However, being
successful in life depends upon two gifts, and two only. One
is, to know where to go for anything you want to get done;
the other is, to be able to get it done for you." He smiled. "I
know who can tell us all about speeds of sailing. Benson. He
lives in Norwich, you know. He knows everything about the
Broads and yachts and the way they're sailed. I'll get him on
the phone."

Finbow returned in a few minutes.

"He says between two-and-a-half and three miles an hour.
He's quite certain about it. Wherries apparently move very
smoothly, and don't depend much on the fine points of sailing. And he says the wind is very constant to-day."

I did a little calculation.

"That makes the earliest time for the murder between 9.7
and 9.10," I said.

"You said William somehow thought it must be later than
9.15," Finbow reminded me.

"He didn't know that there was such a long straight
stretch," I told him—and then suddenly I wondered.

"You're becoming suspicious," Finbow said. "Anyway, this
clears you; because everyone told Birrell that you were in the
small cabin from before nine until you left it with Avice."

"I always told you I hadn't done it!" I retorted. But
Finbow had begun writing again:

"(d) Time chart:

	8–50	Ian calls to Roger and hears an answer.
	8–55)	
	9–0)	Tonia and Ian enter small cabin.
	9–5)	
9–7 the earliest time possible for the murderer to have left tiller (say 9–5 at the outside limit).	9–10)	Philip and William enter cabin.
	9–12	C h r i s t o p h e r leaves cabin.
	9–15	Christopher enters cabin again.
	9–16	Avice enters cabin.
	9–18	Tonia leaves cabin.
	9–22	Philip leaves cabin.
	9–24	Avice and Ian leave cabin.
	9–25	Roger found dead.

Bewteen 9–0 and 9–5 William says he was trying to seize the bath behind Philip's berth. Heard P's voice all the time. After two or three minutes went into P's room. P. did not go back.

"That's roughly the scheme, don't you think?" Finbow asked. "It's made up of what they all told Birrell and of what you told me. It can't be accurate to the minute, but it gives the general plan."

"William put the earliest time for the murder at 9.15," I said thoughtfully. "If that were true he'd be cleared straight-away. While as it is——" I began to feel excited.

"As it it," Finbow broke in quietly, "everyone but you can be suspected at present."

"Everyone?" I said.

"Everyone," said Finbow. "The facts I've just written are reasonably certain—I'm pretty sure of (a), (b), (c) and (d). There are two other pieces of material evidence that I'm not so certain of. I'm going to set them down as questions." He wrote another sentence:

"(e) What is the significance of William's finger-marks on the tiller?"

Finbow paused and spoke:

75

"You see, it's very probable that, when Roger was shot, the tiller didn't stay in its old position. That is, the boat must have altered its course. Unless the murderer readjusted the tiller, you'd have found yourselves with your bows in the bank. Well, the boat didn't run into the bank; so I think it's pretty certain that the tiller was touched. If that's so, then *either* the murderer avoided finger-prints, and William impressed his own when he steered the boat later; *or* William made finger-prints twice."

"You think William may have done it?" I asked excitedly.

"Anyone may have done it—except you," Finbow replied calmly.

"The other queer fact I want explaining is:" and he wrote down:

"Why are the log-book and pennant missing?"

"I don't think it's just a coincidence," he said. "They must have been thrown overboard for a reason. But why? In the name of sanity, why? I could invent explanations for the disappearance of the log-book, I suppose. For instance, it might have contained some news that would direct suspicion."

"Yes," I said, "I told you, Roger said that he'd quarrelled with William over lunch yesterday."

"I wonder why none of the others mentioned the quarrel," said Finbow. "They said nothing to Birrell about it. It must have ben a very mild affair. It's possible the log-book contained something a great deal more serious than that—for someone. It doesn't seem very likely, though. A record of a friendly expedition like this is usually merely an excuse for the keeper of the log to demonstrate an execrable prose style."

"Why should the pennant be lost as well?" I asked.

"I haven't an idea. As a shot in the dark, I might suggest that it had been used to wipe off finger-prints, and then dropped into the river. I'm not very proud of my guess, however." Then he stretched his legs. "There's just one other concrete matter to be jotted down, before I begin to consider the people in the party. The concrete matter is the actual geography of the wherry itself."

He started to sketch a plan of the wherry, marking in our berths and the cabins. On page 13 is a reproduction of Finbow's drawing with its edges smoothed off.

He marked the wash-basins with a neat "W.B."

"I suppose you and Christopher used the one near the fore-hatch, William and Philip the middle one, and the two girls the one in their room," he murmured.

"Yes," I said. "That must have been true."

"Pity some of you hadn't got into the habit of a cold dip in the early morning. I never have myself, but it strengthens the character—and would have prevented at least one murder," he said, looking at his plan. Then he stared at me: "Ian, why did you say 'must have' been true? Don't you know?"

"You forget that this was the first morning I'd spent on the wherry. I hadn't time to find out the usual arrangements. The others have been on for a week now."

"It *is* true: at least they all told Aloysius Birrell that *was* where they washed," Finbow said, and laughed. "But my dear Ian, your last words make it even clearer that you couldn't have killed Roger."

"Why?" I asked.

"Simply because whoever did was extremely well acquainted with the morning routine on the wherry. Think, man—think of the risk, if you didn't know the habits of everyone!" he said.

"You'll soon be sure that I'm not a murderer," I chaffed

77

him. He laughed, and lit a cigarette. His glance was far away as he spoke:

"I just wanted to see what I could do with the facts, when I proved you were innocent. People talk about material truth and psychological truth as though, if you are interested in the one, you can't be interested in the other. Of course that's nonsense. If I had all the material facts, I shouldn't want any psychological facts. That is, if twenty-eight different and reliable witnesses had seen Roger shoot himself dead before their eyes, then I should believe it, though it's psychologically improbable that anyone like Roger would shoot himself. In exactly the same way, if I knew all the psychological facts about—say, Aloysius Birrell—and they made it quite certain that he was bound to kill Roger, then I should believe that, though it seems to me materially improbable. But the point is, one never has *all* the material facts or *all* the psychological facts. One has to do what one can with an incomplete mixture of the two."

I nodded.

Finbow smiled: "Yes, I must tell Aloysius Birrell that. He carries a notebook in which he writes down all the great thoughts on criminology. Anyway, all that I can say from the material facts so far is that any one of five people may have killed Roger. Any fool could have arrived at that. The important thing is to find some of the psychological facts."

"Such as, I suppose," I said, "why anyone should want to kill Roger."

"That will be one of the easier questions to answer, I think," he said.

"What are the difficult ones?" I asked. "Do you know already?"

"I promise you I'll tell you anything I know. Or even anything that I suspect," Finbow answered. "The only reason people preserve an air of mystery is because they have nothing else to preserve. Personally, I'm not in the least ashamed of being wrong. So far as I can see, any of the five may have killed Roger. But I'd make one guess; I don't think Philip did."

"Avice can't have murdered anyone. You can rule her out at once," I remonstrated.

"She is a very lovely girl," he said slowly. "By the way, do you know anything about Tonia?"

"Nothing," I replied.

"She's rather attractive, too. Curious to see anyone with a face as strong as that made up so exotically. A sort of cave-mannequin, in fact."

I laughed, for Finbow was hurt if his quips were not appreciated. Then I said:

"But what *are* the puzzling things to you?"

"I'll be bold, and write them down," he said.

Soon he gave me a sheet of paper, and I read with a nervous interest:

"(1) Why was there no attempt to throw the blame on to any single person?

"(2) Why did the murderer not take the offer of a con-spiracy of silence?

"(3) Why did Avice and Christopher not seek each other's company after the murder?

"(4) Why did Philip and Tonia seek each other's com-pany so demonstratively after the murder?

"(5) What emotion is William concealing?"

"There they are," he said as I read them. "And I confess they interest me a good deal more than a lot of facts which any efficient inspector from Scotland Yard would analyse in about half the time it took me."

"I notice," I said, "that you've asked at least one question about all the five. So that the questions must involve who-ever happens to be guilty."

"That," said Finbow, with a smile, "is the true art of detection."

CHAPTER SIX

William Smiles

Lunch was a difficult meal for us all. We gathered together in the small dining-room, from whose open windows we could see the river and the flat marshes green in the sunlight. But the freshness of the day only made us aware of the constraints and silences which had sprung up between us in so short a time.

We sat close together round a table barely large enough for six. Awkwardly, we refrained from any allusion to the subject which occupied all our thoughts; there was no mention of the murder, and the omission seemed more pointed than any talk could have been. Finbow chatted casually on cricket and music, but the rest of us ate hungrily and with little conversation. Despite all that had happened to us, we had immense appetites. Despite, did I say? That is a conventional stupidity. The effect of strong emotion is often to make one crave food, and probably we ate the tough roast beef ravenously because of the murder rather than despite it.

While he ate, Finbow talked smoothly on. It lessened the strain perceptibly, but there was always the unavoidable thought that this atmosphere of tense anxiety must persist and get worse and worse until it broke. It was not a pleasant lunch. The presence of Mrs. Tufts, which in normal times would have been funny, was itself a contribution to our uneasiness. We tried to smile at each other, but we were more oppressed than amused by the small fat implacable woman. She gave us food grudgingly and waited on us with a marked exasperation, which heightened to a climax when she came in with a fruit-tart and saw Philip stroking Tonia's arm. She put the tart on the table with a thump, and said very loudly:

"Young man, what do you think you're doing?"

Finbow and I both tried to calm her, but she asked again:

"Young man, what are you doing with that girl?"

Philip was taken aback. Tonia came to the rescue:

"He was stroking my arm. And I like him to. And, anyway, what does it matter to you?"

Mrs. Tufts fumed:

"Morals nowadays—they're enough to call down fire from heaven to burn us for our sins. The way girls like you carry on. You want whipping——"

Finbow got up.

"My dear Mrs. Tufts, these young people are all very, very good indeed really. Their manners are a bit different from those we had when you and I were young, that's all. Don't be too harsh——"

Mrs. Tufts stood like a small, fat basilisk.

"I shall think what I like and I shall say what I like, and as long as I give you your food and keep the house, I've got a right to my own opinion on painted women. And I shall say what I think of them as long as I live."

She flounced out of the room.

"I'm sorry," said Finbow. "We ought to push her quietly into the river, but we've got to humour her for a while. If she goes away, she might gossip."

Tonia laughed, but there was an unpleasant hysterical note which surprised me.

"It's a little hard," she said, tightening her red mouth, "to run across a police-sergeant and a housekeeper who both think that I'm worse than I look."

"She probably thinks you did the murder as well," William said quietly.

It was the first time the murder had been mentioned since we had met for lunch.

Tonia gave a twisted smile, and her voice was not steady as she replied:

"That's a rotten joke, William. I mean, one of us has done it, after all. Never mind. Let's sing," and she got up from the table and sang 'You Are My Heart's Delight' huskily.

Finbow watched her.

I spoke to William.

"Does Mrs. Tufts know about the murder?"

"Of course." he answered. "Birrell's been talking to her for half an hour."

"I've told Birrell to keep her quiet at all costs," said Christopher, "I think he will. She seems fond of him."

"Those two are friendly, are they?" Philip commented, with a forced brightness. His eyes had been anxiously following Tonia's nervous movements. "I shall regard it as my duty to arrange a match."

Tonia turned from the piano, and drew her fingers through his soft hair.

"Arranging matches, are you?" she said, but still with a curious jerkiness. "I wouldn't trust you to arrange your own marriage."

He pushed back his hair, which had fallen over his eyes.

"I'll leave that to you," he answered, smiling more happily.

The day wore on, slowly and with a brooding irritability over us all. No one could find anything to do, and yet no one could keep still for long at a time.

For most of the afternoon William read in the sitting-room, but often he would walk to the river aimlessly, and then go back to his book. Christopher lay on the sofa with a novel in his hand, several times throwing away cigarettes before they were half smoked; twice he returned to Avice, who sat miserably in her room, and tried to persuade her to take a stroll.

Twice I heard in reply Avice's low voice: "Oh, my dear, I should only make you wretched."

Philip and Tonia made a brave attempt to philander in the garden, but several times Philip left her, and came in for a cigarette and a purposeless chat. I sat on the veranda, forcing myself to a composure which I was far from feeling. Finbow sat by me for half an hour, murmured: "Don't be surprised at any of my conversations. I'm tackling this in my own way," and then went into the lounge in order to talk to William and Christopher. When he came back to the veranda, Philip, who had left Tonia on the pretext of asking me for a match, was standing beside my chair.

"Hallo," said Finbow. "Sit with us for a few minutes, won't you?"

"I'd like to," Philip answered. "It's rather . . ." but he did not finish the sentence. Tonia was lying by the bank, trailing one hand in the water; with a set face she watched Philip draw up a chair betwen me and Finbow.

"Don't worry," Finbow raised his voice in order that it should reach her. "I'll bring him to you soon. He's staying here with us so that he'll appreciate how much he'd prefer being with you."

I saw Tonia's lips move into a smile; and then she turned, and lay with her face away from us.

"Your Tonia is a fascinating young woman," said Finbow softly.

"Yes," Philip said eagerly. "I've never met anyone like her. She's got more vitality than anyone I've ever seen. I think that's why I fell in love with her as soon as I saw her." I had a trace of amusement at the thought of Philip, the incorrigibly indolent Philip, captivated by sheer 'vitality'. I told

myself that perhaps it was just the lack of any forcefulness
in himself that made him esteem it so highly in Tonia.

"If you hadn't fallen in love with her, you'd never have
deserved to kiss another girl in your life," Finbow smiled.
"When *did* you fall in love with her, by the way? Soon after
you met her?"

"As soon as I met her. It was in Paris," Philip answered,
with an excited flush on his face. "I was trying to write a
little, but the words wouldn't come. And then one night I
went to a studio party in the Rue de Vaugirard—do you
know it?"

Finbow's lip quivered.

"I know it," he said gravely. "There was a Paris, even in
my day."

Philip went on:

"I saw Tonia there, for the first time. I knew I'd fallen
at last."

"At last?" Finbow asked.

"I'm twenty-five, and I've never been in love before,"
Philip explained. "I didn't think I ever should be."

"When one gets as old as that, one does tend to give up
hope," Finbow agreed. Philip looked suspiciously at him,
but continued:

"She was dressed all in black. I couldn't keep my eyes off
her. And she seemed interested in me. In a couple of hours
we were standing outside the Luxembourg, telling each other
that we were utterly in love!"

"That," said Finbow, "was remarkably quick work."

"So we had eight or nine weeks in Paris together after
that. It was a wonderful time. We went everywhere," Philip
said.

"Did you do any writing?" Finbow asked.

"No," said Philip, "with Tonia about, I hadn't got the
energy. And I never should be any good. I've practically

given up trying." He had been carried away in his delight
at being able to tell all about Tonia, but now there crept back
the sort of careless laziness which made Philip the dilettante
he was.

Finbow murmured: "So."

Philip laughed.

"After all, what does it matter? I had two splendid months
in Paris, and then I brought Tonia back to England for this
party."

"I suppose," said Finbow, smiling, "you wanted to show
her off to your friends. Most of the joy of being in love with
a pretty woman is the envy we arouse in all our intimates."

"You're too cynical," Philip gave his sudden charming
smile. "But I *did* want the others to see her. We all know
each other so well. Naturally, I wanted Tonia to meet my
friends. I wrote to Roger asking if I could bring my fiancée
on to the wherry, and he said he'd be delighted."

"And you'd have had a perfect three weeks together . . ."
Finbow said.

"If only this hadn't happened," Philip said. "While as it
is we've got to wait for all this business to be cleared. If only
it hadn't happened! We were getting on superbly. When
we first started, I thought Tonia wouldn't enjoy it, but——"

I saw an almost imperceptible tightening of Finbow's
face. Though I did not understand, I admired the skill
with which he had conducted this casual-seeming dialogue.
He broke in,

"Why did you think that? Your friends liked her?"

"Yes," Philip said thoughtfully, "but she wasn't herself,
somehow. I suppose I oughtn't to say so now, but Roger was
rather tactless, I think. He was sometimes rather boisterous,
you know. With strangers it jarred slightly."

"I can understand that," I agreed.

"Yes," Philip continued. "Tonia didn't know him, and

she didn't like it when he made jokes about her and me. Sort of hearty jokes, you know."

"Only too well," said Finbow. "I am never amused."

"Tonia was a little upset. But she soon got used to him, and we were all very happy," Philip said, and added:

"Poor old Roger! I wish he were here." Then he saw Tonia beckoning him, and said quickly: "I must go down to her."

He ran down the terrace and dropped on the grass by Tonia's side. Finbow gave a long interested "So!"

He went on to say:

"The desire of most human beings to discuss their love affairs has only one redeeming feature. It makes it possible to collect information which otherwise we simply couldn't get. By flattering someone on the attractiveness of their lover, it is usually possible to learn all one wants to know. Particularly if one uses in addition the art of the irrelevant question, which has never received the attention it deserves."

I could not gather what knowledge he had derived from his talk with Philip, but I saw from his manner that it had a serious bearing on the case. I wondered which he suspected? Tonia? But if so, why? He said nothing more, until after five minutes he remarked:

"I'm just going to add myself to Philip and Tonia for a while."

"Isn't that rather indiscreet?" I asked. It was obvious that they wanted to be left alone.

"I'm sure it is," he smiled, and walked slowly down the fifty yards of grass between the veranda and the bank. He stretched himself on the ground near them, and soon they were all laughing together at some joke of his. My attention, however, was distracted from Finbow, for Avice had at last been enticed out of her room and was walking with Christopher along the bank. She was pallid and melancholy, and I watched her drooping gracefulness with anxiety. I saw that Christopher was looking after her with an obvious concern.

There was a loud laugh from Philip and Tonia at a remark of Finbow's He got up shortly afterwards and joined Christopher and Avice, who were standing together, looking moodily into the water. His voice drifted to me.

"I've been telling Philip and Tonia that they ought to go to the Balearic Islands for their honeymoon."

"Oh," said Christopher dejectedly.

"And what about yours?" Finbow asked—I thought a trifle tactlessly.

"We can't arrange anything yet," Avice looked at him. "until we——" and her voice broke.

"My dear," said Finbow, "don't let this business interfere with your life. It's bad enough as it is, without any more tragedies."

Christopher and Avice began to talk to him, but they spoke so quietly that I could not catch the words. He had contrived, however, to bring some shred of reassurance to Avice, and the three of them came in amicably to tea.

"Philip and I can't have you two stealing our nice Finbow," Tonia said across the table to Christopher and Avice.

"I am, of course," said Finbow smoothly, "an essential part of the house furniture of any young married couple."

"When I'm married," Philip smiled at him, "you'll be forbidden the place."

"I shall console myself by drinking tea," Finbow replied. He brought out his small canister, and made his own tea in his ceremonial way.

"Best tea in the world," he said as he took the first sip.

During tea-time, Mrs. Tufts entered noisily, put a newspaper on the table in front of me, sniffed, said: "That may interest you," and hustled out again. I read:

"MYSTERIOUS DEATH OF HARLEY STREET DOCTOR"

"Specialist Found Shot On Yacht

"TRAGEDY OF BROADS PARTY"

"At nine-thirty a.m. this morning, Doctor Roger Mills, the well-known cancer specialist, who is, of course, the nephew of Sir Arthur Mills, was discovered killed on his private wherry, *The Siren*. The cause of the death is alleged to be a bullet-wound in the chest. Among the party of the wherry there are alleged to have been Miss Avice Loring, who will be remembered for her striking costume at the Chelsea Arts Ball last year, Mr. Philip Wade, son of the Newcastle shipping magnate, and Mr. Ian Capel, a well-known clubman.

"The case is in the hands of Detective-Sergeant A. Birrell, of the Norwich City Police Force. The authorities are confident that a definite statement upon the mystery may be issued at any moment."

I handed the paper round without a word. Everyone read it silently, and it seemed that all of us were waiting for a lead as to whether we should give vent to our fears, or whether we should try to laugh it off. A flippant remark of Philip's set the tone.

"If ever I write prose instead of poetry," said Philip, "I shall try to write like that."

"I thought on the whole you did," Tonia murmured, and he pretended to throw a knife at her.

"I particularly like the 'of course' in the second line," Finbow said reflectively. "It's interesting how the language changes; 'of course', which in my young days meant 'of course', now means 'as we have found out with considerable difficulty and effort'."

"And also Ian being a well-known clubman. What *does* that mean?" asked Christopher. "Is he well known in a club or clubs, or does the general public know him well as a clubman, or what, or why?"

"Also," Finbow inquired, "I am intrigued by what Avice wore at the Chelsea Arts Ball for which she is to be remembered."

"I fancy," said Tonia, with her queer eyes narrowed, "that she'll be chiefly remembered for what she didn't wear."

"Cat," said Avice, blushing faintly.

"What's this definite statement?" William asked sharply. He had been silent through the afternoon, owing, perhaps, to a mistrust of Finbow, which I thought I could detect. "What have they found out?"

"I don't think that it's anything more than Aloysius Birrell's exuberance," answered Finbow. "I have a feeling that he's got his eye on Ian, but a present there is not enough evidence to convict that well-known clubman."

"But Ian can't have done it," William said contemptuously. "He was in the cabin when the murder——"

"Do you want to talk about murder?" Finbow interposed gently. "It's an over-rated topic of conversation."

William compressed his lips, and picked up the book which he had been reading. I glanced at the cover and saw that it was *The Universe Around Us.*

After tea, we took deck-chairs on to the terrace, and lay smoking and watching the yachts go slowly by. The breeze had lightened to the softest of airs; it was a warm night, and I was reminded of the time we had spent in Italy three years before. I remembered sitting on a terrace with the party, just as we were sitting now, except that then the terrace overlooked the blue Ionian Sea—and except that then Roger had been there, genial and noisy.

Christopher had the same thought.

"Do you remember, any of you," he said, "how we used to sit on the terrace of the villa at San Pellegrino?" Those nights when everything seemed so perfect."

"Rather," Philip answered brightly. "We used to look out and see the lights on the coast of Sicily. They were the most beautiful nights I've ever known"—with a smile—"if only Tonia had been there."

"I didn't know you then," Tonia said huskily, and repeated: "Not any of you. I was studying music in Nice, like a sweet, respectable child."

"Roger spent one or two holidays in Nice. You might have seen him," Avice said.

"Don't be a fool," Tonia replied roughly. "You don't think I knew everyone in Nice, do you?"

Philip changed the conversation:

"And where was our Finbow three years ago?"

Finbow smiled, and said:

"Drinking tea in peace in my house in Hong Kong."

We chatted perfunctorily with gaps of uneasy silence, until the sun had gone down red beyond the reeds. Then Avice said that she was feeling cold, and we moved into the dark sitting-room. Through the window the sky glowed from yellow to a luminous blue; in the room Tonia's eyes caught some of the light and shone like a cat's. No one spoke. The dark, quiet room, lit with the sunset glow, seemed to have within it undertones of gloom and treachery and death.

With relief, I heard the clattering footsteps of Mrs. Tufts. She stood in the door, looking dimly white.

"Dinner will be late," she announced hostilely.

"Oh, that doesn't matter a bit," said Christopher at once.

"It does matter," said Mrs. Tufts. "I don't want to be up all night."

"No," Finbow agreed sympathetically.

"I can't get the lamps to work," she explained.

"Can I help? I'm rather good at gadgets," William asked.

"No," said Mrs. Tufts, and went away.

There was a slight laugh after Mrs. Tufts had gone, but the prespect of waiting for an indefinite time in a dusky room did not tend to relieve our cheerlessness. We sat sombrely. The sky darkened, and the room became a mass of blurred and unknown shapes.

Christopher said suddenly:

"This time last night we were sitting in the cabin—and Roger was talking."

"And now," Avice said, very low, "Roger is dead."

Finbow struck a match to light a cigarette, and the flicker of the flame threw shadows on the faces near to him. I had a moment's picture of Christopher, brown and stern; but I forgot that in the shock of seeing William. One elbow was on the arm of his chair, and his chin was in his hands; as the light played on his face, I saw his thin upper lip drawn up to show his strong white teeth. It was unmistakably a cruel and triumphant smile. Almost as soon as the match flared, the smile had gone as though it had never been; and William looked himself, thoughtful, unmoved and strong. Finbow lit his cigarette carefully, and blew the match out.

Why Did Five Pleasant
People Hate Roger?

When we had arranged ourselves round the small table and had begun our meal, I could hardly believe what I had just seen. Opposite me was William, giving a quiet reply to some remark of Philip's. The white glow of an incandescent paraffin lamp in the middle of the table lit up his strong intellectual face, and I tried to convince myself that William always looked like this— that I had never seen his face break into a vindictive smile—that it was a trick of the matchlight and the shadowy room.

Our wait in the dark left its mark on the party. No one except myself had seen William smile—if indeed I had seen William smile—but everyone had heard Avice's "And now Roger is dead", and the effect was to destroy our convention that the murder was not to be mentioned. Whilst we were eating the roast beef (for Mrs. Tufts was an unoriginal if determined cook, and dinner was a copy of lunch with the addition of a synthetic soup) Christopher remarked:

"There's one thing that puzzles me more than anything else in this murder."

"And that is?" asked William quickly. The other conversations stopped; we were all forced to listen to opinions on the murder, even though we wished that they were never spoken. It was like the obsessive desire to bite on an aching tooth.

"The matter of the log-book," Christopher replied. "I suppose it must have disappeared for some reason: but what possible reason could anyone have?"

"What was there in it?" Finbow inquired casually.

"Just an account of each day's proceedings," said Christopher. "With a few bad jokes thrown in: Roger used to fancy himself as a humorist." His face grew grave. "Poor devil," he finished up.

"Roger must have written something which the murderer didn't want anyone to see. Something directly incriminating," William said briskly.

"That theory doesn't explain the pennant," Tonia objected. "Why should the pennant be missing as well?"

"I can't see any reason at all," William admitted.

"I wonder," Christopher suggested, "if it were thrown overboard just *because* there was no reason. Suppose there were a good reason for getting rid of the log-book, and the murderer had to throw it away—and then threw the pennant away as well, with the idea that everyone would assume there was a connection between the missing articles. I think one could explain the facts in that way."

"Ingenious," William commented.

I had listened to the argument, fascinated by the bitter irony of the situation. For one of us *knew* why the log-book and the pennant had disappeared! One of the persons at the table had a complete understanding of the whole puzzle! And yet the room was as placidly domestic as though we had merely dashed down for a week-end. I glanced quickly round. William was emphasising his approval of Christopher's point by draining a glass of beer; Christopher was eating up his last piece of beef; Avice had pushed her plate away, and was crumbling bread in her thin fingers; Philip was mixing beer and cider in order to give Tonia a shandy, and she was watching him with animation. Finbow's eyes met mine. I wondered what he had gathered from the discussion which had just ended. In the background Mrs. Tufts stood disapprovingly and impatiently, waiting to take away the meat.

During the rest of the meal the conversation veered to books.

Mrs. Tufts began to remove the cheese. Suddenly Avice shivered:

"I'm awfully cold," she said.

"Anything the matter?" Christopher asked anxiously. "You're not feeling well?"

"I'm all right," she answered. "I'm just cold. Mrs. Tufts, I wonder if Miss Gilmour and I could have a fire in our bedroom?"

"A fire?" said Mrs. Tufts indignantly. "At this time of year!"

Avice's pale troubled face set into curiously hard lines.

"I want a fire, Mrs. Tufts," she said firmly.

Mrs. Tufts took a step nearer to the table.

"You can't have one," she retorted.

Christopher stood up:

"Mrs. Tufts," he commanded, "you will light a fire for Miss Loring, at once."

"I shall not," said Mrs. Tufts. "Healthy young women oughtn't to need fires on a summer night. And she can't have one, anyway. There isn't any coal."

"Can't we get any from the village?" Christopher asked, frowning.

"No," said Mrs. Tufts. "I wanted to get a couple of bags to-day." She bustled aggressively out of the room.

"I'm sorry, darling," Christopher said to Avice. "There doesn't seem to be anything we can do."

"There must be coal somewhere in Norfolk," she answered, the corners of her mouth drooping petulantly.

"It wouldn't be easy to find it at this time of night,"

Christopher said. "And it isn't *very* cold, my dear. You'll be quite warm after you've had a drink."

"I want a fire," Avice said again. "Are you going to get me one?"

"You can't expect the man to go to Norwich and bring back some coal. Why, we haven't even got a car here! How's he going to get there?" Tonia interposed. There had been signs during the day that she and Avice were not on the best of terms, and Tonia's manner and Avice's reply began to make it obvious.

"I was talking to Christopher," Avice said. Her white cheeks had a faint bad-tempered flush. "It doesn't affect you others. Christopher, I don't often ask." Her tone was more appealing; Christopher shrugged his shoulders hopelessly, and said:

"I'd do anything, darling. But you must see how unreasonable you are."

She gave a forced smile.

"I suppose I am. It must be the worry," she murmured. "I think I'll go to bed at once, and try to get warm. Good night, everybody."

She got up from the table, and we watched her go out of the room with long graceful strides.

"I suppose she's very tired," Christopher apologised. "It's understandable after a day like this."

"We've all had a bad day," Tonia replied. "What would happen if we all behaved like temperamental ballet stars?"

Finbow put in:

"That reminds me of the remark that sergeant-majors used to make to youths who'd got dirty buttons. 'What would happen if every soldier in the British Army came on parade with his buttons as dirty as yours?' There is only one answer, but so far as I know it was never made: it is, of course: 'There

would be a number of dirty buttons in the British Army."
Tonia laughed. Finbow went on:

"As a line of argument, it's not worthy of you, Tonia."

Avice's temper got forgotten in arrangements for bridge,
but I was left uneasy. Often I had seen her sad and languid,
but never before had she shown any sign of sulkiness. I felt
a stronger apprehension.

With this mood weighing me down, I took my place at the
card-table in the sitting-room, cut with Finbow, dealt and
bid mechanically. To my relief Finbow won the bid, and I
was freed for a moment from the pretence of concentration.
On the sofa, behind Finbow's back, I could see Tonia and
Philip talking intimately, their faces near together. I brought
my eyes back to the game, and saw Finbow skilfully accom-
plishing a risky 'Four Spades'. I played the next hand badly,
but soon I lost my fears in the cards.

I have played bridge most of my life, and I think I may
say without boasting that my memory is good enough to
make me better than the average. I was not, however, up to
the standard of the table. In Hong Kong I had heard Finbow
called "the best player east of Singapore"; he could hardly
help being good, with his quick mind and the practice
gained in monotonous evenings of exile. Both William and
Christopher were also quite first-class, and I think it would
have been difficult to say which of the three was the finest
player. Their styles were an interesting contrast. William sat,
rubbing his chin, rarely saying a word, calculating chances
with a mathematical accuracy, and never departing from the
reasonable line of play. Finbow's game was a mixture of
beautifully correct bridge with a dash of poker; as he said
after one outrageous bluff: "Bridge is a poor substitute for
conversation. But I've never found the conversation that
gave me the satisfaction of getting away with a bluff like
that."

Christopher smiled:

"From the little I've heard of your conversation, I should have thought you often *did* get a rather similar satisfaction." Christopher himself had a touch of flair which I could recognise, although I was devoid of it myself.

I forgot my suspicions as long as the game lasted. I did not remind myself of our dismal wait in the twilight. I may say that, though the other three were all in form, I held good cards and won a pound.

At about half-past eleven the third rubber ended, and we all went to our rooms. I was beginning to take off my coat when Finbow stopped me.

"Not yet," he said. "I'm going to take you for a row—I want to talk."

In most circumstances I should have protested, for regular habits become a large part of one's life when one reaches my age, and going for rows at midnight has never been a custom of mine—at least, since I was twenty-three. But all my vague theories and fears returned with Finbow's words. Excitement and anxiety can triumph over age, and I said, genuinely enough:

"Splendid."

"We must wait half an hour," said Finbow softly, lighting a cigarette, "to give those young people a chance to go to sleep. You'd better read a book; I don't want to talk now."

I tried to read Maurois's *Disraeli*, which I had packed in my case when I left London, but my candle burned unsteadily, and the letters were indistinct in the yellow light— and the drama that was related there seemed remote and unimportant compared with that in which I was now an actor. My eyes strayed to Finbow's slightly equine but distinguished profile; he was sitting at his dressing-table with a sheet of paper in front of him, on which he was writing a few words. I returned to my Maurois, but with even less success.

98

At last Finbow got up quietly.

"We'll get out by the veranda," he whispered.

We padded out in our socks, opened the french windows as noiselessly as we could, and got out on to the terrace.

"You wait here," said Finbow. "I'll get the boat."

His long form disappeared through the bushes to the right of the garden. The moon was very bright, and I stood in the black shadow of the bungalow. After a moment I walked slowly to the place on the bank where Finbow could pick me up. As I moved, I heard a noise across the bushes, and saw with an unpleasant thrill, that there was a dark figure lurking in the cover.

It is not easy to be proof against nerves on a day when one of your friends has been murdered, and when you are living in the same house as the murderer. The sight of a dark figure in a moonlit garden was enough to make me uncomfortably aware of the beating of my heart. Yet I dared not say a word, for fear that my expedition with Finbow should be disclosed. I forced myself to walk slowly to the river-bank, but I had the unpleasant feeling that the dark figure was moving in the bushes, following me.

When I got to the bank, I turned and waited for whoever it might be. I was frightened; once that day I had seen a man with a bullet in his heart. The dark figure came out of the bushes and towards me, and I was ready to make some sort of a fight.

Then it came into the moonlight, and I almost laughed aloud. It was Aloysius Birrell. When he got close to me, he said:

"Where are you going, Mr. Capel?"

"For a row," I answered.

"Oh, are you?" he asked, with a challenging look.

"With Mr. Finbow," I said innocently.

Birrell's face fell.

"Oh, I suppose that's all right," he admitted unhappily.

I heard the muffled splash of Finbow's oars, and soon he drew up to the bank.

"Good evening, Sergeant Birrell," he said amiably.

"Good evening, sir," said Aloysius Birrell.

"Will you persuade Sergeant Birrell I'm not going to escape?" I asked Finbow.

"We're just going for a row," Finbow explained. "Old men like us want a bit of exercise before we go to bed."

"That's all right, sir," Birrell said. "The fact is, of course, I've got to keep an eye open on the bungalow to stop the next murder."

"The next murder?" Finbow asked, puzzled.

"I'm pretty certain this is a serial murder," Birrell replied, beginning to get excited. "The plan is to pick the party off, one by one."

"Oh, you must stop that," Finbow admitted gravely. "You'll stay about here until anything happens, I suppose."

"That's the idea," said Birrell. "I've got to find that automatic, and I've got to be on the spot if anything more is tried."

"Good luck, Sergeant," Finbow murmured, as we stepped into the dinghy. He rowed very quietly past the bungalow, and then, when we had turned up Kendal Dyke, he began to chuckle.

"That man," Finbow said, "will be the death of me."

"It seems more probable that he'll be the death of me," I said wistfully.

"Yes, it *is* splendid, Ian. You in the rôle of the murderer of a party," Finbow laughed as he rowed. "Birrell's been reading Mr. Van Dine, apparently."

"Why did you drag me out?" I asked. "You could have talked perfectly well in our room."

"The walls are very thin," he said quietly. "And I didn't

get a chance to test whether one can hear through them. So I thought I wouldn't take the risk of talking there."

He rowed with strong sweeps along the Dyke; over the bank to the left one could see miles of fields, pallid in the moonlight; here and there, the occasional light of a house. In calmer days, I should have been content to rest, and find pleasure in the intimacy of this level land; but at the moment it seemed only an irritating contrast to the jagged uncertainty of the revelations to come. I looked at Finbow, expectantly.

He smiled in reply, and continued to row vigorously against the current. I controlled my impatience, and lit a cigarette. At last we came to the clusters of reeds and channels of water at the entrance of Heigham Sound; across the broad there stretched a golden bar of moonlight, whose smoothness was only broken by the dark intrusion of the leaves of water-lilies floating in the water. In the distance, a wild bird cried.

"Well," said Finbow, resting on his oars, "there are some quaint sides to this murder of yours."

"What have you found?" I asked.

"Not a lot, I'm afraid," he said thoughtfully. "I have just added one or two questions to those I put down this afternoon. The first is—Why is Tonia as much upset as Avice?"

"She's not," I answered.

"She is, only she's got herself under a tighter hand. But look at her, Ian. When William said something about the murder at lunch-time, she almost shrieked; and then when Avice talked about Roger going to Nice, she lost her temper. You heard Philip tell me how upset she was on her first day with the party. Why's that? And what happened at Nice? Of course, it may be nothing to do with Roger at all. It may just happen that she's got some unpleasant memories of Nice —being thrown over by a man, or not having enough money to buy a lipstick. But I would be inclined to bet that there's a good deal in Miss Tonia that we haven't been told."

"Do you think Philip knows anything that we don't?" I inquired.

"I think," Finbow smiled, "that he might know even less. I said this morning that I thought Philip didn't kill Roger. I'm quite certain of that now."

"Why?" I was a little piqued. After all, I admired Finbow, but I had seen everything that he had, and I knew these people so well. "Some of your involved psychology—because he was fond of his step-aunt at the age of two, he can't have killed Roger at the age of twenty-five."

"No," said Finbow cheerfully. "On good, solid material grounds—that is, if hair is good and solid."

"You found somebody's else's hair on Roger?" I asked, with a slight shiver.

"Of course not," Finbow said. "One doesn't thoughtfully butt someone before shooting him. Just watch Tonia stroking Philip's hair."

I was lost, and could not see the connection between that no doubt charming sight and Philip's innocence; but Finbow had begun to talk again:

"It's interesting that Tonia wants to marry Philip straight away. Did you hear me telling them to go to the Balearic Islands?—As you may have guessed, I wanted to see how they reacted. She wants to marry him at once."

"And Philip?" I asked.

"So far as he wants anything, he wants to marry her. He doesn't count for much; if she wants anything, she'll get it," he said, looking intently into the water.

"Look here, Finbow, do you suspect Tonia?"

"That's not a fair question," Finbow reproved me smoothly. "I'm more honest with you than anyone else would be in a business like this— and I'm thinking aloud for your benefit. I just don't know whether I suspect Tonia or not. All I know is that she's very frightened, and that she means to marry Philip as soon as she can drag him to a register office. On the other hand, Avice doesn't want to marry Christopher just yet. That is rather curious, you know."

"Be fair, Finbow," I protested. "You draw lots of inferences because Tonia *does* want to get married. It's absurd to draw the same inferences because Avice *doesn't*. You can't have it both ways."

"I can," he said. "In fact, I'm going to. It isn't so much the wanting or not wanting to get married: it's because, in some way, both the wanting and not wanting are caused by Roger's death."

A swan moved slowly through a channel among the reeds. It added to the sinister quality of Finbow's words. Then I remembered the flare of a match, and a fleeting sight of a cruel and twisted smile.

"Finbow, did you see anything when you lit a cigarette to-night? Avice was talking about the murder in the dark," I burst out.

"Do you think it was altogether an accident that I lit a cigarette just then?" he inquired gently.

"You saw the expression on William's face, then?" I asked.

"The expression on William's face was—rather striking," he replied.

"Just as if he was gloating," I said, as the picture came to my eyes once more.

"I think he *was* gloating," Finbow said. His voice was strangely troubled. "And yet I'm not clear about it. There is something missing every time I think of William. I keep having the feeling that I've seen some positive fact which will settle William one way or the other. It isn't the finger-prints —or his grabbing the tiller—or going into his cabin before you had your conference. It's not any of those; but for the life of me I can't think what the fact is. I'm going, however, to pay a visit to Guy's to-morrow."

I felt knowing.

"To see how William's future is affected, now that this has happened?"

"To see," he said quietly, "how Doctor Roger Mills spoke of his promising young colleague, Doctor William Garnett."

"I haven't seen a smile change a man's face as much as William's did," I remarked.

"Nor have I." Finbow dropped one hand in the water, and let the boat drift with the stream. "And I feel, if I weren't extraordinarily dull, that I shouldn't have to go to Guy's."

"Yes," I said. Then I recalled an episode at tea-time. "Why did you snub him so badly when he talked about the murder at tea?"

"I'm only human," Finbow answered, smiling placidly. "And I was annoyed with him for puzzling me—when I was quite convinced that I ought to know the answer."

"Do you know the answer now?" I asked.

"No," he said, looking into my eyes. "But I shall to-morrow."

He began to row towards home. After a few strokes he let the oars rest, and we floated slowly down the Dyke. He stared at the bottom of the boat intently, and said in a voice which startled me:

"There's one other little question to which I should like an answer."

"And that is?" I said sharply. My nerves were on edge. Finbow replied:

"The question is: Why all these five young people loathed Roger like the plague?"

CHAPTER EIGHT

Lord's

When I awoke the next morning, Finbow had already left our room. I found that I had a slight headache, but it was lost in a depressing recollection of the question Finbow had asked before he had rowed back to the bungalow. Why did the five young people loathe Roger like the plague? I had pressed Finbow for his answer as we returned, but he had been unwilling to tell me anything more definite.

I got up feeling heavy in the head, and as I washed and shaved I thought round and round the question. Or, to be more honest, I did not think: the question merely recurred maddeningly, inevitably.

The rest of the party were at breakfast when I walked into the dining-room. I said "Good morning" to Mrs. Tufts, who grunted. Finbow greeted me cheerfully.

"Hallo, Ian. I was just telling these people about your eyes and that we've decided to go up to London to see an oculist."

"Yes," I said dully.

"Do they worry you much?" Avice asked sympathetically.

"A bit. I ought to have had them examined before I came down."

I wished, with an early-morning bad temper, that Finbow would give me warning before expecting me to lie.

"Where are you going?" asked William sharply.

"Oh, I'm taking him to a friend of mine. The man he usually goes to is distinguished without being competent," interposed Finbow suavely. "A state of affairs which is only tolerable in the Civil Service, where it doesn't matter. In medicine, it rather does."

William laughed loudly; I was surprised, for the remark seemed to me one of Finbow's weaker efforts. Mrs. Tufts prevented me dwelling on the point by saying:

"If you eat your breakfast, I shall be able to clear away."

After breakfast, Finbow made me hurry to catch the 9.48 from Potter. I did not want to run, for Finbow is long and lean and I am not so long and not so lean; and I felt strongly that the spectacle would appeal over-much to holiday-makers in motor-boats. We had to walk, however, inconveniently fast. On the way over the fields we met Aloysius Birrell, who smiled respectfully at Finbow, but who still looked suspiciously at me.

"He's seeing after the inquest to-day," said Finbow, when he had passed. "He's going to get the coroner to adjourn it for a week."

"Oh," I said. Walking at that pace made me dislike the process of conversation.

"I was talking to him before breakfast," Finbow explained. "He's seen the Chief Constable of the county, and they've telephoned to Scotland Yard."

I was worried.

"What will that mean?" I asked.

"Chiefly, that we must pay a visit to Scotland Yard to-day," Finbow said.

My anxieties were drowned so long as I had the physical discomfort of trotting by Finbow's side, but when we were in the train and plodding slowly through the flat country towards Stalham, they began to rise again.

"Why did you say that all those five hated Roger?" I asked uneasily.

"Don't you think it's true?" Finbow said.

"I don't know. I feel as though I were going round in

circles," I said hopelessly. "But you don't mean that those five made a plot to kill Roger—with everyone knowing?"

"My dear Ian," Finbow laughed. "You'll have to go into partnership with Aloysius Birrell. That's a splendid idea. Five people are suspected of murder. Who did it? Answer: everyone. It might happen, of course, but in this case—it didn't."

"What did you mean," I persisted, "about them all hating Roger?"

"Exactly what I said," Finbow replied.

"How do you know?" I asked.

"By looking at them," he said. "Do you think they're behaving like people who've had a close friend killed?"

I saw a gleam of hope.

"It isn't often you're wrong on people, Finbow." I felt not only relieved, but proud. "But I'm sure you're wrong this time. I didn't hate Roger. I was quite fond of him."

"Granted," said Finbow.

"Well, since he was killed, *I've* not been anything like as miserable as you might expect. I've been worried; but chiefly about Avice and the way she's taking it. And several times I've been amused and interested, just as though Roger's death had never happened. Yet he's only been dead twenty-four hours."

"It is one of life's major consolations," Finbow murmured reflectively, "the ease with which we bear other people's misfortunes. What you say is absolutely true. You're behaving quite normally about Roger's death. You're amused by the absurd Birrell and Mrs. Tufts; you're interested in my theories, just as you would be in any sort of mental problem; you're concerned about your health, and you wonder whether you'll catch cold when you go out on the marshes late at night; and you enjoy your breakfast. All exactly as though Roger was in Harley Street fleecing women patients. But my point is: what happens when you *do* think of Roger?"

I tried to be honest.

"I fancy I get a picture of him doing one of the things that he used to do. Playing bridge very noisily, for instance. I wish he were there, and I feel rather sick," I said. "Chiefly, I think, because he's not there—because an amusing person's been taken away."

"For your generation, Ian, you tell the truth remarkably well," Finbow said. "That, I think, is exactly how we all react to the death of a fairly casual friend. It's a selfish emotion. Someone who could be amusing and useful can't be amusing and useful any more. The rest of them aren't taking it at all like that."

I thought over the last day, and inquired:

"What have they said?"

"Do you think Tonia looks as though a friendly host, whom she's just met, has been killed? If there were nothing else in it, she's be vaguely sorry—and that's about all. A young woman of her sort doesn't get frantic because a man she doesn't know has been shot rather near to her. Instead of that, look at her; she's frightened. What's she frightened of? Why does she make love to Philip as though she were frightened? Why does she play the piano when the murder's talked about? I don't know why she's frightened, but I do know why she played the piano. Because she couldn't stop her eyes looking vindictive."

I had a vivid picture of those different coloured eyes. Finbow went on:

"And Avice? She's crying, but not in the right places. She's afraid, too—afraid in a queer complicated way which I can't understand yet. But you might imagine she had a kindly feeling for a man who was in love with her. A young woman treats 'em hard while they're alive, and remembers them kindly when they're dead. Avice knows that she ought to look sorry: she thinks she ought to act as though she rather liked him. So she cries, and makes a deep mournful noise at intervals. But it's wrong, Ian—it's acted."

"You can't say that!" I was horrified.

"I can," he replied gravely. "You remember when I struck that match, and we both saw William's face. Do you know whose face I really wanted to see?"

The air of the carriage seemed to have grown cold.

"No," I said.

"Avice's," said Finbow.

"But she was talking about Roger sorrowfully," I objected.

"In the dark," said Finbow. "I wanted to see how she looked while she was talking sorrowfully. She was behind me; but there was a mirror over the mantelpiece."

"How did she look?" I asked.

"As though she'd squashed a beetle with her foot. Disgusted, frightened—and rather satisfied," he answered calmly.

"That can't be true," I said.

"Avice is a very lovely girl," he said irrelevantly, as he had said it before. "She is also a goodish actress. But she's genuinely frightened all the time. I don't understand it all."

We came to North Walsham, and Finbow gazed at the woods and rolling fields.

"The only countryside worth while," he said, "is one which is completely flat. This is too damned suburban. The real fenland where we've come from I should rather like—in midwinter. Chinese rice-fields and the Trans-Siberian Railway are better still, because they go on for ever."

I was not interested in Finbow's perverted æsthetic tastes. Peevishly I demanded:

"What about the others—Christopher and Philip?"

"Philip isn't capable of very vigorous hating," Finbow smiled. "Or, I'm afraid, of very vigorous loving either. As probably Tonia will find. That young man was born for romantic love-affairs. Beginning in Paris studios, and ending as soon as he touches real life. You remember my talk with him yesterday: he's very pleasant, but he's very soft. So far as he is capable of disliking anyone, he disliked Roger, though. You remember how he read that newspaper account of the murder?"

"Yes," I said. "I was afraid some of them might be upset, but they all joked about it."

"*Who* began to joke about it?" Finbow said quietly. "Just as though it were an account of something vaguely amusing, but perhaps not very important. Philip's no more sorry about Roger's death than Mrs. Tufts is. And he was just the same when he was telling me that Tonia didn't like Roger. He practically said that he'd have been surprised if she could have liked him."

I have a rooted dislike of the impalpable. I protested:

"Finbow, those are such *little* things. You can't say they killed Roger on grounds like those."

Finbow smiled.

"Do you expect them to go about showing their teeth and champing? I've got to argue from little things. We're dealing with people, not the perpetrators of an Aloysius Birrellish crime."

"And Christopher?" I asked dully.

"Christopher, of course, has got his job and his young woman, and is very cheerful, naturally. Like a gentleman, he doesn't parade his cheerfulness. But you remember the time he mentioned San Pellegrino and Roger?" Finbow asked. "And then at dinner, when he began to wonder where the log-book went; he mentioned Roger as a humorist in a perfectly indifferent way. He did a conscientious 'Poor devil' at the end, but I'm sure that was for decency's sake. Do you remember?"

I did. Christopher's voice on both occasions had been level and matter-of-fact.

"I don't think he'd claim any great regret," Finbow continued. "But I think he carries indifference too far to be convincing. And William—Ian, even you'll admit that William wasn't very fond of Roger?"

I saw again a match flare and William's expression.

"I'll grant you that, at least," I said. "If you're right, why did they all hate Roger?"

"I'm beginning to wonder what Roger was like," Finbow answered.

At Norwich Station Finbow bought a copy of *Judith Paris,* and gave it to me.

"This seems to be the longest book within reach," he said. "I *do* hope you'll enjoy reading it."

"Why?" I asked.

"Because I want to think," he said, smiling. "I'll also get you some newspapers. We can see what they say about the murder. I suppose I ought to be able to give up thinking about the murder for a couple of hours, and read some Chinese poetry. In detective stories the best people always did something like that, I remember. They must have been nit-wits. Our thoughts don't run continuously for long—and whilst I was reading the poetry, I should come across a word that would remind me of Avice or William. And I should begin to worry at the problem again."

Between Norwich and Liverpool Street he spoke only once. Near Cambridge we saw the thin pinnacles of King's Chapel, and the frown of hard thought disappeared from his face.

He laughed softly, and said:

"It has been one of the ambitions of my life to stand that curious structure on its end."

I looked inquiring. I was at Trinity, Oxford, and I have

always admired the Chapel as the only thing in Cambridge which Oxford cannot equal. Finbow, I knew, was a Kingsman, and I expected some disclosure in which the Chapel was involved. He, however, merely muttered:

"It would look so much better," and sank into silence.

Within a quarter of an hour of arriving at Liverpool Street, we were tramping down corridors in Guy's, where Finbow expected to see a friend of his, Professor Boothby. Finbow belonged to that curious class of Englishmen who, without position, money or often any qualifications at all, move quite naturally in the most dissimilar circles. They lounge in Bloomsbury, never having any tendency to write 'belles lettres'; they dine with scientists or Cabinet Ministers, never having seen through a spectroscope or been seen through by an electorate; they are received equally warmly by financiers or actresses. Not belonging to this class, I was sometimes a little jealous of Finbow, who had been one of them since he was twenty; but I had several times been grateful for his wide acquaintance.

We found Boothby in a ward, sitting at a small table and shouting cheerily at an emaciated, dejected-looking man who was facing him.

"You won't die yet. Go away and don't let me see your face for a year."

I had never before been in the ward of a public hospital, and I was grimly fascinated by the long rows of beds with their grey coverlets. I was also surprised that Boothby did not moderate his cheeriness; in dismissing the emaciated man, or shouting to a young doctor, or greeting Finbow, he sounded rather like the heartier sort of cricket captain trying to put some life into the game. He was a brisk, bald little man.

"Hallo, Finbow," he shouted. "What's the matter with you?"—from a distance of two feet.

"Nothing, thank God," said Finbow. "I always feel that if you once got me in here, I should never get out again."

Boothby laughed heartily.

"Well, what do you want?" he said, with a loud and cheerful rudeness. "I'm not one of you damned *Tatler* photographers. I have to do some work."

"This," Finbow replied smoothly, "is Mr. Capel—Professor Boothby. It's serious, Boothby. We've come about the Mills murder."

Boothby's bird-like little eyes darted round, under his bushy eyebrows.

"You're mixed up in that, are you?" he asked.

"Yes," said Finbow. "Capel was on the boat when it happened."

"How can I help?" Boothby said. He gave me the impression of a noisy, rollicking efficiency.

"I want to know what you thought of Mills as a doctor," Finbow answered, very quietly.

Boothby guffawed.

"I suppose I oughtn't to speak evil of the dead—and you mustn't tell the G.M.C. what I say, or else they'll probably throw me out," he said. "He may have been a good fellow, but he was a damned bad doctor."

"How did he get his reputation?" Finbow asked.

Boothby laughed again.

"Push and luck and a sort of vigour. And two or three years ago he published some good work with young Garnett. Garnett must be rather good: even Mills couldn't spoil it all."

Finbow gave an interested "So," and said very quickly:

"Look here, who's likely to know anything about Garnett's share in that work?" He dropped his voice. "There's a chance that he may be mixed up in the murder."

Boothby whistled.

"Oh-ho! I've got two people here working on the same sort of stuff as Mills and Garnett. They're both quite able; one of them's so nervous that you won't get him to speak. The other one's very bright. His name's Parfitt. I'll send for him."

Parfitt was a thin young man with large horn-rimmed spectacles.

Boothby hailed him with a shout:

"Parfitt, Mr. Finbow here wants to know what you think of the work of Mills and Garnett."

Parfitt smiled bitterly, and said:

"Mills was a medical man and Garnett's a scientist."

"Using medical man scornfully, I imagine," said Finbow.

"As it ought to be used," Parfitt replied.

Boothby guffawed. Finbow asked suavely:

"Do you know Garnett himself?"

"I've talked to him about his work," Parfitt said. "I don't know him well."

"I suppose you're in the same line exactly?" Finbow said. "Who'll take Mills's practice on? Will it come to you in the end?"

"Not yet." Parfitt polished his thick lenses, and replied thoughtfully: "Garnett might do it, if he threw up this Foulerton that he's just got."

"So!" said Finbow. "What's the advantage, if he does?"

Parfitt became suspicious, and leapt to a conclusion.

"Was Garnett on the yacht when Mills was murdered?" he asked.

"He was," Finbow answered.

"Then I can't tell you any more," Parfitt announced.

I saw Finbow stiffen beneath his courteous manner.

"You must surely see that you've told me far too much already," he said smoothly. "And also I can find the rest of the story very easily if you don't tell me. I don't see why your conscience should put me to a certain amount of unnecessary work."

Boothby interposed.

"Don't be a melodramatic ass, Parfitt. If you young medicos knew as much about people as Finbow does, you might be some good. He's pumped you enough already to hang Garnett—and you, too, if you're not careful."

Parfitt flushed. Finbow pressed on:

"What would be the advantage of Garnett going to Harley Street?"

Parfitt replied sulkily:

"He'd make five thousand a year instead of a few hundred. And be made for life, financially. It would mean cutting down his proper scientific work. But"—he sneered—"most doctors aren't unduly sensitive about that."

"Yes," said Finbow. "One last thing: what about this collaboration of Mills and Garnett?"

"That was a low trick," Parfitt said hotly. "Garnett hadn't any money and wanted to do some research. Mills heard of him, found him a scholarship somewhere and then took half the credit for the work Garnett did. Mills didn't do a stroke of it. He was an utter fool scientifically. Noisy and opinionated, and usually what he said was either wrong or meaningless."

"They published the work together," Finbow said. "Mills and Garnett—is that usual, Boothby?"

"Some senior people publish conjointly with young men working under them," Boothby shouted. "But they reckon as a rule to do a certain amount of the work."

"Mills hadn't the mentality of a newt," Parfitt protested. "He just couldn't have done any of the work. And worse than that, when it was done he often used to call it 'my work'. When Garnett wasn't present at scientific meetings, Mills would talk about 'my results'—and he got away with it. God, it made me sick."

"How did he talk of Garnett, when Garnett was there?" Finbow asked.

"Rather as though Garnett were an example of what a fairly bright young man could do when in the hands of someone of real flair. If I'd been Garnett I'd have hit him."

"I wonder if you would," Finbow murmured softly. "That's everything, thank you very much. This has helped a lot. Good-bye. Good-bye, Boothby. I like you very much, but I hope I never get in your clutches."

When we got into a taxi and were on our way to Scotland Yard, Finbow said in a hard voice:

"The low hound."

"I expect you mean——" I put in hesitantly.

He went on, more moved than was customary with him.

"Now I'm not surprised why your young friends are pleased that Roger was killed. What a cur! Being genial and hearty, and encouraging young men and stealing their work, all in a back-slapping open-hearted good old-fashioned Dickensian way." He calmed down to his normal detached self. "Oh, well, we all have our vices. But I must say that Roger's sort of semi-unconscious dishonesty, masquerading as Santa Claus, is the vice I'd least soon indulge in myself."

"What about William?" I asked.

"I'm still worried," he confessed. "He ought to have done it, certainly. Anyway, I've got some idea of the sort of man Roger was. It ought to be easy to sort out the tangle of motives, now we've got something concrete. What a low dog he was!" he smiled as though he were looking at the world from a height, and was mildly amused by it. "A scientist once told me that there was as much petty dishonesty and mean trickery in science as in high finance. I shall soon think that he wasn't altogether wrong."

At Scotland Yard Finbow left me in the taxi, and went to talk to Detective-Inspector Allen, who was another of his odd acquaintances.

It was an hour later before he came back, and my patience was in tatters. When he told the driver to go to Lord's I was recompensed for my long wait, for I could hear from his voice that the visit had gone well.

"So!" he said as he sat down. "A good afternoon's work."

"What's happened?" I asked.

"I persuaded Allen that unless he came himself there was no point in one of their men going down to Norfolk yet. He may come down himself to-morrow or the next day to have a look at the wherry and the body. Meanwhile, they're leaving matters to Aloysius Birrell, bless his soul. And Allen's promised to put one or two inquiries through for me," he said amiably.

"Splendid." I was enthusiastic. I dreaded the cold approach of a competent official detective.

"How did you manage it?"

"By describing the entire case. It's obvious they can't act at once," Finbow replied.

"What are the inquiries?"

Finbow smiled.

"The first is: whether they can discover anything in Nice about Miss Tonia Gilmour's music lessons and Roger's holidays. I fancy they'll find a connection.

"The second is: the terms of the will under which Avice and Roger were to benefit."

I was taken with dismay and anger.

"You've put them on to Avice!" I accused him.

"My dear Ian, don't you realise they'll find it out in half an hour if I don't tell them? We're not having a game of make-believe with comic-opera policemen. Allen isn't Aloysius Birrell. On the contrary, he's a very intelligent man," he answered calmly. "The absolutely essential thing is that I get the whole matter straight before they've amassed all their facts."

"I'm sorry," I admitted. "You're right. But Avice——"

"That extremely desirable young woman is very capable of looking after herself at a pinch," said Finbow. "And there's Christopher to console her, as well as you."

I smiled; then I remembered that we were being driven to Lord's.

"Why are we going to Lord's?" I asked. "There's no match on."

"We're going to Lord's *because* there's no match on," he replied. "Since cricket became brighter, a man of taste can only go to an empty ground, and regret the past. Or else watch a second-class county match, and regret the future."

"You mean to say that you're taking me to a deserted cricket ground?" I said incredulously.

"I mean just that," he answered.

We sat at Lord's, at the corner of the ground between the tavern and the Pavilion. The wind blew over the grass; the sunshine was pale and melancholy. Opposite, the big scoreboard was blank and hopeless, as though cricket had come to an end with the score at no runs for no wickets.

"I once saw Woolley make eighty-seven on this ground," said Finbow. "After that, any innings which could ever be played is an anti-climax. There is no point in trying to repeat perfection. Cricket, having been created and evolved, has achieved its purpose, produced one lovely thing, and ought to die. So, particularly now that buffoons turn it into an inferior substitute for musical comedy, I prefer to sit on empty grounds—or to watch Bucks play Beds."

"I hope you're happy," I said bitterly, "making me sit here like a fool."

"I'm perfectly happy," he replied. "Or at least I should be

if I had some hot water to make tea. Drinking the best tea in the world on an empty cricket ground—that, I think, is the final pleasure left to man."

"I always know when your mind is really busy," I said, "because you talk more arrant nonsense than usual. Come on, Finbow; what are you thinking about William? Did he kill Roger?"

Finbow's face hardened.

"I'm still trying to remember the point that will decide for me. I *know* somehow that he didn't; but I'm damned *if* I know *why* I know. By all the rules, he ought to have done it. Motive: it's there—or at least enough to make murder plausible. Career and revenge: I wonder if they would be strong enough motives. They might, I fancy, for a cold young man like William. The material facts fit him as well as anyone else. His behaviour since the murder: that could be reconciled to the theory of him as the murderer. And the man himself: that cold, clear scientific mind is just the right sort to bring off a murder successfully. It would leave lots of facts unexplained, of course, if we assumed he'd done the murder; but there's a case against him that would take some explaining away."

He looked away towards the sight-screen, and then suddenly he swore very softly.

"So!" he said. "Now I know why I've been convinced all the time that William didn't kill Roger."

I recalled again the strong face smiling cruelly as the flame of a match caught him unawares.

"Are you sure?" I said. "It looks black against William to me. Remember when you lit that match—the smile on his face?"

Finbow replied:

"I have just remembered the smile on the dead man's face."

CHAPTER NINE

Finbow Plays Out Time

Lord's looked remote and unreal as I echoed Finbow's words dully.

"The smile on the dead man's face."

I brought back to mind—as in some dream too vivid to be true—Avice clutching at my arm, and pointing to a stream of blood and Roger's dead body.

Finbow went on:

"I was puzzled by it when I saw the body, and I tucked it away as a fact to be explained. All the time, when I was considering William, I was certain there was a good reason why he couldn't be the murderer. I'd formed a sort of mental picture of how the smile came—and William wouldn't fit into the picture. So, though I didn't know why, I couldn't believe that William did it."

"I can't forget that smile of William's," I objected.

"Wouldn't you be pleased, if you'd been William, and Roger had been killed? A man who'd behaved to you without a shred of common honesty. No doubt Roger professed all the time the sincerest interest in William's career, and curiously enough he probably convinced himself that he *was* interested in William's career. That sort of dishonesty is never completely conscious. I think we would have liked Roger more if he had been an honest rogue, chuckling to himself that he was cheating William quite cynically. As it was, I expect he battened on William thoroughly, and told himself that he was one of the most generous of men. Don't you think William might reasonably be pleased he was killed?" Finbow asked me.

Slowly I said: "Yes."

Finbow said reflectively, taking out his cigarette-case:

"Then, of course, William's no saint. He's an extremely hard, self-centred, ambitious young man who's going to get on in the world. He's emotionally under-developed in lots of ways. He's frightened of the girls, you notice: he hardly ever speaks to them. He gets no enjoyment from literature: he reads popular science. Like a good many scientists, he's still aged fifteen except in just the things that his science encourages."

"They're not all like that," I objected.

"Of course they're not," said Finbow. "Take old——" (and he mentioned a name known to everyone with a nodding acquaintance with modern atomic physics). "He's a large-sized man in quite a number of ways. But he's an exception; and William isn't an exception."

"But isn't he?" I asked. "He's a bit cold, if you like, but he's perfectly competent in all the normal things. The people you mean surely don't exist as soon as they get outside their laboratories. William, though, enjoys games and yachting——"

"My dear Ian," Finbow broke in, "when I say a man's one-sided, you mustn't think I've got the same idea as the comic papers—absent-minded scientists who forget about their meals, and that sort of rubbish. Actually, an experimental scientist like William is pretty well bound to be thoroughly competent at sailing yachts and mending cars. I mean psychologically one-sided: I mean he's at home with *things,* at home with anything where he can use his scientific mind—but very frightened of emotions and people, utterly lost in all the sides of life which seem worth while to most of us. He can run a society, because that's really an absolutely inhuman pastime, although most people don't realise it; but he could never run a love affair. Now do you see what I mean?"

I admitted to myself that it was possible to reconcile William taking control of the party after the murder, with William boyishly bashful and inept when left alone with Avice. The first would be solved in the same way as a scientific problem; while Avice was outside his world of order and design. Slowly, I nodded.

"His mind's very highly trained for his job: and he believes passionately and selfishly in his mind and himself," Finbow went on. "A man like that, with all his emotional energy and mental energy forced into one channel, is the man who does the effective things in the world. And he's also just the man to be very genuinely pleased when chance makes it certain that he's going to get a great deal more opportunity and recognition. It's not surprising, when I strike a match in the dark"—Finbow lit a cigarette as though in memory of the other occasion—"that we find he's gloating over a man who's hurt him, and gloating over a future that's going to be bright."

"I don't think I like William, if your picture's true," I said. Finbow smiled gently and replied:

"People like William may not be as pleasant to live with as kindly old dodderers like you and me, Ian, but they're a devil of a lot more use in the world."

"I suppose you *are* right about him." I was compelled to admit reluctantly that Finbow's statements were fair.

"Of course I'm right," Finbow said in a detached way. "Everything he's done since the murder shows the kind of man he is. He took control after the murder because he was ten times more efficient than anyone on board: he made some intelligent points about the murder because he's got a good analytical mind: he resents my being here because he's a self-centred young man who likes to be appealed to as a sort of intellectual authority: and he smiles in the dark because he very naturally hated Roger more than any human being. They're exactly the actions that William was bound to perform."

"What about the curious points you mentioned last night —how he came on deck with a pair of trousers on, and went into his cabin on the way down?" I asked.

Finbow answered: "It's rather involved. But it's not a serious difficulty. I'll explain it over a cup of tea."

I seized on a fact which had struck me as being significant.

"But why did he suggest that the murder must have been later than nine-fifteen, if he didn't want to clear himself?"

"My dear Ian," Finbow smiled, "when he was discussing the murder, he did it just as he would a scientific problem. It seemed improbable to him that the river ran straight for more than a quarter of a mile, and he worked on that assumption. By a freak, it just happened that this was the only straight stretch for miles. William doesn't know the river: if we hadn't looked at a map, we should have timed the murder between nine-fifteen and nine-twenty-five."

"Then," I said reflectively, "the murderer must have picked that part of the river rather carefully, so that there should be plenty of time for everyone to have done it."

"So!" Finbow murmured. "I should like to know *all* the reasons why that bit of river was chosen. Still, there's William cleared out of the way: you're satisfied, I hope?"

"You haven't told me yet why Roger's smile shows that William can't have killed him," I said. I was convinced that Finbow's sketch of William's actions was the correct one, but a definite proof of his innocence utterly escaped me.

"The most interesting feature of the body itself," Finbow replied, stretching a long leg on the bench and gazing over the ground, "was, of course, that curious smile. It wasn't a contortion or a grimace or a nervous grin: it was a smile of friendly amusement. It seemed a bit difficult to account for. Most people object to being shot. But the explanation is really very easy. Ian, if ever you're going to commit a murder, choose one of your friends. It makes the technique of the deed so much more simple."

The smooth words sounded as bleak as Lord's, bare and deserted in the melancholy sunshine.

Finbow continued:

"One very easy way is to go up to a friend, and prod him with an automatic in fun. He smiles; it's like boys pretending to kill each other. While he's smiling, you shoot him."

"You think that's how it happened?" I asked.

"Very much like that," Finbow continued. "That's why it can't have been William. Imagine Roger saw William pressing a gun against him. He knew perfectly well William loathed him; and then if he saw William's face—do you think Roger would have smiled pleasantly?"

I thought of William's face, strong and hard as though it had been cut out of metal.

Finbow added:

"I fancy the murder was done like this: someone whom Roger thought was fond of him sauntered down into the well, holding an automatic and joking about it. I think the joke was probably something which Roger had written in the log-book. And 'whoever it was' read out one of Roger's hearty jokes, and playfully threatened him with the gun. Roger laughed—you say Roger always laughed at the slightest provocation. Then—whoever it was—said cheerfully: 'I'll shoot you, Roger!' And I expect Roger laughed again. Then—whoever it was—asked: 'If I were going to shoot you through the heart, Roger, where should I put the gun?'—Whoever it was—wasn't a doctor, of course, and didn't know exactly where the heart was. And Roger smiled and put the muzzle over his own heart, just as though this were an early morning joke. Then—whoever it was—shot him and threw the automatic and the log-book overboard. In your murder, Ian, take care your friend's a doctor. It helps a lot. He shows you where to shoot."

"William, being a doctor, would have known: and Roger wouldn't have helped him to place the revolver," I said thoughtfully.

"And wouldn't have smiled during the process," Finbow said "It wouldn't be anything like such a good joke unless— whoever it was—pretended not to have much idea where the heart was. But the main point is that Roger couldn't possibly have smiled, if William was standing near him with a gun. William is just the last man he would have laughed at, in the circumstances."

We got up, and began to walk out. I had an unpleasant emptiness when I turned back and saw the deserted ground, forlorn and cold. I knew that I should not be able to forget the words which I had heard there, nor to forget Finbow's image of a murder under the guise of a friendly joke. I do not think that I shall ever go to Lord's again.

Finbow took me to his flat in Portland Place, and after the desolate chill of Lord's I was glad to relax in a warm room, where the firelight intermittently reddened the dark walls. I sank into a deep arm-chair, sipped Finbow's best tea, and appreciated the effortless taste which showed in all his possessions. I said:

"Finbow, I've never seen anyone live more tastefully than you."

He said:

"Living tastefully is the consolation one gets for not living at all," and, though he smiled, I think that he was in earnest. But he never talked much of himself, and he continued:

"Well, Ian, I'm not getting on with your murder as fast

as I ought. I know now that William and Philip didn't do it;
but I haven't much idea who did."

The words renewed my fears. I could not help but remember that the elimination of possibilities would go on,
until only one was left. And I dreaded facing the time when
Finbow had got to the final stage. More to take my mind
away from this anxiety than because I was particularly
interested, I said:

"You still haven't told me why Philip couldn't have done
the murder."

He smiled:

"Oh, you ought to have seen that. It's really very simple."

"No doubt," I said. "But I'm an even simpler man."

"If you look at the time-table, you'll find Philip went out
just before you and Avice, and couldn't possibly have done
the murder then: that is, about nine twenty-four. If he did
the murder at all, he must have done it before he came into
the cabin for the first time. You described very carefully how
he came in, how he put his arms round Tonia . . . and that
his hair was nice and smooth. Now if you notice his hair,
you'll see it falls about whenever it is touched. I told you to
watch Tonia stroking it—it's ruffled in a second. It's so light
and soft that he always brushes it when he gets out of bed,
before he washes, because otherwise it's all over the place.
Well, if he'd been on deck shooting Roger, with a decent
breeze blowing, do you think it would have been nice and
smooth when he came back?"

I tried to think of a flaw in the argument.

"He might have gone back to his cabin, after he'd done
the murder."

"We know perfectly well that he didn't. William had been
trying to shift him in order to use the bath between nine and
nine-five, and he heard Philip's voice all the time. He
actually went into the room about two minutes after Philip

had gone, and Philip didn't come back. So William went across to his own cabin, and Philip was there. It leaves two minutes at the most unaccounted for."

"Long enough," I said, "to shoot a man."

"But not long enough," said Finbow, "to shoot a man, and to get very soft, fine hair into perfect trim without a mirror or a brush. He couldn't possibly have done it without a brush."

"I'm afraid you're right," I admitted.

"Afraid?" said Finbow. "Would you like Philip to be guilty? He's rather ineffectual, but he's a very charming young man."

"Of course I shouldn't like him to be guilty. I shouldn't *like* any of them to be guilty. But unfortunately it's got to be one of them." I imagine that Finbow saw the anxiety which I could not put into words. He knew me intimately, and I fancy that he was aware of the prayer which was beginning to form itself in my mind—"Anyone except Avice! Anyone, but not Avice!" He answered my unfinished thought:

"And, however much it hurts, you'd rather it was Philip than one or two of the others." Then he changed the subject: "You weren't convinced about the finger-prints on the tiller, were you, Ian?"

Glad to be discussing something concrete, I said:

"I still think it's strange that there should be only William's."

Finbow replied: "The significant point is that Roger's finger-prints weren't there. That can only mean one thing; that the tiller must have been rubbed clean after Roger had last touched the tiller. Unless the murderer was an ass, he'd remove his own finger-prints as well."

I nodded slowly.

"You see, Ian," Finbow continued, "this removes the idea

of William dashing up to get hold of the tiller as soon as you called, in order to leave his finger-prints quite naturally. If *that* were true; if William had deliberately left prints so that he could explain them as being caused by himself steering *after* the murder: then Roger's would have to appear as well. Actually the tiller must have had *all* its marks removed before the murderer went below; then William made his finger-prints in a perfectly normal way."

It was an obvious deduction. I said:

"Yes, that's clear enough. Oughtn't you to have seen that argument before?"

"I ought, as a matter of fact," he said reflectively. "But I think one can be forgiven for missing an odd detail in a complicated case like this. And, of course, it isn't important; all one can say is, that there was nothing suspicious in William dashing up as soon as you called him and taking control of the tiller. It was quite in character, as I said before; and there is no justification for thinking of an ulterior motive."

"I agree entirely," I said, "but why did he go into his own cabin, while the rest of us went straight into the large cabin?"

"He went," said Finbow with a lurking smile, "for a very good reason."

"And that was?" I asked quickly.

"To put on a shirt," he answered.

"Was that all?" I said.

"Quite all," said Finbow. "He came on deck without a shirt, and he wanted to put one on before he sat in the cabin. For some time I wondered why he came on deck without a shirt; it looked rather as though he had done it deliberately, so as to have an excuse for going into his cabin again on the way down. It sounded suspicious: the unfortunate defect is, that there's nothing he could conceivably want to do in his cabin—except put on a shirt. He couldn't wash, because there's no wash-basin; he couldn't have hidden anything, or else Birrell would have found it; and so I dismissed the theory. It's a pity to have invented a clever device for some-one, and then to find that it never happened; but I'm afraid the truth is, that William ran up on deck without a shirt just because he happened not to be wearing one when you shouted; and that he went into his cabin for the prosaic reason of putting on his shirt."

I laughed, but Finbow continued, smiling faintly:

"That's all quite easy. There is, however, one problem left, which I didn't solve until recently. And that is: why ever was William not wearing a shirt when he heard you shout?"

"I'm not to take that problem very seriously?" I said.

"You ought to," said Finbow. "If I hadn't been able to find an explanation, I should have thought there *must* be something behind it. I expect you'll think the explanation far-fetched—but it's the only one which seems to make sense."

"This is nonsense, Finbow," I protested. "Just nonsense. Surely a man can have his shirt off without your going into a tangle of complicated reasons. After all, one does take one's shirt off, you know."

"One does," Finbow replied suavely. "One also puts it on. And the odd thing is that William had not put his shirt on. Think of the circumstances. He came back to the cabin, when you were all listening to the wireless; he'd washed, he was in pyjamas, all he had to do was to put his clothes on. It is odd that at any stage of the process of dressing he should be wearing trousers only."

I thought a little. I tried to reconstruct what I had done in the morning on the yacht. I had gone into my own cabin after washing, wearing pyjamas, just as William had done. I could not remember the details of how I had got into my clothes, but it seemed probable, when I thought the matter over, that I had taken off my pyjama jacket, put on my shirt and so on. I began to see that Finbow's argument might not be utterly meaningless. I asked:

"It is a bit odd perhaps. But people dress in all sorts of ways. What's your reason for it, anyway?"

"The reason is," and Finbow gave a pleased smile, "that William was educated at a Birmingham secondary school."

"Absurd," I exclaimed.

"You told me so yourself," he replied blandly.

"It's true that he was at a secondary school," I said with irritation. "And I think it was in Birmingham. But what has that to do with it?"

"Everything," said Finbow. He lay back in his chair and tapped the end of a cigarette with a long finger. "Ian, you've heard some of your stupid friends talk of a man's not being a 'gentleman'. If they didn't know his past history, how would they decide?"

"Purely by externals," I said. Finbow pounced on the absurdity at once. "As the entire idea of 'gentlemanliness' is one of externals, that's hardly a profound remark," he said. "The whole point is, which externals?"

"Accent, perhaps," I suggested. "Manners possibly—all that sort of thing."

"Too indefinite," he answered. "Usually those tests would keep out men who weren't gentlemen; but they'd often let through people whom your stupid friends would exclude if they knew their history. Accent, for instance: anyone with a decent ear can acquire standard English just as he can learn a foreign language. Even if he starts from Lancashire, he can learn to speak the civilised tongue. And be quite indistinguishable from you or Philip. With very little effort, he can achieve English which will pass anywhere; he probably never could manage the curious bleat of the minor public schools, but that is a special gift of Providence, like sword-swallowing—which in fact it closely resembles."

I share Finbow's dislike for young men who make a twittering noise in the roofs of their mouths, and we chuckled together. Finbow went on:

"No, accent's no good as a test. Nor are manners. I've met at least two gigolos from remote parts of the provinces who would outshine any Wykehamist I've ever seen. I'd defy anybody to tell them from young men just going into the Diplomatic Service. No, Ian, your stupid friends wouldn't be able to decide on those externals."

"How would they?" I asked.

"They wouldn't," said Finbow. "They're always liable to treat a man as one of themselves, on the evidence of all these tests of 'gentlemanliness'; then they find out that he came from Nuneaton, and say to each other in Old Berkleyan tones that they really knew all along that he wasn't 'quite a gentleman'."

"I daresay you're right," I said. "But where's the connection between gentlemen and William's shirt?"

"It's simply this," Finbow smiled. "Your stupid friends aren't capable of it, but with a little ingenuity we *could* invent tests which discriminate between the sheep and the goats. The sheep being Old Berkleyans and their kind—and the goats, all the rest of this democratic state of ours."

I ought perhaps to mention that Finbow always professed an amused detachment upon English institutions. He had the sort of political and social agnosticism which I have found in several Civil Servants. Once he defined his attitude in a phrase: "Old-established English traditions—there aren't any such things! They're usually extremely new, they're rarely English, and as for traditions—we always change them whenever there's a selfish end to be pursued. The only thing than can be said for them is that they're unutterably comic."

"Let me show you," he went on, "one or two real differences between sheep and goats. Any difference, of course,
must depend on habits which they form in early life. That's
clear. One of them is the habit of taking exercise more as a
religious rite than anything else. If you find anyone who
does that, you can be certain he's a sheep. Anyone who takes
exercise regularly and proudly and talks of it as though it
were a moral duty, he's sure to be a sheep: simply because
he's been brought up to look upon exercise as a moral duty
through most of his childhood. There's absolutely nothing
like that in the goats; if they take exercise, it's because they
want to, not because they ought to, and they don't feel con-
science-stricken if they don't play a game for a month."

"In that case, the goats, as you call them, ought to be a lot
more unhealthy than the sheep," I suggested. I confessed to
myself that, ever since I left school, I had tried to play at
least one game of squash each day. Finbow smiled:

"The relation between exercise and health is more a pious
hope than an actual fact. Anyway, exercise is one difference
between sheep and goats. There are several more; the one
which concerns William is the difference betwen the ways in
which crowds of sheep and goats undress. You see, sheep live
together for a great part of their childhood; and half owing
to the force of public opinion and half owing to the actions
of schoolmasters (who in their humorous way think it assists
morality), they get used to taking off all their clothes in each
other's presence. That is a fact—for instance, neither of us at
school would have thought of putting on a bathing-costume
when we went for a swim."

I could not see where the argument led, but I assented.

"Well, that isn't so with the goats. They live at home, and
physical things are much more private. They do *not* get into
the habit of removing all their clothes. I went to Benson's
secondary school when I was in England last, and I was in

the dressing-room when the football team was changing. It was rather like watching film actresses; those boys showed a complicated ingenuity in never being completely dressed, and never being completely undressed. There is an enormous difference between the sheep and the goats in this way, Ian: it's the difference between people who've lived together in crowds and people who try to hide their private lives."

"Oh," I said doubtfully, "but you're surely disproving your own case? William must have taken his pyjamas off before he got his trousers on."

"Yes," said Finbow, "the curious thing about William is, that he reached a state of nakedness without any necessity for it at all."

"Well," I said triumphantly. "All your theories are wrong. According to your views on sheep and goats, he ought to have done just the reverse."

Finbow sat on the corner of his chair and smiled complacently.

"I'm being much more subtle than that," he said. "Remember the sort of man he is: he's making his way in the world and he's very intelligent. He's certainly very conscious of the differences between the way he used to live and the way he's expected to live now. He's bound to be conscious of it; all clever men are, and most of them try to conform to their new surroundings. William has observed all these differences more closely than I have; and he tries to behave in a way that won't distinguish him from the people round him. Usually he does it very well; but sometimes he conforms a bit too much. He's overcome his habit of not undressing in public to the point of always undressing in public. So there you have the explanation of William's trousers," he said with an amiable smile, "an ambitious young man trying to hide his social origins."

I was indignant. Often I have seen Finbow's fantastic

reasoning prove right even when it seemed to challenge my common sense; and most of his deductions about the murder of Roger and the motives involved afterwards proved to be correct. But I have never accepted the preposterous twists of his remarks on William's trousers. I prefer to think, and I am sure I am right, that it was merely an accident that William happened to dress in that way. Finbow's theory seemed, when I heard it, to be an example of a clever man carried away by his own ingenuity; and it still seems so.

"This is ridiculous," I objected strenuously. "I've never heard you as absurd as this before."

"I have, however, whiled away half an hour to my own very great pleasure," Finbow replied. "I enjoy conversation so much more when no one else says anything at all. And I've also been playing out time. I've contrived to keep you from fretting about the murder, in the only sensible way. If I'd talked on anything further removed from your worries, you'd have been wondering all the time what dark speculations I was hiding from you." He looked at me whimsically. "Wouldn't you now?"

I admitted that I might have. Then I asked:

"But how did you know that I was worrying?"

"My dear Ian," he replied, "you've got an excellent taste in neck-ties, but you're an extremely poor actor. And when I saw your face become miserable-looking after I mentioned that William and Philip are cleared, I think I'm justified in assuming that you're worried about the murder. Or perhaps you think the chain of reasoning too fantastic?" he asked.

We went to my club for dinner, and Finbow insisted on a leisurely and protracted meal. He explained over the soup:

"It's most important that our friends shouldn't have any idea that I'm trying to find out who did the murder. Some of them may suspect: but I flatter myself that I do give a tolerably good imitation of a friend of yours who has just dropped in to hold your hand at a critical moment. If we go rushing back to Norfolk as though I were anxious not to miss anything that's done or said, there'll be a lot more suspicions in the air. And so, though I *don't* want to miss anything, we've got to stay here, like two elderly gentlemen enjoying a night in town."

I was anxious to get back to the party, but I could see the necessity for averting any tendency to guess at Finbow's activities. He continued:

"I don't mind much when my death happens, but I have a curious fastidiousness as to the manner. And it would be too absurd to be killed in a bungalow on the Broads, and be found by Aloysius Birrell and Mrs. Tufts. Even if *you* were killed, Ian, it wouldn't help a great deal: I should have a little more data, but it would probably only confuse matters. So, on the whole, I can't see any strong argument for your being murdered." He dropped his banter suddenly: "Remember this: whoever killed Roger was very clever and very desperate. Another death would only be another incident to 'whoever it was'."

At midnight Finbow was driving me in his car through the northern suburbs. Soon we left houses behind us, and I settled down for the journey to Norwich. Our headlights lit up the straight flat road for a long way in front, and I got that illusion of speed and comfortable detachment which is for me the great charm of driving at night. Finbow destroyed my moment of content. He remarked:

"By this time to-morrow, I ought to know who did the murder."

"What are you going to do?" I asked anxiously.

"Just get a complete picture of all those young people. That's not very difficult. I've done it for William; I really do think I understand him. And Philip; I'm certain I could predict most of the things he's likely to do and say. We've ruled them out. The next thing for me is to get the other three clear in my mind. When I've done that, I think most of the queer facts will fit in. There *are* some queer facts, by the way. I wonder why Avice wanted a fire last night. Still, we shall know soon. There's one advantage in this murder: only five people can possibly have been concerned. So, however stupid I am, I'm bound to arrive at the truth by a process of elimination. That is the beauty of working in a self-contained society. It's rather like investigating a murder committed on a desert island with six inhabitants."

By half-past two we were in Potter Heigham. We left the car in the village, and walked along the footpath to the bungalow. There was a heavy river-mist which made our overcoats damp, but which was low enough to leave the stars clear. I was on edge to be inside the bungalow again, to know that nothing had happened, to be assured that all was safe there at present.

We came to a turn in the path, saw the roof of the bungalow and then the whole building hazy in the mist. There were no lights, and it looked dark and deserted.

"They're all in bed," whispered Finbow. "Be quiet."

We walked the last few yards very softly, and I carefully unlocked the door. The little entrance-hall was opaquely dark.

"Go into the dining-room," said Finbow quietly. "There'll be a candle on the shelf."

I opened the door on the right of the hall, felt for a candle and lit it. I watched the flame until it burned steadily, and then turned round—to meet a shock which sent me cold.

Cowering in the corner of the room, her eyes watching me with fright, was Avice.

CHAPTER TEN

Ordeal by Night

"Ian," she cried helplessly, and came slowly towards me. I had an indistinct glimpse of bare feet under wide pyjamas: but my eyes were held by her strained and pathetic face. I had a sudden sick dread, and then forced myself to speak.

"We've just got back," I said inanely.

Finbow heard our low words, and entered the room. I put the candle on the table, and watched miserably as she gave him a pretence at an indifferent smile.

"Hullo," she said. "I was incredibly thirsty: so I got up to fetch a drink of water."

"So," Finbow replied suavely. "I'm afraid you must be developing a cold. Last night you were chillly: and now you're thirsty in the middle of the night. You must be careful."

Avice stared at him uneasily.

"Yes," she said, "I will."

"Good," said Finbow. "Let's move into the sitting-room: you mustn't stand here in bare feet."

I carried in the candle and stood it on the card-table. Avice wrapped a rug round her body and drew her legs up on to the sofa, throwing quick glances at Finbow and myself. Finbow sat near to her, and lit a cigarette with the deliberate casualness of an actor in a modern comedy. I brought up an armchair into the candle-light, and saw painfully how lines of utter tiredness were disfiguring Avice's face, and how completely exhausted she seemed. If there is anything to be said,

I thought, why can't it be got over quickly? Unhappily, I suggested:

"Wouldn't it be better if we all went to bed? Avice is tired, I'm sure. And we've had a long day, Finbow."

Finbow smiled amiably:

"Oh, there's no need to sleep yet. This is the time when everyone really wants to talk. Talking in the day-time is a duty: but talking at two o'clock in the morning is a necessity and a pleasure."

Avice gave a quavering laugh and said:

"You manage to perform your duty in the day-time very conscientiously, Mr. Finbow."

I heard the light, mocking remark; then I looked at her pathetically white face, and admired her courage. She was under some great strain, though what it was I did not know: she had placed herself in a suspicious situation, for even I, with all the good will in the world, could not believe her story about wanting a drink. Yet here she was, bantering with Finbow as though he had just dropped in at her flat for tea.

Finbow replied:

"If you only knew the effort that I have to make in order to utter a word——"

She said:

"I suppose you're really a very strong silent man!"

Finbow answered:

"I've felt ever since I met you that you were a sympathetic soul."

My cheeks burned dry and hot as I waited for some open reference to whatever part it was that Avice was playing. Instead I heard only this irrelevant back-chat. I saw Avice on the sofa, her slim body muffled in the rug and her mouth twisted whimsically as Finbow made a flippant reply. To my astonishment, the talk went on and on, and in trying to follow Finbow's purpose I grew more irritated and more sleepy. I recognised dully that he was talking very well, but it seemed grotesquely unsuitable that he should choose this occasion to entertain us. I knew that he had some reason, but still I resented his smooth voice as it continued its well-modulated disquisition on the drama. Somehow he had led the conversation from our journey to London to plays in general. Avice had just admitted that, despite herself, she could not help enjoying various sorts of sentimental plays.

Finbow smiled:

"One of the tragedies of life is that one usually likes precisely those things which one despises oneself for liking. It's the same in love; more often than not, you're quite sure that the person you're in love with is stupid or dull or worthless or all of them at once, but—one is in love just the same. All dramatic criticism is a battle between the things your emotions approve of and the things your cultivated tastes know to be ridiculous. Usually the emotions win—not only in the low-brows but the æsthetes too. I'm afraid I'm heretic enough to suggest that it's just as unworthy to be carried away by *Hamlet* as it is by *Peter Pan*. In fact, they do seem to me to be rather similar."

I hoped he would not expand the reason for his opinion. I had heard him argue it out in Hong Kong, and I remembered the complicated path by which he arrived at his literary judgments.

I was too sleepy to challenge him; and I still could not see what he was leading up to; Avice gave a little "Oh!" of protest. Finbow went on:

"But we're all the same. We're all as bad as one another. During the last twenty years, I have watched plays everywhere when I've had nothing better to do. I'm quite certain of the plays I admire. I'm sure that there isn't a better play in the world than *The Cherry Orchard*. But do you know the play I have the most vivid memories of? *La Dame aux Camélias*. It's one of the worst plays ever written, of course. And yet I was affected by it more than anything else I've ever seen. I saw Duse as Marguerite. In Rome it was, a long time ago. I don't even think she was a great actress—at least she may have been great in her style—but I'm certain that the style's all wrong. But I shall never enjoy anything like that again. I had taken someone I was in love with—that helped, of course."

I saw Avice's drooping eyelids lift. The last words had attracted her attention. She said quietly:

"I should think that would alter everything."

"Yes," said Finbow; "in love you enjoy a good play because it's good, and a bad play because it's bad."

"What do you mean?" she asked. Her great eyes were now gazing at him. "I suppose you mean that it's fun to go anywhere, or to anything, when you're in love. You can talk about it together, and make fun of it if you want to, if it's bad. Oh, I wish it had happened to me. Men have taken me to shows since I was seventeen, but there's never been anyone who made me enjoy them more. If I were in love I should want a man to take me into the gods sometimes, and we'd enjoy it more than the stalls."

"I doubt it," said Finbow; "I doubt it very much."

She sat up and went on excitedly:

"And then I should have wanted to have a box at the silliest show in town—and oh! it would be something to live for instead of going on as I have done. Never having a man to tell what I *really* felt. Never having anyone who really interested me. Roger used to take me to plays. I'd far rather never have gone at all."

"Being at a play with someone who doesn't appreciate it can be irritating," Finbow sympathised.

"Irritating! It was loathsome." Her dark hair had fallen over her forehead, and she was leaning forward. "Men don't understand how boring life can be. I used to long and long for something to happen. I can't do anything—I've got no training. I'm just as badly off as a Victorian young lady, except that I do know a bit more. All that can possibly happen in my life is a love-affair. It's the one interesting thing I can hope for. And it's never happened"—her voice became high-pitched—"and I don't think it ever will. Christopher's the best of them, and I like him a lot, and I'm praying that I shall fall in love with him one day——"

"It's not an easy thing to do to order," said Finbow. Avice started to speak again, but suddenly a voice came from behind our backs.

"I won't stand this," said Mrs. Tufts.

For a moment I noticed the shadow of a scowl on Finbow's placid face; but it passed at once and he turned to her:

"Won't you sit down, Mrs. Tufts?" he said.

"I can't stand this, I shan't stand this, and I won't stand this," said Mrs. Tufts. She was wearing a black overcoat over a night-gown, which half covered a pair of red-flannel slippers; her hair was screwed into a number of curling-pins, and added considerably to the formidableness of her expression. "I won't stand this. Being woken up in the middle of the night, and finding a young woman in a room with two men old enough to be her father. It's disgraceful. I'm ashamed of *you*, Mr. Finbow, I didn't think you were capable of it. As for you"—she fixed me with a fierce glance—"it's just the sort of thing I expected from you as soon as I set eyes on you." Her words got faster and faster. "You've lost all notion of right and wrong, all the lot of you. Old men like you—calling yourselves gentlemen, I suppose—and young women like this—I expect *she* calls herself a lady—

carrying on in a way that the brute beasts wouldn't dare to do. I say that gentlemen are only gentlemen when they act like gentlemen."

She paused for breath. Finbow interposed.

"Don't you think it would be better if you went back to bed, Mrs. Tufts?"

She resumed. Apparently she had just seen that Avice had only pyjamas on underneath her rug.

"You dare to sit here with those disgraceful clothes on? Things no self-respecting woman would wear in her bed without being ashamed of herself. You dare to show yourself like that, in front of men like this"—again she pointed to me: I seemed to have assumed the proportions of a symbol of sin, for which I can only disclaim my qualifications—"with trousers on your legs and no stockings on your feet." Mrs. Tufts was shaking with anger. "I'll fetch you a dressing-gown and slippers from your room, young woman, and I shall wait here until you've put them on, so that you can walk decently to your room and go to bed. And then I shall stay until there's respectability in this house."

"You can't go into our room. You'll disturb Miss Gilmour," said Avice, who was biting her lip with nervousness or amusement, I could not be sure which. But as most of us are more affected by abuse than we like to think, I imagined that it was through nervousness.

"If I disturb every man and woman in the house, you're going to wear a dressing-gown before you walk in front of these men," said Mrs. Tufts, and bustled in her determined way to the door of Avice's room. Finbow remarked with a chuckle:

"It's curious how Mrs. Tufts's conversational style seems to be moulded on the Book of Common Prayer. A work which has been responsible for a great deal."

A shout from Mrs. Tufts broke into his sentence:

"Where's that other young woman? What is going on in this house?"

Finbow and I ran to the door and looked in. Mrs. Tufts had lit one of the candles on the dressing-table and was standing speechless for a moment, looking at two empty dishevelled beds. Avice followed us in, slipped on her dressing-gown and slippers, and said:

"She's not here."

"I want to know," said Mrs. Tufts, recovering her powers of speech, "what devilry is going on in this house to-night. Has that red-haired young woman escaped—or is she doing something worse than that?" She thrust out her under lip and stood, small and fat, looking up accusingly into Finbow's face.

"Well," Avice commented quietly, "she can't have escaped very far. She didn't dress. Her clothes are here."

"I'll find her if she's in the house," grunted Mrs. Tufts. "And if she's not she'll be locked out all night. There are two ways in, and I'll see they're both shut."

She fastened the french windows of the lounge, and bolted the door in the hall. Then she said:

"She's not in the kitchen; I thought the noise came from there when your goings-on woke me up. I looked in, and she wasn't there. We will try the bedrooms. Mr. Finbow, knock on that young man's door."

Finbow had taken Mrs. Tufts's tirade in perfect calm. He knocked sharply on Philip's door. There was no answer. He knocked again, and then went in and struck a match. Philip's bed gaped untidily empty. "So," Finbow murmured.

Mrs. Tufts entered with a candle, and Avice and I went in after her. There was something absurdly funny about the four of us—staring stupidly at a deserted bed; Finbow, tall and carefully dressed, with a benevolent smile playing round his mouth; Mrs. Tufts in her overcoat and nightdress, breathing outraged morality; Avice graceful in her Chinese dressing-gown, white and tired, but with an amused gleam in her eyes; and myself looking to anyone but Mrs. Tufts my entirely respectable, adequately-groomed self.

"They're together, and God knows what may happen! God knows!" Mrs. Tufts burst out. "If they're not in the other room, they'll not come back into this house to-night."

I was beginning to protest, but Finbow silenced me:

"That's all right, Mrs. Tufts. Leave them outside, if they *are* outside."

We moved back into the lounge, and Finbow rapped on the door of William's and Christopher's room. After a time, there was a mumbled noise from inside, and Finbow put a head in.

"Philip and Tonia aren't in here by any chance, are they?"

"Of course they're not." William's voice was thick with sleep. "Why the devil should they be?"

"No reason at all that I can think of," said Finbow.

"What do you want them for?" William was waking up and becoming more irascible.

"I don't want them particularly," said Finbow. "Mrs. Tufts does, though."

"Tell her to drown herself," William said. "Good night."

Finbow closed the door and smiled at Mrs. Tufts, who was annoyed by William's replies. Before she had got into her stride again, Finbow said:

"That's all now, Mrs. Tufts. They must be outside, and they'll come back in the morning. I want you to promise that you'll say nothing of this when you see them."

"I won't promise," Mrs. Tufts begun.

"It'll be difficult for Sergeant Birrell if you don't," Finbow murmured.

"Oh," said Mrs. Tufts savagely, "it's against my conscience, but I will say nothing until I've seen Sergeant Birrell."

"Good," Finbow replied, "we'll all go to bed now."

In a few minutes I was watching Finbow take off his collar.

"Can we talk?" I said.

"Yes," he answered. "I tested the room before we went to London. It's the only room in the bungalow that it's safe to talk in. It's not connected with any of the others by thin walls."

"So our row last night was quite unnecessary," I grumbled.

"Quite," he chuckled. "But I didn't know then; and, anyway, it gave us both a pleasing feeling of mystery."

"Tchah," I exclaimed. He continued meditatively:

"A not unamusing night. Decidedly, a not unamusing night."

"Amusing," I said indignantly. I was longing to go to bed, but I could not rest until I learned the purpose of his conversation with Avice. "Whatever made you talk so long to Avice? You could see she was tired out."

"I talked to her just *because* I could see she was tired out," Finbow replied.

"Not a very pleasant trick," I said, "to amuse yourself by keeping her awake."

"My dear Ian," Finbow said gently, "that sort of amusement isn't in my line. I talked to Avice just now because I wanted to learn something about her—and because it was certain to be a lot easier, if she were tired when we were talking. You see, most people talk when they're tired very much as they talk when they're drunk. A point which isn't sufficiently realised, but which is useful to a man who's anxious to find out how human beings' minds *do* work. One talks fluently after a few cocktails because one's losing the conscious restraints; and the small hours act in the same way as the cocktails. Think of the confidences you've had after midnight! Think of the confidences you've given after midnight! Think how ashamed you've been the next morning, when your conscious mind is beginning to criticise again!"

Finbow went on:

"It's a little odd that the daily cycle of consciousness hasn't been realised more often. I suppose it's because most people are so unaware of their own mental processes that they never see any differences in them. The only man I've met who really makes use of the difference is a novelist I know. He always writes late at night, when his unconscious mind is getting active: and then rewrites the next morning, when the critical part of himself is busy. He gets three times as much work done, he says. He is, however, an extremely bad novelist."

My patience left me. I implored him:

"For God's sake, man, stop talking generalities and tell me *why* you were talking to Avice. And *what* you found out. Can't you see I'm aching to know? And what was she looking for when we found her? What does it all mean?"

"Sorry, Ian," Finbow said. He sat down on his bed opposite to me. "I know you're worried. But you've got to be calm for a couple of days more. I still don't know who did the murder. And I don't know why Avice was walking about when we came. I imagine, to burn something—you remember she wanted a fire last night."

I was anxious at once:

"Do you think it means——"

Finbow cut in:

"It might mean anything or nothing. Remember, there are all sorts of emotional conflicts in this little party of yours, and some of them can't have anything to do with the murder at all. Either Tonia or Avice is a possibility—but both of them can't have done it. And yet they're both behaving as though there was quite a lot to conceal. I'm trying to disentangle all these complications. *That's* why I talked to

Avice to-night. It was really rather a skilful conversation, though you didn't appreciate it. I began with the theatre, on the grounds that any young woman like Avice has had a secret desire to act at some time in her life. I led on to amorous melodrama, which I was sure would appeal to her— as it does to most of us at her age. If she'd been musical I should have talked about operas. I was aiming at creating at atmosphere of romantic love. Then an actual allusion to a love of my own—and all I had to do was to sit back and let Avice tell me the story of her life, with particular reference to all the men she's not been in love with! "

I had an unwilling and resentful admiration.

"You're a very clever man, Finbow," I said.

He smiled.

"I'm also not averse to flattery, thank you very much. Like most people who flatter a good deal, I'm susceptible to the process when practised on myself. Still, I deserve it this time. I should have heard all I wanted from Avice, if that damned Mrs. Tufts hadn't come in and spoiled it all. Which means I shall have to have another chat with Avice to-morrow. As it was, I learned a certain amount. I'm not quite convinced how much trust I can put in it. But it looks like this: she wasn't in love with Roger——"

"I knew that," I said.

"I thought it was just possible that she might have loved him and hated him at the same time. Those attractions have a knack of happening with men like Roger. But I was wrong," Finbow admitted. "What is very much more important, she's not in love with Christopher. I must think over the consequences of that. Good Lord, your pleasant yachting party had a curious assortment of personal relations —Roger in love with Avice; Avice engaged to Christopher but not in love with him; Philip and Tonia in love with one another—with some undercurrent involving Tonia, I'm pretty certain; William hating Roger. I must find out what Christopher thinks of his engagement to Avice."

"I think he's passionately fond of her," I said. "If he isn't" —I saw a possible reason for some part of the involved story— "if he isn't, he may want to marry her for her money. And Finbow, *he* may have murdered Roger so that she'll get a great deal more."

"That's ingenious, Ian," Finbow remarked. "It might even be right. But I don't know. I think we'd better go to sleep." He looked at his watch. "It's nearly half-past four."

I got into bed: then suddenly I remembered:

"Finbow," I said, "what about Philip and Tonia? We can't let them stay out all night."

"We can't," said Finbow, preparing to lie down. "And they won't."

"Why?" I asked. "Who'll open the door?"

"No one," Finbow answered; "they won't need the door opening. They happen to be in the house."

"How do you know? Did you see them?"

"No," he said. "But one would have to be quite insane to stay outside in pyjamas for an hour in the middle of this mist. And, though they're in love, they're not mad."

"Where are they then? We looked everywhere," I said peevishly.

I had an irrational, disquieting fear of Tonia and Philip lurking invisibly in the dark.

"As they're not outside, they're inside somewhere," Finbow yawned. "Ian, *do* you want me to get up and work it out? I shall have to draw plans of the bungalow, and it'll be the devil of a nuisance. I'll promise that you'll see Philip and Tonia safe at breakfast."

"We don't know what may have happened to them," I objected. "We don't want another——" and I stopped.

Finbow smiled good-naturedly.

"Damn you, I suppose I shall have to pacify you." He sat up in bed, reached for his coat, took a pencil and paper from the pocket, and began to draw. When he had finished, he gazed thoughtfully at his plan of the bungalow. I lay on my side, and watched him tap his pencil impatiently on his knee. Suddenly he laughed: "It's all right. I thought for a minute that they might have been outside after all. But of course they can't be. I take off my hat to Miss Tonia; in her way she's the cleverest of all of us."

"Where are they?" I asked.

"I think I know; but it's obvious that they don't want to be disturbed," he answered.

I could not rid myself of my anxiety.

"Better to disturb them, than to find Philip as we found Roger," I said.

"Don't be silly," said Finbow. "Tonia is quite capable of killing various men, but she's more likely to kill herself than to kill Philip. Look here, Ian; will you be convinced if I go across to Avice's room and ask her this question—did Tonia go for a swim after dinner? If the answer's Yes, then Philip and Tonia are both in the house, and you'll promise to go to sleep in peace."

The likelihood of a swim after dinner seemed so remote that I agreed he might go and ask his question. He went, taking the candle, and I was left alone.

The room was black before my eyes. I was too tired to make an attempt at answering the questions that pressed on me. What had Avice been doing? Where was Tonia? Were we to find another horror blacker than the first? Slowly my eyes became used to the darkness, and the window-space grew full of a diffused grey glow. The misty gloom added to my nervousness, and with a sudden impulse I sat up in bed, clutching at the pillow and listening.

For a moment I heard a murmur—I reassured myself that

it was Finbow talking to Avice. And then, just as I was be-
genning to relax my tension, there came a groan which tore
at my nerves in the way that a note from a violin breaks a
glass. I shuddered; and then I could not be certain that I had
heard a sound. For it had lasted so short a time that I told
myself that it might have been my own invention, made out
of the strain and the dark silence. I lay in a cold sweat.

Finbow opened the door, and I welcomed the ironical smile
which the candle-light revealed.

"Did you hear?" I asked anxiously.

"What?" he said.

"A sort of groan," I answered. "A sort of dry groan."

He smiled. "No," he said. "I didn't hear it. But I shouldn't
worry if I *had* heard it."

I did not understand the answer; but I tried to persuade
myself that I could rely on Finbow.

"What did Avice say?" I asked.

"I asked her if Tonia had gone for a swim after dinner,"
Finbow answered.

"What did she say?" I repeated.

"She said Tonia *did* go for a bathe just before she went
to bed," Finbow replied, with a complacent smile.

"You think everything's all right?" I was amazed that his
prediction had been correct.

"I'm quite certain," he answered.

"How did you guess about the swim?" I asked. I was nearly
asleep. Whatever the mysteries going on around me, I was
now too tired to bother. All I wanted was sleep.

"Because," said Finbow, "of a very simple fact. Tonia is
a young woman of the world."

CHAPTER ELEVEN

Uneasy Morning

The next morning I woke and saw Finbow in a dressing-gown, standing by my bed with an amused smile on his face.

"It's nearly twelve o'clock," he remarked. "Mrs. Tufts is on the verge of apoplexy."

I was dazed and puzzled for a moment, and then the adventures and fears of the disturbed night crowded upon me with an unpleasant vividness. It was like dreaming that one was lying ill in bed—and waking up to find that it was true. I remembered Avice cowering in the corner of the dining-room, Finbow's interminable conversation, Tonia's empty bed—and a groan in the darkness. I sat up with a jerk and asked:

"Are they all right? Is everyone here? Finbow, go and look."

Finbow answered casually: "Everyone's perfectly fit, except that Avice says she's got a headache. William and Christopher have had breakfast hours ago, Tonia's just starting. Avice and Philip are still in their rooms."

"Have you been up long?" I asked, relieved. I began to wash.

"A quarter of an hour," said Finbow. "My capacity to remain awake at night is only equalled by my capacity to remain asleep in the morning," he added sententiously.

I turned from the washstand:

"I'm glad you were right about Philip and Tonia. How did you know?"

"I told you last night," said Finbow, "because Tonia is a woman of the world."

"What does that mean?" I asked.

"I have heard various definitions," Finbow replied, "most of which were rather silly. Personally, I should call anyone a woman of the world when she has acquired one branch of knowledge——"

"And that is——" I asked.

"How to use her scent. If she knows that thoroughly, it means she has to know almost everything else as well. As you no doubt noticed when we came into this room last night, Tonia is a mistress of the art," Finbow said.

"I didn't notice any scent at all when we came in here," I said mystified.

"That," said Finbow, "is precisely what I mean."

"They had been in here?" I asked.

"Of course they had been in here," Finbow said calmly. "When we were all searching the house, they were in here laughing at us. Look at my plan of the bungalow. We know they weren't in the kitchen when we first entered the house; and they weren't in the sitting-room, because we went in there straightaway. They can't have been in Philip's room, because there's no way out of the passage—and we should have found them when we searched. So they were either outside in the cold, which is ridiculous, or they were in our room all the time we were talking in the sitting-room and while were were looking round the house. Then, as soon as we were all safely side-tracked outside William's door, they dashed across the lounge into Philip's room."

"Whatever was their idea?" I inquired, laughing despite myself. Finbow chuckled:

"They must have been wanting to get each other alone all day, and I expect the other two and Birrell and Mrs. Tufts kept getting in the way. So, when they found we hadn't come

back by the last train, they probably decided we were staying the night in London, and Tonia had the inspiration of
arranging a rendezvous in our room."

"Why our room?" I put in. "Why couldn't they go to
Philip's?"

"Because ours is the only room that one can make a noise
in without much danger of being overheard. Tonia is a clever
young woman. She didn't want the things they were saying
to each other to be known to anyone else in the party."

"Usually," I suggested, "she likes making love in public."

"That's the point, Ian," Finbow commented. "They
weren't making love, at least not all the time. In fact, I think
they had some serious confidences to exchange. I rather think
that if I knew what they were, I should be a bit more at ease
over the Roger business. But anyway, that was the scheme;
they wanted to get alone, they came into our room when
everyone was asleep, and Tonia wasn't going to leave any
traces. As I say, she's a young woman of the world, and she
knows the first rule about scent. Which is: that it's more
important than clothes. And the second, which is: that
generally one should be sure that one's lover goes away with
enough of it to remember one. And the third. Which is:
that sometimes it can be fatal for him to go away with enough
of it to make other people remember you. Tonia knew that
if we came in here and smelt her scent, we should have a
suspicion which wouldn't be far from the truth. So she had
a swim, and got rid of as much of it as she could."

"You guessed all that?" I said, with a definite admiration
in my voice.

"I've met Tonia's sort before," he smiled. "They're clever
enough to be interesting. She'd have been successful in this
case, if it hadn't been for shocking bad luck. She didn't
realise that we might return by car."

"That was rather stupid," I said.

"We said we should probably get the last train, and I don't suppose she could see any reason why we should charge back if we missed it. And on the whole she must have thought that the risk was worth taking," Finbow suggested.

"Yes," I said. "But why ever didn't they come out when we were talking in the sitting-room? They knew that we should go to bed sooner or later—and they they were completely caught."

"I leave the answer to your imagination," Finbow chuckled. "Have you ever been in love? And they knew we were a pair of kindly old idiots who like to see young folk enjoying themselves."

I laughed. I think I am old enough to say that I still firmly believe that conventions are made only to be broken—except the codes of manners and of honesty between friends, without which any unconventionality becomes merely a coarse and sordid caricature of decent living. I should indeed have been glad to see Philip and Tonia enjoy themselves in happier times. But immediately I felt a twinge of uneasiness.

"How was it that Avice didn't realise that Tonia was out of their room? She can't have realised it, or she wouldn't have gone out herself," I asked.

"Avice must have gone out first," said Finbow. "Tonia was probably waiting for her to go to sleep. I expect Philip had been in our room for some time. And when Avice got up and slipped out, I imagine Tonia took her chance."

"She must have known that Avice would come back and find her gone," I objected.

"What did she care?" Finbow replied. "She could threaten Avice that if anything were said, two could play at that game."

"You think Tonia wouldn't mind blackmail?" I was a little shocked.

"I'm quite certain she wouldn't," said Finbow. "In fact,

she'd rather like it. She hates Avice, and she'd like to see her cringe."

I brushed my hair in silence and then said: "You think she really hates Avice?"

" 'Resents' would be a better word," Finbow said, "just as Avice resents her. Two girls as different as they are—and as attractive—are bound to get on one another's nerves. If you're ready, we'll go to breakfast, Ian. I want to get things straightened out to-day, and there isn't too much time. I must talk to Avice and Christopher. Before I get their relations clear, I can't settle anything at all."

I smoothed my coat down. Finbow looked impatient at my careful dressing, but went on: "Of course, it's a little difficult finding all I want, without being able to ask a direct question. Except that it would be a good deal more difficult if I *were* able to ask a direct question. These young people are a lot too clever to give much away to nice blunt honest questions. You know, the sort by which detectives are supposed to get hold of intricacies of motive. It would be harder for a real detective than it is for me."

"Would you like me to keep out of the way while you talk to them? It might help if you had them alone," I suggested.

"Nonsense," said Finbow. "While you are somewhere near, they're not so likely to think that I've got anything more than an innocent curiosity. You're a sort of investigatory chaperon."

We walked through the lounge on our way to the dining-room. William looked up as we passed:

"Good morning," he said, then he asked suspiciously: "How are your eyes, Ian?"

"Finbow's man thought there was nothing to worry about," I said, and told myself that my lying had improved.

"Good," William commented, with a trace of irony, I thought. "What the devil were you all playing at last night?"

"Hunt the slipper," said Finbow blandly. "It's such a good game, William, you should try it; it would prevent your getting old before your time."

Tonia was lying on the sofa; I saw her eyes flash at Finbow's reply. "Hullo," she said combatively, as though expecting a reference to the night before. Christopher had an amused smile, which creased his brown face into pleasant lines. "Good morning," said Finbow, disregarding the strained atmosphere completely. "We got back rather late, Ian and I, and I'm afraid we overslept ourselves. I'm glad that you others didn't wait breakfast. We're going to have ours now."

At the breakfast-table Philip and Avice were sitting silently. Both were looking rather pale, but mustered smiles as we sat down.

Mrs. Tufts gave us plates of bacon and eggs. "They're cold," she said.

"That," Finbow remarked, "is not very extraordinary. We had a late night, Mrs. Tufts—oh, of course, you may remember."

Mrs. Tufts snorted. "Mr. Finbow," she said grimly, "I've kept my promise and I haven't said a word that's in my mind about those shameless doings that went on under this roof last night. Standing here, allowing these young men and women to eat as though nothing had happened, and not telling them what I think of their sinful ways, it's been the greatest trial of my life. Don't think it was because of you, Mr. Finbow, that I made my promise. I only promised you because I was told to oblige you in every way I can. I was told that by the one man I can trust."

"Who?" asked Philip.

"Sergeant Birrell," she said. "But if Sergeant Birrell had told me the goings-on that you encourage, Mr. Finbow, I never would have said to him: 'Aloysius, I'll do all I can for Mr. Finbow.' I promised you last night, Mr. Finbow, but never again. Never again! I went to bed ashamed, and I got up ashamed this morning."

"So!" Finbow answered, cutting up a cold egg. "Remember your promise."

"I've been struggling with my conscience." She looked fat and fierce. "Is it right to keep a promise if it means that evil is being done, and no voice raised against it? Is it right?"

"Ask Sergeant Birrell," Finbow suggested.

"I will," she snapped, and went out of the room.

Avice had listened to the tirade with a smile in her tired eyes. But I watched her long fingers spinning a napkin-ring, spinning it time after time mechanically; and the contrast between the nervous fingers and the controlled face was so great as to make me feel both the anxiety she was suffering, and the attempt she was making to hold herself in check. Her tension communicated itself to me, and I sat strained and worried through Mrs. Tufts's angry speeches. There are times, I think, when farce is a relief from strong emotion: but there are other times when it adds to the pain which one is enduring. I could see that Mrs. Tufts was making the party more hysterical.

When Mrs. Tufts had gone, Avice looked at Finbow with just the same expression that Tonia had worn in the lounge. She too expected a reference to the events of the past night. I told myself that, if I had been there alone, they would have treated me like a good-natured uncle, kissed me and assured me that I need not worry. But Finbow, though they liked him, was a man to whom they subconsciously felt that they owed an explanation.

Finbow, however, munched his cold egg with complete indifference, and began to discuss the financial situation. He explained to Avice the origin, significance and disadvantages of a gold standard. He explained it clearly, and even brought in a trace of wit for the only time in any economic exposition that I have ever heard; and yet I was certain that Avice wanted to shriek. But she listened politely, and asked an appropriate question or two. I watched her pale sad face and the rings under her eyes. Finbow finished:

"It's not a difficult thing. It's a good deal easier to understand than this mess you people have got into."

I was shocked at the smooth and calculated brutality. Avice's great eyes stared at him. Philip answered, with an uneasy attempt at a laugh:

"I think ours is rather a commonplace business."

"Not so very commonplace," said Finbow quietly. He spread some marmalade on his toast, and gave us his views on Japanese imperialism. I might mention that, though he was a well informed man of affairs, he had no curious special knowledge of the kind one used to meet in detective fiction— except perhaps on a few Chinese subjects, but that I am not competent to judge.

At length we joined the others in the sitting-room. They were still there, detained by the inertia which is the second stage of anxiety. First, one worries actively and cannot keep still. Then, one gets to a point where the fears immobilise one utterly; and the only longing is to hear the worst. Tonia was still on the sofa, her hands joined at the back of her neck. William was reading a detective story—I think it was called *Unnatural Death.* Christopher was scribbling notes on the back of a letter. Avice and Philip sat down without speaking. Finbow addressed the room cheerfully:

"We've just been arguing about the position in the Far East."

"Oh," said William, glancing up uninterestedly from his book, "are you interested in it?"

"Of course I'm interested in it," Finbow replied. "Anything which affects the lives of a few million Chinese interests me."

"Sorry to be selfish," Christopher interposed. "But at the moment, my own life interests me the devil of a lot more than any number of Chinese."

"When you and William get older," Finbow said, "you'll find your attitude will change."

"Nonsense," William cut in. "Your generation exhausted England's supply of social conscience. You were all damned keen on the future of the world; and look what you did with it! Look at Christopher and me. Our first real memories are of war-time hysteria, nerves, foolery of all sorts. We were adolescent in the post-war years, the silliest years that ever have been, I should think. And now just as we've got our lives more or less arranged, we get a financial crisis that may upset everything. It's a legacy of your generation, Finbow, and your damned social consciences. Do you wonder we've got no hope left? Do you wonder we concentrate on our own lives, and let the rest of the world go to hell in their own way?"

The bitterness of William's attack was in harmony with the mood of the party. It reflected the ordeal they were going through—and I think it was a symbol of something deeper. Finbow looked thoughtful. Christopher nodded:

"I agree entirely, William. My world doesn't get further than a few of my friends. You understand, Finbow?"

"I think I do," Finbow replied. "On purely selfish grounds, though, you will lose a good deal if your lives are as narrow as you say."

"That may be," Christopher smiled. "Anyway, I shall see millions of Chinese in Malaya, and they may broaden my mind. That reminds me: the Board want to interview me for the last time to-morrow. Do you think Birrell will mind if I go to London?"

"I'll go and ask if you like," Finbow answered. "It'll be easy; I have a certain influence with him."

Finbow found out from Mrs. Tufts that Birrell had gone to the Bridge Inn for lunch, and suggested that I should accompany them into the village. Gladly enough, I left the others silent in the sitting-room. William had gone back to his book after his outburst. Philip and Tonia were strangely uninterested in each other, and Avice sat apart and melancholy. It was good to escape from that fear-ridden atmosphere, even for only half an hour.

Finbow, Christopher and I walked slowly along the footpath.

"What's going to happen in your interview?" Finbow asked Christopher.

"Oh, first of all they'll send me to the Company medico. He prods me, and sees that I shall be able to stand the climate. I don't mind that," he laughed. "I've never had one, but I've always felt that medical examinations were the one sort of examination I could be pretty sure of passing."

"Don't be modest." Finbow smiled. "I've no doubt you'd have got through any examination that you wanted to take. What else do the Board do to you to-morrow?"

"They say in their letter that the Managing Board will ask me certain confidential questions. That's not so pleasant, but I daresay I shall be able to survive. Then they send me back to the medico to arrange about inoculation."

"Will you be back the same night?" Finbow said.

"Oh, yes; it won't take long. I'll catch the five-forty-nine," Christopher replied.

We crossed a plank bridge. Finbow remarked:

"I was very interested in what you and William were saying before we left. The people round you are the only things which concern you?"

"Yes," said Christopher. "Is that very unusual? Are you passionately keen on the fate of nations?"

Finbow ignored the question. "I suppose," he said meditatively, "most men would feel rather as you do, if they were in love with Avice."

Christopher's thin face hardened. "I felt exactly as I do now long before I met Avice," he said.

I noticed that Finbow's conversational technique had been defeated. Christopher had refused the bait. Finbow continued: "A curious disease, being in love."

"I have been told so," said Christopher, with a slight smile.

"I wonder if the odd hours of pleasure are worth the days of utter blinding misery," Finbow mused.

"I wonder," said Christopher.

"When we're not in love, we think they are; but when we are, it seems more doubtful," Finbow said.

"Not unnaturally," Christopher replied.

"It varies a lot according to your temperament. A cheerful man forgets the pain as soon as it's happened. I expect Roger was like that: he seems to have been a very cheerful man," Finbow said quietly. Christopher smiled.

"Poor old Roger had a bad time," he said. "He was cheerful, as you say. But he'd have had to be incredibly cheerful to survive the coldness which he always got from Avice. Still, he persevered. He was the most persistent man I've ever seen. It annoyed Avice."

I could not decide whether Christopher was speaking deliberately, or whether Finbow had led him to the topic unawares. Finbow said:

"She is an astonishingly attractive young woman. I should think she's been cold to quite a lot of men."

Christopher smiled, a little twistedly I thought.

"Most women as pretty as she is have more men around them than is exactly necessary," he said. His one burst of confidence had left him secretive again.

"I suppose you've known her a long time?" Finbow asked.

"Between three and four years," Christopher said.

"Different from Philip and Tonia," Finbow murmured. "They apparently have known each other for about two months. During which time they've settled everything."

"They're rather simple creatures," said Christopher. "I should think they've both been in love before—and they'll be in love again."

"Yes," Finbow agreed. "I imagine it comes pretty lightly to youngsters like that."

Christopher did not reply, and Finbow gave up the attempt to talk over Avice's emotions. Instead, I joined in a pointless discussion on films, which lasted until we entered the bar at the Bridge and found Aloysius Birrell.

Birrell was leaning against the bar, with a whisky-and-soda in front of him. From his previous moral views I should have expected it to be a lemon squash, until I remembered that the combination of puritanism and abstinence is entirely an English invention, and that in Ireland it is possible to drink whisky and remain as pure as Aloysius Birrell. Finbow approached him: "Good morning, Sergeant," he said.

"Good morning, Mr. Finbow," Birrell replied, looking at him with a troubled expression. "Mrs. Tufts has been telling me horrible stories of things that happened in the bungalow last night. If anyone but Mrs. Tufts had told me, I shouldn't have believed them. But Mrs. Tufts is a good woman."

"More than good," said Finbow. "No harm was done, Sergeant, however."

"That depends," said Birrell, "upon how you look at it."

"Remember the state of mind they're all bound to be in," Finbow said smoothly, "after being watched by a man as astute as you. You can't expect them to be responsible for their actions."

Birrell was serious and gratified.

"Mr. Finbow, I have got everything ready for action," he said in a whisper which reached a yard or two along the bar. "Perhaps you'd like to hear?"

"Certainly," said Finbow. "It's good of you. I'm enjoying your handling of the investigation enormously."

"It's a pleasure," said Aloysius Birrell excitedly, speaking very fast. "Well, the whole of the wherry has been searched from bow to stern, and there's no sign of an automatic or the log-book. There are no finger-prints anywhere near the body. The autopsy didn't show anything interesting—the bullet was fired from a small automatic, probably a *.22*. I've got my diving-suit coming down from Plymouth; it should arrive late to-morrow. So I shall dive for the automatic the next morning and then I shall be able to take steps. The Chief Constable's written to Scotland Yard, telling them everything I've done. He won't let me arrest anyone till he's heard from them."

"You're a marvel, Sergeant," Finbow told him. Birrell's fresh face looked very happy. "But it's a difficult case, Mr. Finbow," he said. "It's a difficult case. There's very little to go on. These problems may seem easy to outsiders, but when you're in it, it's different."

"I'm sure you'll win through," Finbow encouraged him. "And now I wonder if you'll mind Mr. Tarrant here paying a visit to London to-morrow. He's got to be interviewed by the Board of the firm which is going to employ him."

Birrell studied Christopher with a judicial air, and asked: "May I see the correspondence which fixed this interview?"

Christopher smiled and gave him a letter, which Birrell glanced at.

"It all seems in order," he said. "I think you ought to report at a police station during the afternoon, so that if I'm asked any questions——"

Christopher shrugged his shoulders: "If you like," he said. "It's rather a nuisance. Where shall I go?"

Birrell answered uncomfortably: "I forget the names of the police stations in that part of the town."

I realised that he knew nothing of London, and suggested Vine Street, with sudden memories of indiscretions on Boat Race night. Birrell leapt at it.

"Vine Street's just the place. I'll get them over the phone and tell them to expect you, Mr. Tarrant."

On the way back to the bungalow, Christopher smiled in his characteristically twisted but pleasant way. Aloysius Birrell," he said, "gives me the impression of having learnt detection by a correspondence course." Finbow laughed; I was too worried to be much amused. Every time I returned to the party, I found it more of an effort to conquer the anticipation of what I might see there. Every journey back to the bungalow took me to a place where I must hear distressing news. There could be no possible happy ending. At the best, there could only be an ending which some day I might forget. At the worst—but I dared not think of that.

When we returned, the others were already sitting down for lunch. Avice pushed her meat aside, and toyed with a slice of bread. Tonia was almost as sad looking, though her eyes had a glint in contrast to the clouded gloom of Avice's. William ate with an emphatic silence, and Philip seemed as broken as he had been on the morning of the murder. There was very little said for some minutes after Finbow, Christopher and I had taken our places. Suddenly Tonia gave a prolonged yawn: "I *am* sleepy," she said.

"That's a pity," said Finbow sympathetically, "I should lie down after lunch if I were you." The words seemed to infuriate Tonia. She broke out:

"For God's sake say something! You all know I was out of my room last night. You all know it. Why don't you ask me?

Do you think I was going to do a murder? *Do* you?"

Philip took her hand. "Of course not, darling. They're just not interfering."

"Why haven't they said something? They could see we *wanted* them to say something. Finbow, why didn't you mention it? Don't you believe I just wanted to tell Philip some news?—some news that I couldn't keep until this morning."

"It's not my business,' Finbow said blandly. "I'm sure you do everything for the best possible reasons." Tonia buried her face in her hands, and we could only see a mass of red hair.

Avice asked in a low voice: "Do you think that of me too?" Her white face was thrust forward towards us. Tonia flared up again:

"Yes, what was *she* doing? She was out of our room as well. Why shouldn't I please myself? Why don't you ask her?"

"You were out of your room too?" Christopher asked sharply across the table. Surprise and concern strengthened the lines on his lean face. Avice gave an almost inaudible "Yes." Finbow intervened smoothly: "You're both of you worrying a great deal too much. Ian and I have both attained years of discretion. Which means that we tend to lose our senses after midnight."

CHAPTER TWELVE

Avice's Proposals

Finbow's remark drew a smile from most of the party, and for the rest of the meal there were no more outbreaks. But there were angry, bitter glances and awkward silences; and it was clear that nerves were near the breaking point.

After lunch I took a deck-chair down to the river bank, and sat there trying to make sense of all that I had seen and heard, of the words I heard spoken and of the inferences which Finbow had drawn. Soon Finbow joined me, and to my surprise began to play patience on a newspaper which he spread on the grass. He saw my amazed glance.

"It's all right, Ian," he said. "I've not gone mad. I'm simply trying to act my part as a kindly but rather silly friend of yours. After each sign of intelligence which I'm forced to show, I think it's a good idea to let your young friends see that I really am just inane. Unfortunately I've never learned how to play this wretched game. I suppose if I put cards down in rows and then pile them on top of one another, it will look fairly convincing."

He made an imitation of playing a hand at patience, talking as he adjusted the cards. His voice was unusually serious, and there was no trace of the flippancy which he sometimes assumed:

"I'm puzzled. Damned puzzled. And I seem to get further off every hour. This Tonia business get queerer and queerer. What did she say to Philip last night? Why is she so frightened that it'll affect him? Why is he so worried? He's not the man to be put off easily, he's far too happy-go-lucky to let much disturb him. It's very very curious. And then Christopher. He's more complicated than the other two, and that makes it more difficult. I wish I could decide how much of his conversation this morning was provided for the benefit of inquisitive strangers. Still, I did get one good concrete fact out of our talk on the way into the village."

"And that is?" I asked, as he put a king of spades on a two of diamonds, which is not allowed in any patience I have ever seen.

"That he doesn't want to talk about Avice," Finbow replied.

"What do you think that means?" I asked anxiously.

"I'm not sure," he said. "If I believe what Avice told me last night, it's fairly understandable. A man doesn't want to talk overmuch about a woman who isn't in love with him. That is, if he's in love with her and if they're going to be married. It all seems quite reasonable; Avice probably likes him quite a lot, he's certainly very much in love with her— you could hear how it hurt when I pressed my questions— and they're both finding the prospect of marriage rather difficult."

"Why did she get engaged?" I asked.

"I don't know. But if everyone waited until they were in love, your annual bill for wedding presents would diminish, Ian. The important question is—how did she regard Roger? She said last night she was indifferent to him, in fact she implied that she disliked him. I accepted that at the time. I told you so, and you agreed. But is it true? It might be: she was too tired to lie very convincingly."

"From what I have seen these last two years, I'm absolutely certain it was quite true," I said, glad to testify to Avice's statement.

"I think the same," said Finbow. "It may be one of the

crucial psychological points of the case. I think we can accept it. She's certainly never been in love; she couldn't have deceived me with her acting last night on that point. There is a limit to lying. She likes Christopher, but she's not in love with him. She was not fond of Roger. Both what she said and what I infer from Christopher agree very nicely. He was quite definite about her attitude to Roger, of course, but I don't want to attach undue weight to that."

"Why?" I asked.

"Because Christopher knows as well as I do that he might murder a successful rival, but that he hadn't much reason to murder an unsuccessful one. *If* Roger had been the successful rival, and Christopher had murdered him, then Christopher might have tried to deceive us by telling us that Roger didn't count in Avice's eyes at all. That is, he might have told the same story as he actually has done. But, if Avice had really liked Roger, it's ridiculous to suppose that she'd shield the man who'd killed him—and ridiculous to suppose that she'd have any reason for misleading us into thinking that she wasn't fond of Roger. No; so far as I can see, Avice was quite indifferent to Roger. I must probe her a little more, soon, but her story and Christopher's coincide rather well as they stand."

"You're taking a lot of trouble over the relations of those three." I said. Finbow shuffled the cards and replied: "If I can establish them, I shall be able to settle Christopher one way or the other. He's a very clever young man, with enough depth to carry off a murder like this. You noticed his bridge? He can gamble. I think he'd be quite capable of killing a man if it were necessary. And then this medical exam worries me a bit. If he doesn't come back, or if he comes back tomorrow night with something a little wrong with him, I shall suspect a connection with Roger." He looked thoughtful.

"But I mustn't see connections everywhere. He's bound to

have a medical exam. Also he seems to have been away from the cabin on the morning of the murder an extremely short time. It's not easy to kill a man, arrange the tiller, and make yourself presentable inside three minutes. I wonder if he saw something or heard something that made him rush into the cabin out of sheer fright?" I refused to admit the picture which Finbow's words evoked. Finbow continued: "However, it's not impossible that Christopher did this murder, And it would seem quite likely if there were any motive of jealousy. If we can rule that out—And I think we can—then it's difficult to see why he should kill an unhappy rival. The more usual course would be to have enjoyed Roger's sufferings."

"There's the possibility I outlined last night," I said. "Christopher might have killed Roger so that Avice would be very rich sometime. The money would come to them both when they were married."

"It's possible, Ian," Finbow said. "But it doesn't seem to fit psychologically. I doubt if a man who is passionately in love would murder for money—particularly when he'll be very comfortably off, and when his whole anxieties are centered in a young woman who's not quite sure whether she'll marry him at all. I'm inclined to think Christopher would have felt that the prospect of more money coming to her might just have tilted the scale, and made her decide that she wouldn't get married just yet."

"What's your final opinion?" I asked.

"I haven't got one," said Finbow. "I'm getting definite pictures of these people in my mind. To finish off the process, I must have another chat with Avice this afternoon. You wait here: I won't be long."

I lay back in my deck-chair and shut my eyes, in the hope that some thoughts would crystallise out of the complex tangle. But all I obtained was a series of fleeting, distressing pictures, accompanied by memories of Finbow's smooth voice. I saw Avice lamenting Roger's death ("she was a good actress," Finbow had said)—staring at me as the light from my candle lit up the corner of the dining-room—telling Finbow intensely of her desire to be in love ("she was too tired to lie convincingly, I think," he had said.) But self-inflicted pain does not go on for very long; and soon I was making theories to myself which incriminated Christopher. Finbow seemed to suspect him; and it was not so hard to imagine his lean brown face gazing on the man he had murdered, as to think of Avice's eyes looking coldly upon a black hole in a man's chest. I tried to arrange all the facts to suit the hypothesis of Christopher as murderer.

After a quarter of an hour, Finbow and Avice came up from the garden. Finbow's long face wore its pleasant smile. He said:

"You look comfortable, Ian."

"I am comfortable," I said.

"That's a pity," Finbow replied, "because we were going to ask you to take us for a sail in the dinghy."

I groaned, but I am rather proud of my sailing; and soon we had fetched the dinghy, put the centre-board down, and were sailing very slowly along the Thurne towards Potter.

"Avice," said Finbow quietly, "I want to talk to you."

Avice's pale face went paler still, but she smiled at him across the boat.

"Nice for us both," she answered.

"About the only subject on which a middle-aged man can possibly talk to a young woman," he went on.

She smiled wanly:

"And that is?"

"Her love-affairs," said Finbow. "One gets other people's love-affairs in the right perspective by the time one gets near forty. It helps one to make a greater mess of one's own."

I avoided gybing round an awkward corner, and then told Avice:

"Beware of him, my dear. He's never had a heart. He merely makes generalisations in order to delude you into thinking that he has."

Avice twisted her lips.

"I don't think," she said, "that I want to talk about my love-affairs."

"You didn't mind telling me of them last night," Finbow replied.

"I wasn't myself last night," she said, with her mouth drawn into a thin pale line. "We all say stupid things sometimes."

"We do," said Finbow quietly. "It's often very good for us to do so."

"And no doubt," she put in, "very entertaining for our listeners."

"It is always entertaining to listen to an indiscretion," said Finbow blandly. "And an indiscretion from an attractive young woman has a charm all its own."

"Thank you very much," she replied. "I hope I was indiscreet enough to make you happy."

"It would need more than a few words to do *that*," said Finbow. "But if you confided in me now, it would give me a good deal of pleasure. I think that you ought to be grateful that it's in your power to give me pleasure."

"I've heard that before," she said scornfully. "Like nasty men who've tried to maul me. 'It'll please me and it won't hurt you.' Mr. Finbow, I think you exaggerate your importance."

I had tried to catch every shade of meaning in this rapid dialogue. I wondered to myself which was the real Avice, the cool young woman who gave Finbow as good as she got, or the fragile creature whose eyes were often near to tears.

Finbow's reply showed me that both were the same person. He said in a level voice:

"I think that you exaggerate your safety."

Avice's face softened to a pathetic appealing misery. She faltered: "You mean that the police may——"

"I mean," said Finbow, "that unless you talk to us two harmless middle-aged gentlemen, you may be forced to talk to people without any of the social graces of Ian and myself."

Avice sat silent for a second. Then she seemed to make a decision, and said quietly:

"*Must* you go into my love-affairs?"

Finbow answered:

"I'm afraid I must."

She bit her lip. Suddenly she broke out:

"I've never been in love."

"That," said Finbow, "is a misfortune for a great many men."

"I've been fond of several men, I'm very fond of Christopher. I may love him, in a sort of way, some time. But do you know why I got engaged to him?"

"I should like to know," said Finbow.

"To stop Roger pestering me," she said fiercely. "To have someone whom I could go to, to keep Roger away. To prevent Roger hanging round me all day, asking me to dinner every night, calling in at all sorts of times. It was intolerable." Then she calmed down. "Roger has wanted to marry me for years, but I never could have stood him. I liked him as a friend, of course—and now this awful thing's happened I only wish I'd liked him more——" Her mouth drooped and her eyes grew sad. I watched her anxiously, with Finbow's words of the day before in my ears: "She's a good actress!"

I remembered Finbow's theory that she hated Roger, and here she was dutifully lamenting his death. In my worry, I

ran the boat very close to the bank. When I had recovered
control, Finbow was saying:

"Of course it must be terrible for you. When did he propose to you?"

"About once a month for the last three years," she said,
with a melancholy smile. "Since I was twenty."

"But you refused him firmly from the first?" Finbow lifted
his eyebrows and smiled at her. "I suppose you did, as you
knew he'd propose again?"

"Mr. Finbow," she protested earnestly and almost tear-
fully, "I never did flirt with him. Honestly I didn't. Four
men have proposed to me in my life——"

"That is too few," Finbow commented.

She glanced at him, and went on:

"Three of them I might have married. One of them's
Christopher, and I think I shall marry him. I don't deny I
flirted a little with the three of them. It's a bit hard not to,
you know."

"I'm sure," Finbow agreed, "that the temptation must be
very strong."

"But Roger I never could have married: and I never
flirted with him. Not once. Not at one dance!" she said
vehemently.

"That's definite enough," said Finbow. "Ian, you'd better
swing her round, or we shall be late, and Mrs. Tufts will
throw plates at us."

We went placidly back, in a light breeze that was lessening
every minute. I knew that Finbow had drawn out the information which he wanted; I wondered nervously what
conclusions he would be led to. Avice seemed surprised that
he had stopped asking her questions, and had an agitated
smile on her lips, as though she was plucking up courage to
say something. When the bungalow was in sight, she sighed
nervously:

"Mr. Finbow, aren't you going to ask me about the will? I'm the heir to quite a lot of money now that Roger's dead, you know."

Finbow answered:

"I really don't think it's necessary to go into the details of that."

CHAPTER THIRTEEN

Dinner in the Shadows

I was heartened by Finbow's last words. As we went in to tea, I told myself gladly that the only conceivable motive for Avice was the heritage; and if Finbow was not interested in the will, it seemed that he must have dismissed the possibility of Avice as murderer from his mind. With great relief, I took a cup of tea from Mrs. Tufts, and went so far as to smile into her basilisk face.

The others, however, were no more cheerful than they had been at lunch. The strain was breaking out in characteristic ways. William ate his food methodically, said almost nothing, and spent most of the time reading detective stories or Jeans; occasionally he would utter a sharp word. Avice lounged in a chair, listlessly, as though the life had gone out of her; she seemed to try to remove herself from the party, and rarely spoke. Tonia was aggressive, and gave husky laughs at her own jokes; but she was clearly near the point of wild hysteria. Christopher was making an attempt to eat his tea in peace, but his forehead was deeply furrowed and his face looked thinner. Philip carried on a running conversation with Tonia and Christopher; dejection appeared to come over him in waves, and suddenly he would sit and look abjectly sad, his eyes fixed on Tonia.

Only Finbow made tea-time tolerable; his refusal to act as though anything unusual had happened made it difficult for anyone else to break through the polite restraints which were still holding. Yet in the end it was Finbow who provoked an open fit of irritation. He made his second pot of tea in his own way, and, as he sipped the straw-coloured liquid, murmured, in the words which he never altered: "Best tea in the world."

Tonia said loudly:

"Finbow, if you say that again, I shall scream."

William added, a harsh note coming into his voice:

"You ought to realise that a mannerism—particularly an absolutely pointless and silly mannerism—is bound to infuriate the people who live with you in conditions like these. Haven't you got any imagination? Or are you doing it deliberately?"

"William," I protested, "Finbow is my guest. I can't have——"

William broke in abruptly:

"Yes, I know Finbow is your guest. I should like to know——" and he paused: "What else is he?"

I saw Philip's pupils dilate and Tonia's hands clutch at her chair.

"What else is he?" echoed Tonia.

"Why did he come here?" William went on. "Any fool ought to see that we don't want strangers when we're all in the middle of the worst thing that's ever happened to us. Why did he come here? Unless——" he sneered, "it happens to be his profession."

Finbow laughed in a way which sounded completely unforced.

"This comes, my dear William," he said, "of reading too many murder stories. You tend to suspect a detective behind every face which doesn't look very intelligent. I assure you that in my case I'm nothing more than I look. I like watching Aloysius Birrell—who wouldn't? In a detective story, however, I should certainly reveal myself as one of the Big

176

Five—or alternatively as the murderer. I do not propose to
do either of those things."

William said brusquely: "What are you doing here?"

Finbow was unperturbed. " I came down as a friend of
Ian's, in case I could be useful to him. I may still be able to
avert a certain amount of official unpleasantness. If you
want any details about me, you can read them in *Who's Who*.
I appear there, mainly because the editor thought my name
would bridge the gap between Finberg and Finburgh rather
neatly. However, if I irritate anyone I don't mind going
away in the least. I can stay in the village."

"Don't be ridiculous," Christopher said. "The suspense
has made William forget any sense he may otherwise have.
Of course you can't go, Finbow."

"Of course not," said Avice quietly. "William ought to
apologise."

"It's all very well for you," William told her, with a bitter
smile, "whatever happens *you*'re all right."

"You'll stay, of course, Finbow," Philip said. He seemed
to be more cheerful than at the beginning of tea.

"I shall stay," said Finbow, smiling, "if only to annoy
William."

"Good," said Tonia. "Look here, we've got to forget all
this. What about putting on the gramophone and having a
dance?"

Everyone approved; at that moment everyone would have
approved of anything that would take our minds off the
murder. Finbow and I watched William supervise the
gramophone, and we listened to a wailing fox-trot. Tonia
and Philip danced languorously together, and Avice walked
round limply in Christopher's arms. The fox-trot beat on
mournfully, and I admired Philip and Tonia, who moved
as though they had only two legs between them. Avice had
let her head drop on to Christopher's shoulder, and her eyes

were dark-ringed, but, as I watched them, I saw that her long legs followed Christopher's with accuracy and grace.

Then I noticed that Mrs. Tufts was standing in the door-way, fat, white and with her lips pursed. As the dance stopped:

"This is shameful!" she said indignantly.

"Don't be silly!" said Tonia, but Mrs. Tufts was in full spate:

"I should have thought that even people who haven't any respect for God's laws"—she glared at me furiously: I for some reason, probably because Birrell had told her that I was the murderer, always received her deepest scorn—"for God's laws, would have enough decent feeling to stop this gallivanting in a sinful dance, when that poor dead gentleman is lying stiff and cold!"

We each waited for someone else to reply. Finbow, usually our stand-by in attempting to placate Mrs. Tufts, was looking out of the window, with the suspicion of a smile of his lips. Christopher broke the silence:

"Mrs. Tufts, if you say anything more I shall be forced to write to Mr. Williamson," he said sternly.

"I shall tell Mr. Williamson that I'm doing my duty!" Mrs. Tufts snapped. "I shall tell him that no one else would stay in a house with a murderer!"

Philip put in, with a flash of the old gay impudence which had been subdued all day:

"You'd better be good, Mrs. Tufts!"

"What, young man?" Mrs. Tufts exclaimed.

"You'd better be good," said Philip carelessly, "or else we shall tell Mr. Williamson you've been seen in compromising circumstances with Sergeant Birrell."

Mrs. Tufts made a bursting noise, and then, to our amazement, blushed a curious dull pink. Philip chuckled, and she bustled snorting out of the room.

"When I die," said Philip, "I hope you'll all remember my one good deed."

The party gave a brave imitation of mutual toleration after Mrs. Tufts had gone. William set the gramophone going, and Finbow and Tonia began to waltz. As Christopher had picked up a newspaper, I danced with Avice. She was light in my arms, and it was a relief just to dance silently, letting myself bathe in the music; the last days had been an ordeal of concentrating on word after word, speech after speech, any one of which might be a sign of the end; and how much more an ordeal, I thought as I felt Avice's hair against my face, for this girl and the others! It was a relief to let my mind be drowned in the waltz.

Dancing and a few songs by Tonia and Finbow brought us safely, if a little precariously, to dinner-time. There had been occasional sharp words, but nothing like the hysterics of the earlier part of the day.

At dinner the undercurrents of strain renewed themselves, and seemed to swell to bursting-point. The paraffin lamps had gone wrong again, and this time had defeated Mrs. Tufts: and so we sat round a table in the room whose long window gave on to the river, and ate by the vague light of candles placed on shelves and tables. Everyone seemed strangely altered in the shadowy room. In the window one could see reflections of candles and faces, and beyond the reflections the sky, dark save for an illuminated strip over the horizon. In normal times the room would have been depressing; but, with our nerves already quivering, it made every word an accusation, every phrase a challenge, every face a secret stranger whom we feared.

There was no pretence at conversation. Through most of the meal, Mrs. Tufts stood by, accusingly. When she had gone out and left us to our coffee, Philip broke out suddenly:

"This is getting on my nerves. All of us being here

together, and everyone suspecting everyone else! I can't
stand it!"

Tonia laughed in a high-pitched tone:

"I shall soon believe we all did the damned murder
together."

Christopher confessed:

"I wish we could do something, myself."

Philip threw back the hair from his eyes.

"What the devil *can* we do?" he asked.

Avice turned her head from the flushed faces at the table,
and looked out of the window over the dark marshes. Her
face was white.

William interposed in the discussion:

"There's nothing *we* can do," he said bitterly. "Finbow has
everything under control, no doubt."

Tonia let her eyes dwell on Finbow.

"What do you think of this business?" she asked him.

There was a hot silence for a moment. Then Finbow
answered urbanely:

"I almost never think. It's a habit one gets out of, after one
has passed your age, my dear."

"What is going to happen to us?" said Philip wildly, getting to his feet. As he moved, a candle fell to the floor; a
corner of the room became black and distant. I felt that the
strain was tearing the veils off the party, that fear was
struggling through the meshes of caution and guile. The
candles flickered in a gust of air, and Philip's voice came very
high and shrill:

"Who did it? God, who did it? We can't stay here being
polite to each other!"

Christopher leaned forward over the table, and a little of
his control had gone as he joined in:

"It would help us all if the person who did it said so, now.
Staying on like this won't do any of us much good."

Tonia almost shrieked:

"Say something, Avice, for God's sake. Don't sit there as if you were too good to talk to us! Are you thinking about Roger?"

"You mean——" said Avice. She had gone livid.

"Are you thinking about Roger?" Tonia repeated, with a broken husky laugh.

Christopher stood up and shouted: "You damned gold-digger, are *you* accusing *her* of a thing like that? You—who've just picked up Philip for his money?"

Tonia quailed before his anger, and then her eyes glinted with rage: "Nice for you, too, to have a wife with some money. A wife with *Roger's* money. And *you* dare say that I picked up Philip——"

"Of course. I imagine you'd had some practice at that sort of thing." Christopher scowled. His brown face had flushed a sullen red. Philip pushed his chair aside and walked across to Christopher.

"What the hell do you mean?" he shouted, "what the——"

"Poor child," said Christopher. "She's got you all right."

"I'll kill you," Philip screamed. "Damn you——"

"There's been enough killing in this party," shouted William. "Pull the fool off."

Philip cowered. "Enough killing——" he whispered. "Oh, God!"

Tonia turned on William. "You madman. You don't think Philip's the murderer, do you?" She hurled the words at him. "If you want to know who did the murder, I'll tell you——"

Finbow stopped her. He spoke calmly enough, but without his customary smoothness:

"That will be enough," he said. "You'll only hurt each other if this goes on. Let's go into the sitting-room and behave like human beings."

In the sitting-room we made up a bridge four, more to avoid conversation than because any of us wanted to. Avice watched and kept my score-card. Philip and Tonia talked in whispers on the sofa. The evening dragged on painfully, and everyone was glad when William said he was tired and wanted to go to bed.

"I think," said Christopher, "we might all turn in. It must be the marsh air that makes me sleepy."

"I've not been to bed at ten since I was at school," Tonia murmured. "Still, I'm all for new experiences."

Finbow and I went to our room and sat on the bed. He lit a cigarette and said reflectively:

"Another eventful night."

"Why didn't you stop them at dinner?" I asked. "It wasn't a nice quarter of an hour."

"I did stop them," said Finbow.

"After they'd let themselves go," I snapped.

"I wanted to hear what they'd say," he admitted.

"Did you get anything useful?" I had suspected that he had had a reason for letting the hysteria develop.

"Nothing that fits into any rational scheme," he said shortly, and went and looked out of the window. I joined him, and we smoked in silence for a time. Then he said in a voice so quiet that I could scarcely hear:

"Ian, I don't like this."

"Why?" I asked, but my heart sank.

"I'm being driven to think that one of two extremely attractive young women is going to have some difficulty in continuing to be extremely attractive," he answered coldly.

"You mean——?"

"It looks too much like Avice or Tonia," he said.

The unemotional words made me feel faint. Finbow went on:

"If either of them did it, I'd rather it were Tonia. On

purely æsthetic grounds. Avice is the loveliest thing I've seen since Olive's days. But I'm forced to narrow it down to them."

"Why?" I asked hopelessly.

"Well, Philip's out of it," said Finbow. "And William's out of it; we saw that this morning. And after our sail with Avice, we can rule Christopher out, too. Three from five leaves two!"

"What did she say?" I was too afraid to be clear-minded.

"Among other things, that she was going to marry Christopher to get Roger completely out of the way. Christopher's no fool: he probably knows that as well as she does," Finbow said.

"You think it's true?" I asked.

"Everything points to it. It's exactly as I said this afternoon. She's not in love with Christopher—so she says, and I fancy it's true. That sort of very delicate, beautiful young woman usually finds it difficult to fall in love with anyone," he answered, with a half smile. "It's your Tonias who fall in love easiest."

"But she can't have been going to marry just because of Roger," I protested.

"People seem to marry for even sillier reasons than that," he said. "And, anyway, from what I've found out about Roger, I personally should have done quite a lot to get to Malaya out of his way, if I'd been Avice. Of course, it wasn't as simple as she said—she likes Christopher a lot, he's an extremely pleasant young man with a career at his feet, and she doesn't love anyone else, and she'd rather like to be married—all those are the main factors. No psychological state is ever as simple a matter as it seems when it's explained. But given all those desires whirling round Christopher, it is quite natural that Roger should decide for her by making himself a nuisance, and getting in the way. He just resolved her uncertainty. So she said that she'd marry Christopher."

I accepted the explanation doubtfully.

"Of course," Finbow continued, flipping a mosquito from his sleeve, "she wouldn't put it like that. She thinks she is unselfishly gratifying Christopher by marrying him—and she cannot admit, even to herself, that she rather wants to get married. The result is, she explains the whole thing by blaming it on to Roger. That's a detail: it doesn't affect the murder; the important fact is that Avice was less likely to marry Christopher with Roger dead than with Roger alive."

"You've dismissed the idea that Christopher might have been jealous of Roger?" I asked.

"It's exactly the other way round. Roger was ludicrously unsuccessful with Avice. Christopher could afford to view him with the sort of generosity that one shows to an unsuccessful rival, as I told you this morning."

I walked up the room and back to the window. "Unless you admit my theory about his wanting Avice's money——" I said.

"I don't," said Finbow.

"There's no motive for Christopher then?" I said.

"We can forget him," Finbow agreed. "He'd not only got no reason for wanting to kill Roger; he'd got a strong reason for trying to keep him alive. Christopher wants Avice more than anything else in the world. With Roger alive the chance of marrying her was pretty good, with Roger dead it's more doubtful."

"Yes," I said gloomily. "And how about Avice?"

A furrow appeared on Finbow's forehead. "I wish I knew," he said. "I'll tell you the idea I toyed with for a while. You know the absurd theory that if you want to hide anything, you should put it in the most conspicuous place? I imagined it might have been possible for Avice to take advantage of the fact that she'd got an absolutely obvious motive. That is, she had such an obvious motive that no one could have imagined that she'd dared to have killed him. After she *had* killed him, she returns to you and me and everyone as though she was afraid that she'll be suspected of killing him for his money—the obvious motive. We all crowd round and pat her hand, and she gets away with the simplest murder in history."

"Finbow," I said fiercely, "you don't believe that anything like that can be true?"

Finbow looked thoughtful.

"She's acting most of the time—but I think that she *is* frightened. If she'd had the nerve to plan a coup of that magnificence, I don't think she'd be as frightened as she is. But I'm not certain. She's one of the most interesting young women I've met since I became middle-aged," he said pensively.

"To-morrow I'm going to investigate a few of the possibilities of that other fascinating young woman—Tonia. If we sit up to-night we shan't do any more good. I'm going to bed."

When we were in bed and I was trying in vain to find a way to exculpate Avice, Finbow sleepily made a last remark:

"There's one curious thing, Ian. It's easy to think of good reasons why these people should want to kill Roger; actually, it's even easier to think of better reasons why Roger should want to kill them."

CHAPTER FOURTEEN

Roger's Love Affairs

The dining-room at breakfast the next morning was very different from the fear-ridden place of the night before. Tonia flaunted a green dressing-wrap which revealed rather than concealed her exotic pyjamas, and Mrs. Tufts was excited to a red-necked indignation. However, she confined her protests to slamming plates down on the table. Apparently she had not recovered from Philip's gibe at tea-time. We were all amused by her pantomime; the room was full of a bright morning light; after last night's crisis of suspicious fear, there seemed to be a general friendliness among us all.

Even I, though I had heard Finbow eliminate suspect after suspect, was able to forget the greater part of my fears. It was a strange inexplicable respite; vaguely I told myself that after all Finbow might be wrong, and for the moment I was satisfied. The others were anxious to show that they regretted the quarrels at dinner-time, that hysteria had been responsible for their own bitter words, that they all wanted to retract and be friends again. And they treated the quarrel as though it had never happened.

No one referred to the angry quarter of an hour in the candle-light. Finbow told a long and extravagant story of how he had once been entrusted to drive a young French honeymoon couple and two tactful provincial friends through France from Lyons to Le Touquet. Tonia, in particular, derived much amusement from the steps taken for the comfort and well-being of 'les jeunes mariés', which was the tactful friends' invariable name for the young couple.

"Finbow," she asked him, "would you like to drive Philip and me somewhere, when we get married? We ought to have someone to look after us."

"I'm a modest man," Finbow replied, smiling. "And that, I fear, is a task beyond my powers."

Christopher was also very cheerful.

"This afternoon I shall give Aloysius Birrell a great pleasure," he said.

"Why?" asked Philip.

"By reporting at Vine Street," Christopher laughed. "If any of you see him, you might tell him that I shall follow all his instructions, and that there's very little danger of my escaping. If he's anxious, you might tell him that I shall re-appear without fail by a late train."

"I'll tell him," Finbow said affably.

"Thanks so much," Christopher said. "Whenever I meet him, I always have an intense desire to poke him in the stomach and say 'Boo!' He's essentially a man who provokes horse-play."

"I'm only restraining myself by an effort," Finbow murmured.

"I hope your Board don't decide to halve your salary from the start. All the old buffers will be talking of economy," William said, drinking a cup of tea.

"That would be a little hard." Christopher smiled. "Wish me luck that I don't get more than a ten per cent cut."

We all said "Good luck," and drank from our cups. Avice clinked hers against Christopher's, and smiled at him affectionately.

Christopher went away immediately after breakfast, and the rest of us spent an idle morning reading, writing letters, talking and at times joining in a game invented by Philip called 'Idiocy Poker'. The rules of the game were rather complicated. First, newspapers were searched for characteristic inanities uttered in public by leaders of English thought. These were written on small squares of cardboard, and play proceeded as in poker, the value of the card depending on the inanity of the utterance. The best hand of the day was one held by Avice, and consisted of a very powerful 'full house' of sayings due to three headmasters and two bishops. Two of the remarks I can still remember; one was included in a speech by a bishop in support of the preservation of Rural England, and ran: "I have never seen people dancing round a maypole in Piccadilly Circus." The other was pronounced by a headmaster: "I am certain that the boy who gets a commission in the O.T.C. and a place in the House Rugger team is going to turn out a better man than the boy with precocious tastes in literature. If more of our politicians had been trained in the Corps or on the Rugger field, England would never have got into the financial difficulties of to-day."

The first hours of the morning might have been extracted from our peaceful holidays of the years before, so marked was the lull in our anxious suspense. Inevitably, however, the tranquillity became broken. Long before lunch-time Tonia was sitting with her reddened lips set in an angry straight line. Minor irritabilities crept in insidiously throughout the afternoon, which turned cold and windy enough to keep us together in the sitting-room. The close contact made our tempers worse. The rain beat against the windows; the wind rustled incessantly over the reeds; grey clouds followed each other across the wide marshland sky.

On the river there was a solitary yacht, beating slowly up against the wind; two young men, with rain streaming down their faces, were sailing her grimly but without any skill, and they crossed and re-crossed the river in front of the bungalow without gaining a yard. I watched their manœuvres dejectedly.

Then there came a chugging down the river, and Birrell's motor-boat flashed by, avoided the yacht by the narrowest of margins and turned abruptly.

"Birrell can drive," Finbow remarked. "He apparently wants to talk to us."

We let him in through the french windows, and he began talking enthusiastically, with no regard to the rain that was dripping from his coat on to the floor.

"Good afternoon," he said. "I wish to ask you all some more questions about the—unfortunate gentleman. I find I can't make a complete schema"—he pronounced the word unctuously—"of the case until I have got some information upon his life before the murder. I shall want you all to tell me everything you can remember about Dr. Mills since you first knew him. Miss Gilmour, I shan't want you, of course, as you didn't know Dr. Mills. I think I'll start with you, Mr. Capel."

"Before you begin, I suggest you take your coat off," Finbow suggested gently. "The police force can't afford to have you laid up in bed. And you are very wet, you know."

"I hadn't noticed," Birrell answered, his eyes sparkling. "When I decide anything ought to be done in an investigation, I never think of anything else at all."

"That," said Finbow, "makes you the man you are." Birrell smiled gratefully. Finbow continued: "You'll allow *us*, however, to be interested in your health," and helped him to take off his coat, and made him sit in an arm-chair by the window. I realised that it was desirable for Finbow to keep on good terms with Birrell, but this exaggerated politeness seemed very much out of place. I took a chair by Birrell and answered bad-temperedly his questions about Roger. I told him that I first met Roger in 1921, when he had just become house-surgeon in his hospital; that I had seen him frequently during the next ten years; that I had twice been his guest at the villa in Italy, and that he had paid a visit to my cottage in Ross-shire. When Birrell asked me whether Roger was a wealthy man, I replied:

"He had an adequate income of his own, and a very lucrative practice as well."

Birrell went on: "He was his uncle's heir, wasn't he? He was expected to come into a lot of money when Sir Arthur Mills died?"

"I believe that was so," I said, not wishing to enlarge on the subject.

"Do you know, Mr. Capel," Birrell said, "whether Mr. Mills ever contemplated marriage?"

"I expect so," I replied. "Most men of his age have, at one time or another."

"I'm asking you for a definite answer, Mr. Capel," Birrell reproved me.

I thought it would be unwise to evade direct questions, even with Aloysius Birrell.

"I have heard rumours of an unhappy love-affair," I said.

Birrell slowly wrote all my replies in a new notebook, which I noticed had on its cover the inscription 'BACKGROUND OF MILLS CASE'. He read what he had written with a puzzled face, and then looked at me distrustfully.

"I don't think this gets me much further," he said.

"I'm sorry," I answered.

He passed the matter off good-naturedly. "Oh well," he said, "it will be useful when I make up my schema."

I joined Finbow and Tonia, who were sitting in a corner of the sitting-room together while the other three waited their turn with Birrell. Finbow said quietly:

"Hallo, Ian. You're just in time to see me tell Tonia's fortune."

"First I knew of it," said Tonia, with a short laugh. "Damned nonsense."

"But I'm sure you'll like it." Finbow smiled. "Be a nice polite girl and fetch me some cards."

Tonia found a couple of packs, and Finbow shuffled them meditatively. I was divided in my attention; by the window Birrell was questioning Avice, and though I knew that he was unlikely to gain any knowledge, I could not prevent my ears straining for her replies. On the other hand, I guessed that Finbow was telling fortunes in order to understand Tonia's emotions and reactions. It was a typical device of his. And I knew that, though I might miss it, he would extract some shred of meaning which would help to solve the real nature of Tonia's agitation. So I watched him deal the cards in two horizontal rows of five and heard him say:

"You were very fond of a dark man before you were twenty."

"He wasn't *very* dark," said Tonia.

"The cards aren't quite decided on the point," Finbow agreed.

[Birrell's voice captured my attention: "You have seen a great deal of Dr. Mills during the last four years, Miss Loring?" I heard Avice's quiet "Yes.". . .]

"But they show several other young men," Finbow went on. "They don't give the exact number, but it's more than two."

Tonia's laugh sounded to me a little forced.

"A brown-haired one at the end—that must be Philip," Finbow said. "Both he and the dark man were in love with you, the cards say." [. . . "my cousin did a lot of entertaining," I heard Avice reply.]

"There's someone before Philip, though," Finbow remarked, gazing at the cards as though they were full of meaning. Tonia broke in quickly: "Oh, that would be Boris. Haven't I ever told you about Boris, Finbow? He was a man

I met in Nice. He was in love with me, but I was too busy learning music to worry about him."

"I don't think the one I mean can be Boris," Finbow murmured. "The one I mean, I don't think you sent him away."

[Birrell was beginning to question Philip—"How long have you known Dr. Mills?" . . .]

"The cards are not telling you the truth," Tonia said.

"They told me of your successes with Philip and the dark man," Finbow murmured. "Why shouldn't they tell me of— other things? It happens to us all, you know."

Tonia got up suddenly—her pupils had dilated so that the brown and grey of her eyes formed only a narrow rim round the black centres.

"This is a silly game," she said. "Thanks, Finbow, but I'd rather you talked to me."

"I've said nothing of the future yet," Finbow smiled.

"We'll leave the future to look after itself," she said. Her strong painted mouth was twitching. Finbow studied her face attentively. "As you will," he replied, and I knew that he had discovered what he had set out to find.

After writing copiously in the notebook for some time, Birrell had a private chat with Finbow and then left.

When he had gone, it seemed that the bitterest feelings had been aroused. Again I had to listen to recriminations that everyone would regret in a few hours.

At tea-time Avice's hand shook as she took her cup, and her face was miserable and drawn. William sat sulkily in a corner, ignoring the others and reading Jeans over his tea. Philip made nervous attempts to talk to Avice. Tonia refused tea with enough scorn to abash Mrs. Tufts, and demanded a stiff whisky and soda. Finbow made his own tea with his imperturbable ritual, and as solemnly as ever murmured: "Best tea in the world."

After tea, tired of it all, I put on a mackintosh and went out in the garden. It was good to feel the driving rain after those hours inside. I listened to the high shriek of the wind.

Soon Finbow's voice came from near to me:

"Pleasant evening, isn't it, Ian?"

"Pleasanter than being in the house," I grunted. "Finbow, don't you find it horrible? Seeing those youngsters all trying to keep some sort of control—and breaking down? Don't you think it's pathetic?"

"I find it—interesting," he said quietly.

"God, man, are you quite inhuman?" I burst out. "Do you enjoy seeing them twist and squirm in front of you?"

"My dear old Ian," he replied, pulling up the collar of his coat and with a faint smile on his lips, "if I wallowed in the softer emotions, I shouldn't be much good at this kind of job. I try to understand people; but I don't see any reason why I should make myself unduly miserable over them."

I looked at his firm face and said:

"Your heart's a lot kinder than you pretend."

He laughed, but did not reply.

A great sweep of wind bent down the rushes over the water, and died away.

I asked Finbow: "I suppose you were trying to analyse Tonia's share in this business, when you were playing the fool with fortune-telling?"

Finbow opened his eyes in a mocking surprise.

"Ian, this is too acute of you."

"Why did you use a roundabout way like that?" I said.

"Because sometimes the easiest way of arriving at the truth is to give up asking questions and to make statements instead," he answered.

"I should have thought it was an unreliable method," I objected. He smiled, and explained:

"The usual views upon the best ways of getting at the truth

in personal affairs are stupider and more naïve than I ever can believe. It isn't surprising that most people never *do* reach the truth in personal affairs. You see, Ian, you and everyone else put an absurd superstitious value on the spoken word. If anyone says such-and-such is the case, then you tend to believe them. Even if you know they're liars, you still think there may be something in what they say. I should lay down one cast-iron principle. If anyone says such-and-such is the case, then we should not worry for the moment whether it's true or not. One should simply ask—*Why* did he say that such-and-such is the case? When you've got the motive, you can usually estimate the value of the fact.

"All the information you're ever told is a mixture of true facts and false facts floating on the surface of a great mass of wishes and fears and memories. To sort it out and find out what it means—you're simply obliged to use more subtle methods than Aloysius Birrell's. For instance, Tonia told us she'd never met Roger, then she told us she was at Nice and flared up at the suggestion that they might have met there. The only value of that statement is—that for some reason she'd hate us to think she was in Nice with Roger. It doesn't mean that she was in Nice with Roger, or that she wasn't: all it means is that she loathes the idea. If I asked her in an Aloysius Birrell-like way—Did you see Roger in Nice? She'd say no, and there's no direct way of finding out. So that one has to rely on a process of association. If I were allowed to write down a hundred words on a piece of paper—like this—

SCHOOL
ARTIST
TUBE
NICE

and so on, and made all the party write down opposite each

word, without stopping to think, the word which it recalls to them, I'd guarantee to show you some amusing results. Well, my method of questioning is just a simplified conversational way of securing people's associations. That's why I don't much mind what turn the conversation takes: I can usually make something of it. That's why I talk to young women when they're tired, and shock you to your chivalrous soul: associations are a lot easier to evoke when the conscious mind is dulled. And that's why I tell fortunes; because most people have a tinge of superstition left in them, and the idea that what I'm saying may be true throws them off their guard."

"How would you have managed if your shots at Tonia's young man had been wrong?" I asked. "You began by saying she liked a dark man before she was twenty; if that had gone wrong, you wouldn't have been able to go on."

Finbow chuckled:

"After observing her temperament, I thought it extremely improbable that she hadn't been fond of some man before she was twenty. And it was an even chance that he was dark. No, rather better than an even chance; fair men as a class aren't so amorous as dark."

I was amused for a moment. Then I said:

"What did you fiind out in the end?"

"For that," he answered, "you must wait a few hours."

There was a scream from the wind. I was impatient.

"Well," I asked. "Do you know who killed Roger?"

He answered gravely:

"I think I know who killed Roger."

"Who is it?" I cried, inflamed with fear.

"I can't tell you yet. Because, if you know, your own attitude may upset a very delicate situation. You see that, Ian?"

"Don't you see that it's unbearable for me?" I said anxiously.

"My dear Ian, I'm trying to prevent what might be even more difficult to bear," he answered, with a trace of regret in his voice.

For me at least, the hours after my talk with Finbow were the worst since the murder. I had to sit at dinner, and look at Avice's mournful, appealing face and Tonia's strong and striking attractiveness, with the knowledge in my mind that one of them had committed a cold and calculated murder.

Finbow sat between them, joking and chatting as though he was taking a couple of pretty young friends to a fashionable first night; and yet I knew that he alone realised which of those charming girls had shot Roger dead. Never have I so much envied him his ease of manner; and never have I more bitterly resented the detachment which made it possible for him to enjoy his masquerade!

Longingly and desperately I wished, as I looked at the three of them, that it was Tonia upon whom Finbow was to fasten the guilt in the end.

After dinner I tried to read, but the words altered themselves into floating shapes which I could dimly see—'Harley Street Specialist Shot by Beautiful Cousin.' I gazed at Avice sitting limp in a deep arm-chair, and I told myself for the hundredth time that I could never think the slightest evil of her. Then a surge of hope would go through me. I would think that Finbow was not infallible, that the case against William had been dismissed on fantastic grounds, that it was still possible that William had done it. I went over the evidence against him again. There was Christopher too, I told myself; even though we could not see the motive, suspicion could justifiably be thrown on him. Tonia or William or Christopher, but not Avice, I assured myself. And then I would feel the weight of doubt return. I hope I shall not spend another evening like it, during the rest of my life.

The return of Christopher was a diversion for which I was
more than thankful. He had driven by car from Norwich,
and arrived at the bungalow just before ten o'clock. He
came into the sitting-room, smiling and happy.

"How did it go?" asked William quickly.

"Splendidly," said Christopher, sinking into a chair. "They
all seemed to approve of me—and they've confirmed the job
and the salary. I knew they would, of course, but it's nice to
see it on paper."

"Congratulations, my dear," said Avice, with a wistful
smile.

"Thanks, darling," he smiled into her eyes, and kissed
her.

"What did they ask you?" Philip inquired, as he handed
glasses round so that we might celebrate.

"Oh, lots of silly questions. What I thought about race-
prejudice and whether I approved of Chinese and how I proposed to reorganise the research, and so on," Christopher
replied, with a satisfied sigh.

"When are they going to inoculate you?" said William.

"Next week," Christopher said. He raised his glass in
acknowledgment as we toasted him. "Rather a good man,
the doctor. I've never been examined before; and I didn't
know there were such a lot of things he would do. He said I
was an 'A.1' life, though."

"Comforting thing to be told," I said. "There aren't many
of them. Here's to Malaya!"

One by one we left the sitting-room, for it was obvious
to all of us that Avice and Christopher had to be left
alone to talk over their future. In order not to make our
tact too apparent, we made various excuses before we
escaped.

Tonia and Philip went into the garden, William to his
room, and Finbow and I walked slowly into the tiny entrance

hall. We were considering a stroll over the fields, when we heard Mrs. Tufts's voice:

"Aloysius, Aloysius, that red-haired hussy's clearing off with her young man. They're taking the motor-boat. Come quick. They'll get away if you don't. You must chase them."

"She's telephoning him," whispered Finbow. "This may be interesting."

We went out of the door, and walked round the house into the garden. In a few minutes there was a great flurry down the river, and the dark blur of a motor-boat made a wide circle in front of the bungalow, and came to a standstill by the bank. A fat shape came to meet it.

"Aloysius," Mrs. Tufts's voice came from the fat shape.

"Here I am, Elizabeth," came from the motor-boat.

"They've gone up towards Hickling," she said, panting for breath.

"We'll soon find them," Birrell answered. "You come with me."

"I'd like to," she said fiercely. "That vixen and her good-for-nothing—trying to clear off under our noses. Trying to escape by sea, I expect."

"Thanks to you, Elizabeth," said Aloysius Birrell, "they won't do it." By a light from the house, we saw Mrs. Tufts's small fat body lumbering into the motor-boat. Very quickly Birrell brought her round, and rushed up towards the Dyke.

Finbow spoke sharply: "Come on, Ian, you've got to sail the dinghy. We must watch this."

Rapidly I got the dinghy under weigh. I beat up the Thurne against a stiff cold wind. The banks were lost against the black sky, and sailing was difficult and slow. Until we got to the Dyke, apprehensions and sick fantasies about Avice had been washed from my mind by the demands upon hand and eyes made by the dinghy at night on the dark, narrow river. Then as we turned, and I let the sail fill with a beam

wind, I had a sudden overwhelming relief. For Tonia had
fled! It was Tonia we were hunting! And Avice, my dark,
pathetic Avice, was in safety in the house.

I eased the sail as we caught a hard gust. Then towards us
there came a familiar choking purr, and a motor-boat dashed
by, turned in its own length and came back to us. We were
rocking in its wake.

"Is that you, Sergeant Birrell?" asked Finbow blandly.

"It is me, sir." I could make out indistinctly his round
face. "I've been chasing two of your party. Miss Gilmour and
Mr. Wade." There was a note of disgust in his voice.

"Shame on them!" said Mrs. Tufts, whom we could not
see.

"Mr. Finbow, do you know what those two went to
Hickling for?" Aloysius Birrell said.

Finbow made an interested noise.

"They went," Aloysius Birrell continued, "to canoodle
each other."

"To fondle each other," Mrs. Tufts added, denunciatorily.

"It's revolting," Birrell cried. "The way they go on; kissing and cuddling and stroking each other's hair——"

"The shameless good-for-nothings!" shouted Mrs. Tufts.

"I told them to their faces——" said Birrell.

"So did I," said Mrs. Tufts loudly.

"What unblushing sinners they were," Birrell added.

"I told them if they were my son and daughter——" Mrs.
Tufts began.

"But if they were your son and daughter, they wouldn't be
likely to want to make love to one another, would they, Mrs.
Tufts?" Finbow interposed.

Aloysius Birrell broke off.

"Is that Mr. Capel with you?" he asked suspiciously.

"He's here safe," Finbow answered, with a trace of a
chuckle.

"To-morrow," said Birrell, "I'm going to dive for the automatic. Now I'm going to take Mrs. Tufts home. I shan't leave this boat until those two wastrels have come back."

"If everyone had your sense of duty, Sergeant——" Finbow murmured, and I gave the dinghy the wind and sailed on up the Dyke.

The Sound was so dark that twice we brushed against beds of reeds which had lurked invisible in the blackness. Time after time birds were roused and screeched protestingly—like Mrs. Tufts, Finbow remarked. Somehow I managed to find a clear stretch of water which led to Whitlingsea. The dinghy heeled before the wind, and the water lapped softly against our bows as we scurried along. We crossed Whitlingsea, and came up to the first of the posts which mark the passage through Hickling.

"Well," I said to Finbow, "what do we do now?"

"Good bit of sailing," he said. "If those two are making love, they're pretty certain to be somewhere near the bank. You'd better coast round very gently."

It was pleasant to be able to correct Finbow.

"As they're in a motor-boat, they'd almost certainly have run her aground if they'd gone anywhere but the centre of the Broad. It's only a few feet deep even in the middle. They must be in the middle," I announced triumphantly.

"Some day I must go for a walking tour through the Broads. Literally through the Broads; through the middle of them," replied Finbow unabashed. "Anyway, why did you ask me, if you knew where they were?"

I sailed on up the Broad. We seemed to move in a silent and unending darkness. Then there was a noise from over the water.

"That's Tonia, I fancy," whispered Finbow. "Voices carry for miles on these lakes. We must get nearer: I don't expect they're making love all the time."

"You think that was put on to drive Birrell and Mrs. Tufts away?" I asked very softly.

"Pretty certainly," Finbow replied. "Tonia's a quick-witted young woman. But even if they are making love, Ian, we're both old enough not to be unduly perturbed." I thought I heard a fragment of a chuckle. With the sail close-hauled, I approached quietly to the direction of the noise, and gradually it took form and resolved into words, and we could hear Tonia speaking.

"My darling, I didn't tell you. It's not the sort of thing which I even trouble to remember. Until this happened."

Philip's light voice carried easily.

"I ought to have been told before I brought you to the party. If I'd known you'd met Roger——"

Tonia's husky reply followed:

"If I'd known beforehand that Roger was giving the party, I *would* have told you. But you just mentioned Roger. I've run across hundreds of Rogers. When I saw who it was, I didn't want to worry you by telling you."

"You ought to have told me," said Philip.

"It was nothing," Tonia insisted. "Nice is a gayish place, and it was hot, and I—well, I had to have someone to have an affair with. And Roger happened to be there, that's all. After a few months, I got tired of him. He was in love with me, of course, but I threw him over."

Philip's voice became warmer:

"Never mind," he said.

Tonia answered:

"You are a darling. I had to tell you, because it's getting on my nerves. And those wretched policemen will find out, and ask me why I lied to them and why I told them I'd never seen Roger before. I had to tell you before they all came and badgered me and tried to prove that, because I'd had a little affair with Roger and thrown him over, I must have killed him." Her voice had risen to a note of hysteria.

Philip soothed her.

"Of course they won't. They won't find out—and if they do, who cares?"

"Don't be a fool, Philip. They'll suspect me. I know they will," the words poured out fiercely. "And everyone will think I did it. I swear to you that's all that happened: Roger and I had an affair two years ago. I threw him over, and didn't see him again."

Philip replied softly:

"You needn't swear to me, Tonia dearest. Oh, don't worry, we'll find a way out. Old Finbow will help us. Let's forget murders and policemen and silly people now," and no more coherent sounds came over the water.

Finbow whispered very softly:

"I rather feel that the conversation ought to be observed from closer quarters or not at all."

The sail home was very quiet. Finbow sat thoughtfully, with a cigarette glowing red in the darkness. He said nothing until we were nearly at the bungalow. Then he remarked casually:

"I'm beginning to get things straight."

CHAPTER FIFTEEN

Aloysius Birrell Dives

It was ten o'clock before Finbow and I appeared at the breakfast-table, the morning after our sail to Hickling. Finbow had just arrived back from an early morning walk. I expected to find the whole party there to chaff us, but actually there was only William, who was reading a long letter and smoking an after-breakfast cigarette, and Mrs. Tufts. By this time I had been acquainted with Mrs. Tufts for three days, during which she had varied in mood from exasperation to extreme exasperation, but I saw at once that any previous annoyance of her was mild compared to this.

"This," she hissed in an undertone, "is the fruits of sin.

"So!" Finbow replied. "Who's been sinning now?"

"You can mock, Mr. Finbow, but you know what I mean." She looked balefully at me. "That red-haired vixen and her long-haired young scoundrel—if they'd not been sinning last night, they'd have been at breakfast this morning. And I had to go with Sergeant Birrell after them, and we left the others alone in the house. Who knows what happened then? In my young days, if one of us girls had been left alone for half an hour with a man, we should have thought the worst."

Finbow sat down, and said absently:

"Mrs. Tufts, you flattered yourselves."

She began to explode, but Finbow interrupted the beginning of her speech, and said brusquely:

"That will do."

She said:

"I shall say what——"

Finbow broke in:

"You will not. You will say nothing at all to any of us this morning. I cannot have Miss Gilmour disturbed."

Mrs. Tufts gripped the wooden arms of her chair and was working up her energies for a new attack, but Finbow silenced her:

"That will be all," he said, and read his letter.

He gave a soft "So!" and handed it to me. It was written from Scotland Yard, and ran:

Dear Finbow,

After you had been here on Tuesday, I wired at once to a man in Nice who is there in connection with another job. I asked him to give me information about Mills's visits to Nice. Last night I had a wire from him. He says: "Mills well known in Bohemian circles in neighbourhood. Regular visitor for ten years, often accompanied by different women. Reputed generous but faithless to his women. Lived for two months with red-haired girl corresponding to description of Miss Gilmour. Left her suddenly. She stayed in Nice, expecting him back. He never came. She got into debt, and left Nice."

Miss Gilmour sounds an interesting young woman. I think I shall have a look at this case myself, if the local man doesn't finish it shortly.

As for the will, the thing is perfectly ordinary. Mills's uncle is worth about ninety thousand pounds, and Mills is heir to all except five thousand pounds. If Mills died, the whole lot passed to Miss Avice Loring. We also had a look at her financial position. She appears to live on about two hundred and fifty pounds a year, and yet she goes to the best shops and moves in circles where the average income is ten times more. There's a minor mystery for you, Finbow.

Anyway, that is all the information I can get you. What

are you going to do with it? Are you amusing yourself as you used to do, just solving puzzles for your own private entertainment? Perhaps I oughtn't to ask. But if you're merely interested and this problem is really subtle, I should be glad if you'd tell me what you think—that is, if I decide to come in. I imagine that you might save me a fortnight's hard work.

Ever,

Herbert.

I knew that 'Herbert' was Finbow's friend, Detective-Inspector Allen, but I was surprised at the informality of the proceedings. I learned later that the two of them had been close friends for years, and that they had several times co-operated on investigations where Finbow's insight could profitably be employed. Finbow himself told me later:

"I never look at anything that one of Allen's bright young men can do better than I can. Ninety-nine per cent of murders are like that. But the odd one per cent is a bit more subtle, and Allen and I together do it about a hundred times quicker than he and his satellites possibly could."

As I read the letter, however, the relations of Finbow and Allen were trifling compared with the news itself. Tonia had been lying to Philip the night before in Hickling! The story of her and Roger was different from the one which she had told! But there was also the disquieting report upon Avice. I tried to persuade myself that it was trivial, and that the letter had gone a long way towards throwing all the suspicion upon Tonia. Still, I had a haunting fear that I was too biased to make any judgment at all.

I gave the letter back to Finbow, who was eating fried eggs with a face completely untroubled, as though he had just received a chatty account of parish affairs from a maiden aunt. Yet it must either have fitted his argument, or destroyed it. My faith in him was great enough to make me sure that, in fact, the letter had merely gone into its place in Finbow's methodical scheme. I was certain that by now he knew the truth.

I almost hated him as he sat there, munching bacon, when two words from him would release my mind from its dread. I pleaded to myself: couldn't he just have said "Not Avice"?

Instead, he glanced with a sly smile at Tonia when she came in to breakfast, and asked her:

"The marsh air does make one a bit sleepy, doesn't it?"

She smiled, a little twistedly, and answered:

"Yes, Uncle Finbow."

"I should like to have heard your chat with Sergeant Birrell last night," he remarked thoughtfully. "I've always felt that my education in the matter of invective could have been improved."

Mrs. Tufts snorted, and left the room. Tonia gave a hearty laugh.

"The poor goop nearly died when I kissed Philip on the neck."

Avice arrived in time to hear Tonia's last remark, and said softly:

"I sympathise with him."

Tonia's eyes glinted. Every day there seemed more friction between her and Avice. She said:

"What do you mean? I suppose *you* prefer to make love on the quiet."

Avice drank a little tea, and replied:

"As a matter of fact, I do. Watching people make love ought to disgust anyone; to look at, it's the silliest activity in the world."

"You think I oughtn't to kiss Philip if there's anyone within sight?" Tonia murmured.

"It *does* get rather tiresome, seeing you mauling him," Avice agreed. They were both angry; Avice coldly contemp-

tuous, with an indifference that I felt sure was assumed;
Tonia with her red mouth distorted and her eyes shining.
It was, of course, a natural expression of the antagonism
which had been obvious to all of us. Avice's light gibe had
only put a match to a fire already laid.

Tonia said fiercely:

"You little devil. Very nice and frail and delicate you look.
If only we knew——!"

Avice winced. I noticed that Finbow's eyes were fixed on
her throughout the quarrel. At this point, however, he
interrupted:

"Tonia, you do Mrs. Tufts credit. At good, solid, well-
timed abuse, you'll soon be as good as she is."

Christopher and Philip came in together, and in a shame-
faced way Tonia and Avice became very distantly polite to
one another.

Later in the morning, a large motor-boat drew up outside
the bungalow. Aloysius Birrell alighted from it and walked
up the garden, with an intense excitement on his round,
fresh face.

"Mr. Finbow!" he called. "Mr. Finbow!"

Finbow had been writing letters in the house, but he came
out quickly, and smiled.

"I'm just going to dive for the automatic," Birrell announced. "Would you care to come?"

Finbow said: "Of course," and they chatted together for
a few moments. I went on reading Maurois on the veranda,
but looked up from time to time. Apparently Finbow was
making some suggestions which Birrell was unwilling to
receive; in the end Finbow whispered into his ear, and a
wide smile spread over Birrell's face. "Yes," he said whole-
heartedly, and went back to the motor-boat.

Finbow came up to me.

"Come and see the fun," he said. "Our Mr. Birrell will

now do his trick of diving for automatics. I've got him to consent to your coming in the motor-boat."

"Is that what you've been arguing about?" I asked, putting my book down.

"Yes," Finbow smiled. "He was a bit against it, to start with."

"However did you talk him round?" I said, as we were walking towards the boat.

"Oh, simply by telling him that you're likely to confess when brought to the scene of the murder and confronted dramatically with the weapon," Finbow answered. "Though how exactly he proposes to be dramatic in a diving-suit, I don't quite know."

I laughed, for Birrell's suspicion of me had become a joke now that Finbow's searching had gone so far. I was glad to get away from my thoughts, even if it meant watching Birrell dive.

The motor-boat ploughed its way rapidly from Potter, leaving a wash which tossed the moored yachts mercilessly up and down. Finbow protested to me:

"I do resent having to do things which offend my sense of suitability. I cannot regard the motor-boat as a suitable means of progression for a man of taste. It goes quicker than a yacht, and it's a lot more efficient; but in a large drawing-room, a bicycle would be quicker than walking and a lot more efficient. Yet no one ever rides a bicycle in a drawing-room: why *will* they drive motor-boats on small rivers?"

I grunted, and looked uninterestedly at the crowd in the boat. There were several policemen in plain clothes, one or two indeterminate and rabbit-like officials whose names and functions I have never learned, and two sailors imported by Birrell to manage the pump and diving lines. How or where Birrell had acquired the technique of diving, I could not imagine, but he appeared to be going through the routine with the same enthusiastic fervour that he brought to the detection of crime.

We rushed through Horning, and Birrell anchored exactly at the spot where we had moored the yacht three days before.

"We'll begin here," he said, and started to put on his diving-suit. With his native modesty, he retired to the cabin to take off his clothes, and reappeared in long woollen pants and a flannel vest.

One of the sailors said briefly:

"You haven't got enough on. It'll be cold down there."

"Yes," said Birrell. "I know that. These are the under-clothes I wear in winter. I always put them on in September so as to be ready for the cold weather." Finbow murmured in my ear: "It sounds like a proverb—'If you remember That cold September Will hurt your chest—Put on your vest.'"

And then he asked: "But yesterday, Sergeant Birrell, you got wet and stood in the bungalow without thinking of your health at all."

"That is when I'm following up a clue," Birrell explained. "Otherwise I always try to look after myself. I am going to put on a lot more clothes this morning, so that I shall be nice and warm in the water." He pulled on pair of pants after pair of pants and flannel shirt after flannel shirt. He began to look remarkably fat. It was the first time I had ever seen a man enter a diving-suit, and I did not know that the process of dressing up was a usual preliminary. I thought that the use of five pairs of pants was an idiosyncrasy of Birrell's. His two sailors hustled him into the suit, and after some hitching and re-adjustments he stood before us, the complete diving man.

We inspected him solemnly. There was something vaguely H. G. Wellsian about the mechanical-looking figure with Birrell's face peering through the thick glass window. One of the sailors shouted to him:

"Are you ready to start?"

His face was blank and uncomprehending. He had heard nothing.

"Are you ready to start?" the sailor bawled.

He looked puzzled. Apparently a little noise had penetrated the suit, but had conveyed no meaning to him. He wore the unintelligent expression of the completely deaf.

Both sailors bawled together:

"Are you ready to start?"

His mouth formed a question. He had still not heard. Then the sailors pointed desperately at the water. Birrell moved his head in assent, and began to clump towards the side of the boat.

One of the indeterminate and rabbit-like officials told us that he was going to walk along the bed of the river until he came to the bend. The official remarked:

"The bed's hard here. That's lucky for him. Most other places on the river, it would be nothing but mud."

"It was, I think, rather considerate of the murderer to choose this stretch," said Finbow thoughtfully.

At last Birrell was safely over the side, and slowly he was let down to the bed of the river. The pump wheezed monotonously. As he walked beneath the water we could see the beam of his powerful flashlight covering the ground. The motor-boat kept pace with him by moving for a few yards and stopping. The beam of light moved foot by foot.

Finbow was amused:

"I ought to stand Aloysius Birrell a drink," he said to me. "Last night I said I'd like a walking tour through the Broads —but I never expected to see someone actually do it."

I was not so easily amused as Finbow, and for me the search was serious.

We advanced, yard by yard. The rabbit-like officials twittered. The Norfolk policemen looked unmoved. Finbow smoked placidly. I gazed at the black still shadow of the reeds; the nerves above my elbows trembled with excitement.

Then, as the minutes passed away, the excitement died. Going yard by yard over a stretch of water seemed a dull pastime which had been going on for ever and would never stop, which had had no results and which could have no results. I stared dully into the water. We had crawled over half a mile.

Suddenly Birrell waved his torch three times. At the signal, my heart leapt. He was pulled up, and in his glove he held an automatic to which there was attached some other object: from where I stood, I could not see distinctly.

Finbow said "So!" interestedly. The police shouted "Good old Aloysius!" The officials made indistinct noises. The sailors spat approvingly.

An official laid the automatic awkwardly on the deck, and the sailors began to remove Birrell from the diving-suit. Finbow and I walked a few yards in order to have a closer view of Birrell's find. When I got close enough to examine it, I had a curious sense of unreality, as though I had just been an assistant at a conjuring trick in which I was expected to believe. For, stretched out along the deck in a long and sodden line, there were a small automatic, a dirty discoloured pennant and a large brown-coloured book.

"It's the log-book," I said to Finbow, and I went on my hands and knees in order to see how the three objects had been connected. It was very simple; the twine belonging to the pennant had been tied in the way shown in the diagram.

In fact, the pennant was merely a means for tying the automatic to the log-book. A long piece of cord would have served exactly the same purpose. The grotesqueness of the arrangement made me feel stupidly hopeless: an automatic alone was to have been expected—but this ridiculous collection left me dazed and bewildered.

"What can it mean?" I asked Finbow, who was standing smiling.

"It means," he said, "that someone had a sense of humour."

Soon Birrell was standing on the deck in his long pants and flannel vest. In a puzzled way he studied the automatic.

"It's a .22. That corresponds to the bullet we found in Dr. Mills's heart," he said.

"Not very surprising," Finbow remarked.

"This cord is tied with a simple knot round the barrel," Birrell continued unhappily, "and the other end is tied round this book——"

"Which is, of course, the log-book. I'm almost sure I recognise it," I broke in.

"I should think these are the missing log-book and burgee," said Birrell, regarding me coldly. He slipped the book out of its cord, and opened it.

"Yes," he said, "it is the log-book all right, but the water's done its work. It's impossible to read much of it." He looked disconsolately at the automatic and the book, his face clouded, a picture of disappointment.

"The water will have washed off every finger-print," he grumbled.

All of a sudden, his round face lit up; he bent over the book and laughed; he straightened himself and surveyed us. He paused for a dignified second, and then uttered the one word:

"Suicide."

CHAPTER SIXTEEN

Aloysius Birrell Makes His Report

There was a commotion on board. One of the officials said: "Suicide!."

Birrell replied complacently: "Of course," and looked round at us all.

Finbow said: "Don't you think it would be better if you explained, Sergeant? We have not all got minds as quick as yours, you know, and what seems obvious to you may be very mysterious to us."

"Right," said Aloysius Birrell. "I will give you all a few minutes. But I have not much time to spare, naturally. I must get in touch with Scotland Yard very soon. There may be wrong ideas to clear up."

Still wearing only his flannel pants and vest, he stood with the automatic between his feet, and we formed a semi-circle round him. He was radiantly happy. It was the hour of his life. He announced: "What else is the reason for tying a book on to the automatic? If a murderer wanted to get rid of an automatic, he would just throw it overboard."

One of the officials muttered:

"That is true enough, Aloysius."

Birrell continued: "Why should he go to the trouble of joining the automatic to a book by the strings of the burgee? When he could just toss it overboard. But when you've shot yourself, you can't throw an automatic away, so, before you commit the act, you tie your automatic to a heavy object, over the side of the boat. Then when you have committed the act"—I saw Finbow smile at the inane phrase—"your grip loosens, and the heavy object pulls the automatic after it into the water. So that the automatic disappears after you have shot yourself. In this case, the log-book was the most convenient heavy object."

"But why should anyone want to do that?" asked an official. "After you have shot yourself, I should have thought you would not take much interest in what happens to automatics."

Birrell pursued dramatically: "The idea in this case," he said, "was *to make the suicide look like a murder.*"

We all exclaimed.

"It's surprising," admitted Birrell, "but it must be true. For some reason Mills"—I noticed that, now the case had become suicide, Birrell dropped the 'Dr.'—"wanted to end his own life. The reason I can easily find out," he said, "but I suspect it to be connected with some matrimonial imbroglio." Again I saw Finbow smile. "I found out yesterday by careful examination of the yachting party that not long ago Mills was concerned in a matrimonial imbroglio." He rolled the phrase round his tongue. Then he looked solemn. "A man will do much on account of an unhappy love."

There was a moment's silence. Birrell went on: "But the story does not stop there. Mills not only wanted to end his own life. He wanted to injure someone else by killing himself. It is a horrible thought; a man dying unprepared—and his last act trying to injure someone else. In my profession, though, we come across the seamy side of human nature. Mills killed himself to ruin someone else. But who I can only guess. The way to do it was simple: to make his suicide look like a murder. I have no doubt that he thought over the matter, and read up the criminological literature and found this device. It's an old one. You'll find it described in Gross's *Handbuch der Criminologie, volume two,* page 247. Fortunately for the interests of justice I happened to know my professional literature."

I was overjoyed. Birrell had convinced me, for what else could be the purpose of the weight? It seemed also completely consistent with the picture of Roger which Finbow had established. He had died as he had lived, cheating his friends, and at that moment I could not bring myself to regret that he chose to end it. The world, I was convinced, was none the poorer; and I thanked God that none of my friends had been involved in a crime. I laughed to myself that I had suspected Avice. Avice! The idea seemed ridiculous now. And I began to think kindly of Tonia, that queer ardent girl.

Birrell disposed of one or two questions easily, and received Finbow's congratulations with a broad, delighted smile.

"Sergeant Birrell," said Finbow, "no one else of your rank in the whole of England would have got to the bottom of this as quickly as you have done! I hope soon to congratulate you on your promotion."

The motor-boat was hurried to Horning, in order that Birrell could put his news through to Scotland Yard. The rest of us waited in the lounge of the 'Swan' while Birrell telephoned. He returned in half an hour with an ecstatic smile. "It surprised the Yard more than anything that they've heard for years. Murder arranged to look like suicide they have heard of, often enough; but they were dumbfounded when I told them I'd proved this was a suicide arranged to look like a murder," he told us. "The next step is for us to make out a formal report. I should be obliged if you gentlemen would stay and certify that I actually found these articles in the way I am going to describe."

Birrell wrote laboriously for some minutes. I was not anxious to hurry him. It was deliciously pleasant to bask in the assurance that everything had come right in the end, that after all their trials my friends could go unscathed.

I felt it was almost worth enduring the strain of the last few days, in order to come at last to this content.

Birrell gave Finbow and the officials a statement to sign. It said, as far as I remember:—

Search for Revolver and Conclusion of Mills's Case

I began the search for the missing revolver in the Mills's Case at 11.30 a.m. on Sept. 4. I used the appropriate method of traversing the bed of the river in a diving-suit. At 12.10 a.m. approximately my search was successful. On investigation it transpired that I had obtained a .22 automatic (corresponding to the bullet in Mills's heart) which was undoubtedly the fatal weapon. It also transpired that appended to the automatic there were, first, a burgee, one of whose cords was secured to the barrel of the automatic, and, second, a book round which was secured the other cord of the burgee. On examination the book proved to be the log-book of the yacht. The absence of the burgee and the log-book had been commented on in a previous report.

The conclusion arrived at from these pieces of evidence is that Mills committed suicide after having connected the automatic to the log-book, which hung over the side and acted as a weight. (Gross's Handbuch, volume two, page 247). Motive will be described in a subsequent communication, together with the automatic, etc., which will be forwarded for inspection.

(Signed) A. Birrell,
Detective-Sergeant, Norwich City Police Force.

We hereby testify that the account of the progress of the search followed the course described, and that the results were as stated.

Birrell had left a space for names. Finbow wrote his signature with a smile and suggested that he and I should go back to Potter and relieve the anxiety of the party, who were still in ignorance of the happy solution. Birrell agreed lightheartedly.

We found that a bus was leaving for Potter in twenty minutes, and we strolled up and down outside the 'Swan'. I could not resist saying maliciously:

"You might have been right about the murder, Finbow—if there'd been a murder."

"It is a surprising thing," he murmured, "how one underestimates the people around one. I never should have thought that Birrell was likely to make a useful discovery."

"And here he's just quietly settled the whole business," I said cheerfully.

"Not exactly quietly," Finbow protested. "I've met few noisier men in my life."

"Anyway, he's settled it. It *is* funny, when we've been thinking all the time that Avice or Tonia might have murdered Roger. It seems utterly ludicrous now," I said.

"It *is* funny," Finbow agreed.

"I suppose you couldn't have been expected to consider suicide as a possibility. I should never have thought it myself, and I knew him pretty well," I told him.

"I never thought of it," he said.

"Well, never mind. We'll have a pleasant little party at the bungalow now." I was feeling at peace with all the world.

"It is odd," Finbow leaned against a wall, and tapped a cigarette with a finger. "Fancy a man going to those lengths. Imagine a man who's so bitter against someone that he's willing to kill himself to injure him—or it may have been her. He doesn't go about it in a vulgar way, and fix the suspicion directly on the person he wants to be found guilty of the murder. He just knows that the evidence of motive will be enough to convict the one he's aiming at. So he arranges everything dramatically, so that apparently lots of people might have been concerned, and stages an absolutely convincing murder. Imagine him sailing on that last morning, with the automatic weighted so as to carry it away and leave no doubt that he'd been shot by one of his party. Imagine his satisfaction when he thought of Avice—I wonder if it was Avice he was aiming at—being finally tracked down, and sentenced, and carried, shrieking, to have her pretty neck broken. Imagine his delight when he's got everything planned —and then, when all's ready, he pulls the trigger and dies with a smile on his lips."

"And the automatic goes overboard—and the rest of the story we know," I added.

"The automatic goes overboard, leaving a scratch when the cord bit into the paint. Oh, I'm sure there's a scratch on the boat where the cord bit into the paint," Finbow continued, and then, in a low tense voice, he said:

"So! Distinctly clever!"

"Roger was a clever man," I agreed.

"I'm afraid I wasn't thinking so much of Roger," said Finbow quietly, "as of the person who killed him."

CHAPTER SEVENTEEN

Five Pleasant People Are Relieved

The words came to me as the greatest shock of the whole mystery. For an hour I had been uplifted by the thought that, after all, the happiness of our party could be restored, and that no longer would we all dread the weeks to come. In one sentence Finbow swept the hope away from me.

"The person who killed him?" I said dully. "You don't believe it was suicide?"

"Of course I don't," Finbow replied. "Though it may be convenient if the authorities do."

I stared up the road, sick at heart: our bus was coming slowly in. Desperately, I exclaimed:

"But it *must* be suicide. Think of that log-book! Why the devil should a murderer want to tie the log-book to an automatic?"

Finbow smiled, climbed into the bus, and stretched himself on the seat. Then he began to talk:

"My dear Ian, you may remember I made a point a day or two ago that no man knows *all* the material facts or *all* the psychological facts. It was a platitude, of course; and like most platitudes, it happens to be true. I said at the time that if twenty-eight reliable witnesses had seen Roger shoot himself, then I would accept that—and I should try to find what psychological point I'd missed, because at present for Roger to commit suicide seems utterly incredible.

"But we haven't got twenty-eight reliable witnesses to vow that Roger killed himself. Instead, we've got one piece of evidence that recalled to Birrell a rather ingenious device of a malevolent suicide. Naturally it was *meant* to recall that sort of device. On the other hand, there's masses of psychological evidence that make it extraordinarily unlikely that Roger could ever have killed himself. Very few people *do* kill themselves, you know: and those who do aren't usually cheerful optimistic successful men with growing practices in Harley Street."

"You're usually a bit more subtle than that," I complained. "He wasn't really successful—he probably knew that William was going to steal his thunder: and he must have been miserable because of Avice. It's not pleasant to be in love with a girl who doesn't love you, you know."

"But not a reason for suicide," Finbow commented, with a flickering smile on his lips. "Roger probably had a wretched time, being in love with Avice: but I'm quite certain that he never gave up the hope that she was really in love with him after all. You see, Ian, for almost *anybody* it is just the most difficult thing in the world to realise that someone you love is not in love with you. With the most honest of people, the feats of self-deception that can be performed are quite amazing. One devises all sorts of explanations why she won't admit that she's in love with one. One even says to oneself that she *isn't* in love with one. But one never believes it. That, I think, is true of everyone. It is even true of the most complete of realists—such as myself"—and I thought I could see a shadow pass over his pleasant face—"how much more must it have been true of a man like Roger, cheerful and dishonest with himself and everybody else and—by the way— used to having a certain amount of success with women. Not that *that* means anything. I should say it was absolutely certain that, most of the time, Roger was convinced that sooner or later Avice would go up to him, and tell him that she'd loved him for years."

I had to admit that his reconstruction of Roger's attitude to Avice was in complete agreement with what I had seen for myself in the last year. I made one last suggestion:

"What about William? Roger must have been worried about him," I said.

Finbow said, smiling:

"Roger was certainly worried about William, but there were a great many things he could have done—and would have done—before he committed suicide. Roger held the cards, you know; he had an established reputation, and people have an enormous respect for established reputations, even if they suspect that the holder of them isn't really much good. No, if every doctor or scientist of the Roger type were to kill himself because of his young rival, there'd be quite a high death-rate among doctors and scientists; what happens, in fact, is that the young rival is only very slowly allowed to run into an established reputation. Then *he* repeats the process on *his* young rival, and so we go on until we get to Mr. Wells's scientific Utopia."

"There might be things in Roger's life that you know nothing about," I said reflectively.

"That's quite true," Finbow replied. "And if there were strong material evidence for suicide, I should have to admit that I hadn't gone deep enough into him. At present, though, the psychological facts agree with the material facts: together, they make it impossible that Roger can have killed himself."

"The material facts?" I objected. "They all make it conceivable that he *could* have done it."

"There's one material fact that you have overlooked," he said softly.

"And that is——?" I asked.

"Yourself," Finbow replied.

"What?" I shouted.

"Think a minute," he went on. "If this were a suicide, it was an extraordinarily cunning and calculating one, done with the definite object of looking like a murder. You'll agree to that?"

"Yes," I answered.

"Well, it wouldn't look much like a murder if Mr. Ian Capel suddenly wandered round the deck and saw Roger taking a careful shot at himself. You see, for all Roger knew, you were sitting on deck all the time . . . and one unknown factor can't possibly be reconciled to a well-thought-out suicide. Ian, this is important: Roger couldn't possibly have known your movements. Only the people below could be certain where you were!" said Finbow.

"I suppose that's so," I said.

"It's obvious. Roger might have known where everyone else was at that time of the morning; parties do fall into a sort of routine. But he couldn't know where you'd be, until you'd been on the yacht a day or two," Finbow explained.

"He might have risked it," I protested.

Finbow replied smoothly:

"He might—if there'd been any real reason for hurry. But there wasn't. There was nothing he wanted to stop within the next day or two. Assume it was Avice's wedding: that's arranged for some indefinite time in the future. Or William's career; that could be smashed by killing himself within a month as easily as on Tuesday, September 1.—No, Ian, as Aloysius Birrell would say, the tempo's all wrong!"

"You were wrong to abuse Aloysius Birrell's word, weren't you?" I said.

"The only justification for stupid terms is that an intelligent man can use them as a sort of shorthand," he said, smiling. "Whoever did this—was desperate: and whoever did this—knew where everyone was on that Tuesday morning."

"Why tie the log-book on to the automatic, then?" I asked, with a dark realisation that Finbow must be right, and that soon I had inevitably to hear—things which would pain me beyond feeling.

"The person who did it was cleverer than any of us," Finbow replied. "If the murder had looked like a suicide from the start, in a vulgar sort of way, with letters of fare-well and a revolver near the body, I think everyone would have doubted it. Instead of that, the murder was arranged to look like a murder—for a time; and a very mysterious murder, too, with five people equally possible, and a strongish case against all of the five. Then when the revolver is found. You remember it is conveniently dropped on to a part of the river with a firm bed, so that it isn't too difficult to find? Not too vulgarly easy; nothing in this business is too easy or too underlined. When the revolver is found, what do they conclude? That it is a suicide, but a suicide looking like a murder. This must be the first case in history of a murderer making his murder look like a suicide arranged to look like a murder. Don't you see what a very beautifully worked-out piece of work the murder was? Suspicion against five—that was important, in case the suicide didn't work. And also I think so that Roger's character should be dis-covered in the investigation. Then the suspicion averted by a malevolent suicide. Oh, it's very, very clever! It's the murder of a person of taste, nothing vulgar, nothing too obvious, everything balanced and in harmony! The one person of taste left in this journalistic world!"

I was silent. Finbow continued:

"The real importance of Birrell's find is that several of the puzzling facts have disappeared. We know now why the log-book and pennant were missing. The log-book, I'm sure, was used as I suggested at Lord's—to amuse Roger while he was being shot. And it made a very convenient weight. The pennant was probably the most convenient thing to tie it to the automatic; it happened to be lodged on the same shelf, you remember.

"Also, we now understand the queer business of no one confessing when you promised a conspiracy of silence. Obviously, if—whoever it was—was looking forward to the death being proved to be a suicide, there wasn't going to be a confession."

We had arived at Potter Heigham, and walked slowly back through the straggling village and over the fields. I was numb with pain: it was a murder after all, and the unravelling was yet to come. Before we got to the cottage, Finbow said quietly:

"I'm going to tell the party that I believe in Birrell's theory. You must try to look as though you were convinced, too. You must act, Ian; try to be normal and happy, just as you would be if it had been a suicide."

I promised that I would, but never have I felt less like pretence.

The party had an air of concealed strain when Finbow went and sat among them in the garden. Philip and Tonia were lying on the grass, with their faces turned to each other; Avice and Christopher lounged quietly in deck-chairs: William sat in a wicker-chair, reading absorbedly. When Finbow and I took our places, however, it was clear that all of them were aching to ask the question which had been in their minds since someone had heard Aloysius Birrell announce his quest.

Yet the convention that one dissembles one's interest in anything that is really important proved very strong; and there must have been a feeling also that too strong an interest would be unwise. Accordingly, whilst all the five had only one topic, one question, in their heads, they listened politely to a discourse by Finbow on the relative merits of local lines of the L.N.E.R. compared with German district railways. Christopher and William both gave their views on railway systems in different countries.

Finally Philip burst out:

"Finbow, what about the automatic?"

"Oh yes," said Finbow calmly, looking down at him on the grass. "Aloysius Birrell found it."

"Did he?" murmured Christopher.

"Yes," Finbow answered. "He found it. About half a mile from Horning. It had the log-book attached by means of the strings of the pennant. Everyone's satisfied that Roger shot himself, and had arranged the log-book so that the automatic was pulled overboard to make it look like murder. Birrell has explained to Scotland Yard that it was just a rather curious suicide."

There was a second's stillness. Then Avice gave a gentle "Oh!", and her pale face softened into a smile. Tonia and Philip wreathed their arms round one another, and kissed with a long and quivering intensity. Christopher looked pleasantly around, and touched one of Avice's hands lightly. William uttered a harsh and jeering laugh.

"That's a good joke," he said. "Everyone suspecting everyone else—and the damned fool killed himself."

"I think it's funny," Finbow agreed.

"You're convinced that I didn't do it?" William added. "You thought I did, of course?"

Finbow smiled.

"As a matter of fact, I always knew you didn't."

"I don't believe you," William laughed. "Why did you know?"

"I'll tell you some time, perhaps," said Finbow. "It's connected with the fact that you're a rather aggressive young man."

The whole ghastly farce was torment for me. It was abominable that I should have to sit while Finbow told them all that there was no more need to worry. I had to try to be placid, when I knew that it would soon be known by whom the murder had been done. Avice's low voice broke into my thoughts:

"It's good to feel free for once," she said. "These last few days—Lord, I think I've aged ten years!"

"It's not been very nice," Christopher agreed.

"I never want to go through anything like it again," said Tonia, raising her flushed face from Philip's. There was a murmur of "Nor I!" from the party, and I felt pity for them all, and a greater pity for the one who would be living for the next few hours in a fool's paradise.

"I know!" said Philip. "Let's tell Mrs. Tufts."

Mrs. Tufts was called and, after a few minutes, appeared, disapprovingly and unwillingly.

Philip commenced:

"Mrs. Tufts, you'll be glad to hear that none of us did the murder."

"Who says so?" said Mrs. Tufts suspiciously.

"Sergeant Birrell," answered Finbow.

Mrs. Tufts's face showed a touch of warmth.

"Well, if *he* says so," she said. "He's a clever man, is Sergeant Birrell—and a gentleman, which is more than can be said of lots who call themselves gentlemen." She glanced at me; she seemed to resent me very much, independently of whether I had done the murder or not.

"It's perhaps as well that none of you did it," said Mrs. Tufts. "You'd have been wanting to stay here longer. When shall you be going?"

"At once," Avice murmured.

"This afternoon," William said.

"We ought to stay at least one more night!" Philip protested, "just to show that we're friends again, and that we can hope to enjoy a holiday together some other time."

"Good idea!" said Christopher. "We'll stay until to-morrow evening or the morning after that, Mrs. Tufts."

"H'mf!" said Mrs. Tufts.

The afternoon was a long-drawn-out ordeal for me. The party was behaving with a spasmodic childish gaiety, rather as people will who feel that they must conscientiously celebrate a great event. Finbow observed dispassionately as he watched them:

"It *is* curious that convention should dictate how everyone ought to behave under strong emotion. Look at them all, trying to be gay, just because it's been bred in them to think that they *ought* to be gay when they're relieved from anxiety. While actually the normal reaction to great relief from strain is simply a rather indifferent tiredness."

"How can you go on looking at them as though they were insects?" I said bitterly. Finbow smiled and smoked by my side, while the other five swam a little and basked in the sun in bathing-costumes. Avice looked slim and white and languid: Tonia's legs and arms were browned by the Mediterranean sun, and she and Philip embraced and fought in the water. Avice and Tonia were both more beautiful than an old man had a right to see, I thought. And one of them had killed a man in cold blood. I heard Finbow's smooth and pleasant voice.

"The case of Tonia and Roger is rather interesting," he said. "Of course, she is the sort of girl who falls in love pretty easily and extremely thoroughly. She's very much in love with Philip now. But I dare say she was quite a lot in love with Roger two years ago. The interesting thing is the way she takes it now. She tried hard to conceal from everyone that she'd ever known him at all."

"Because it was dangerous," I put in.

"No. Chiefly that Philip shouldn't have any idea," Finbow continued. "That is the interesting point."

"Surely a young woman normally conceals her affairs from her lover," I remonstrated, not quite realising where Finbow was leading. Finbow chuckled.

"I don't mind betting that Tonia has told Philip about every other affair—except this one. She's certain to have had a good wholesome pride in the men who've been fond of her."

"Then why did she keep this back? Unless she was planning to kill Roger," I said.

"Because she wanted Philip to be in love with her, and she didn't like him ever to see her with a man who'd thrown her away without a thought. Remember all the time that Roger was living with Tonia, he was regularly proposing to Avice. And Tonia knew that Roger was in love with Avice. That is what she can't forgive. That's what she couldn't bear Philip to know," Finbow answered quietly.

"If he loves her, does it matter?" I asked.

"She was probably acting—without knowing it—on the good sound principle that everyone's affections are influenced by people round them. One often likes a woman because other people do; and in the same way, though one likes a woman a great deal, one is definitely affected if other men don't find her attractive. So if Philip saw that Roger loved Avice but didn't care a damn for Tonia, Philip would very likely lose quite a lot of his passion for Tonia. It's absurd that we are all affected by what other people think: but it's true. It's simply because no one is sufficiently sure of himself to dispense with the approval of the crowd—or with its envy!"

"There's something in what you say," I said, and I gazed at

Avice and Tonia as they stood side by side in the sun. I re-flected that any young man who had either of them in love with him could count himself lucky. And yet——

"You ought to have gathered this when you heard Tonia telling Philip the other night," Finbow remarked reflec-tively. "She wasn't much frightened of being suspected of the murder; but she was very frightened of Philip hearing from some other man that she was a cast-off of Roger's. You remember how she insisted that she had got tired of him, and thrown him over. More than anything, she wanted Philip to believe that. That is why she went with him that night and made love to him, and told him the story which she would have liked to be true. And of course that is why she hates Avice. Every time Tonia sees Avice, it's a reminder of her shattered pride."

I looked at Finbow's long face.

"This is convincing and clever as far as it goes," I said. "But what does it prove?"

"It rather proves," he replied, "that Roger dead was far more of a danger to Tonia than Roger living. If he were dead, his affair with her was certain to become known: while if he were alive and still hoping to marry Avice, he would not be likely to let it out that he was living with Tonia at the time that he was proposing to Avice."

"You mean," I said, horrified, "that you think that Tonia didn't do the murder?"

"Of course she didn't," he said calmly. "I should have thought you'd have seen that she was proved innocent as soon as we had found the automatic."

CHAPTER EIGHTEEN

Avice Burns Some Paper

I could not speak. I had only the one thought left—that Avice alone had not been cleared. She was standing on the bank, undecided whether to dive in again or not; her pale face was grave, her slim body graceful, the whole picture one of great loveliness. I closed my eyes in horror.

Finbow explained calmly:

"The position of the automatic determines pretty accurately the time of the murder. Even if we don't allow for the movement along the hard bottom with the current, the automatic can't have been dropped later than nine-fifteen or so. It's just the same calculation as we did on the first morning. Well, that lets Tonia out completely. She couldn't have gone out of the cabin before nine-twenty. She had to pick up the automatic from somewhere, presumably Roger's cabin. Of course she can't have had it on her. You can't conceal an automatic in your pyjamas if you've got a figure like Tonia's. Then she had to kill Roger. It would mean she couldn't possibly have dropped the automatic before nine-twenty, and that's right outside the limits of error."

I had no spirit left to raise objections or to challenge statements. All I could realise was that Avice lay in deadly danger. I struggled with the words:

"So it's Avice? Good God, man, don't do anything. Let them think it was suicide. I can't bear it!"

Finbow's voice did not change from its usual smoothness:

"You've only got to stick it for another few hours, Ian. It'll soon be over. And I'll do what I can."

With that promise I had to choke down forebodings that gave me a physical nausea.

When the party finished bathing and had dressed, Tonia suggested that we should go down the river to Potter Heigham for tea. This struck them all as a symbol that there were now no constraints, and with noise and laughter they packed into the two boats which were attached to the bungalow. Most of them got into the motor-boat, which Christopher drove; I sailed Finbow and William in the dinghy. I had a memory of the last time I had sailed the dinghy; in my stupidity I had thought then that Finbow had brought the crime to Tonia; now that the truth was so unutterably more painful, the memory was bitter.

The others were sitting at a table in the garden of the Bridge when we arrived sedately in the dinghy.

"Come on," shouted Tonia. "This is Murderless Tea."

"Quite a new experience," Philip smiled, "to be sitting down to a meal without the feeling that one's got a murderer within a few feet."

"Life, in fact, becomes utterly dull," Christopher remarked as Finbow, William and I sat down. "I think Ian ought to do something about it—Ian, won't you do a murder just to relieve the monotony?"

I tried to muster a smile, but it was not a success.

"What's the matter, Ian?" said Avice softly. "You don't seem very happy."

"When you get to our age, my dear," Finbow interposed, "you'll realise there are a lot of physical ills both immobilising and not readily mentioned in public. At least, not by a modest man like Ian. Actually—he's got indigestion."

"My poor Ian," Avice exclaimed in a distressed tone. "I'm *so* sorry. Can't I do anything?"

"It'll be all right," I muttered.

"I'll go to the pub and see if they've got any magnesia," said Avice. "An aunt of mine used to take it."

I had to sit through the grim buffoonery. It was all I could do to prevent myself crying out, as I watched Avice walk with long, flowing steps in order to fetch some magnesia for a complaint invented by Finbow. While, in fact, I was being eaten up by dread at the fate in store for Avice herself.

However, my unwilling clowning went on. In a melancholy way I swallowed a little of the powder; and the rest of the party accepted me as a silent spectator at a feast of thanksgiving.

Tonia was inquisitive about Finbow's jest.

"Just now you said 'old men like you and Ian,' Finbow," she protested. "You're nothing like so old as Ian, of course."

"In every respect except calendar years, I'm immensely older," said Finbow. "Actually I was born in eighteen-seventy-nine—a year in other respects, quite undistinguished."

"Why, you're only fifty-two," Philip exclaimed.

"A correct deduction," Finbow answered.

"Young enough for me to marry," said Tonia, lifting her eyes sideways from her cup.

"*Two* young for that job, I should have thought," Finbow replied.

"Beast," said Tonia.

"Isn't it absurd," Philip said, looking round the table, "to remember what we've all been thinking of each other these last three days? I won't tell you who I thought killed Roger —but it *was* awful."

"I'm not a sentimental man, God knows," William answered, "but I'm glad it's over."

"Roger's dead, poor devil," said Christopher. "Let's forget it now. And talk about our next holiday together."

"We might come and visit you and Avice in Penang," Philip said lightly.

"That would be splendid," Christopher agreed, but his face looked slightly worried. "We shan't be married until I've been out there a year or two, though."

"Seems a pity," Tonia burst out. "Why not make it a joint wedding with us next week?"

Avice passed the matter off.

"Oh, there's plenty of time," she said.

Plenty of time, I thought! She must have nerves of steel.

"Let's go to Hyères at Christmas," Tonia suggested.

"I might be able to," said William, "but I'm not one of your parasites. Still, I'll try."

"I think I can manage it," Avice added.

I bit my lips to check an exclamation.

"You can count me out, I'm afraid," Christopher said. "I shall be growing countless tons of rubber."

"What about you, Ian?" Tonia demanded.

"I don't know, my dear," I said miserably.

"You'll feel better to-morrow," she replied.

"Can you come, Finbow?" Philip asked. "We're really quite pleasant people in normal circumstances. You'll like us better when you've seen more of us."

"I wonder if you'll like *me* better when you've seen more of me," said Finbow. I think that I alone knew what he meant.

Tea went on, with chatter and banter and a great deal of eating and drinking. Finbow made himself two pots of tea in his own way, saying "the best tea in the world" to the first cup from each. Philip and Tonia played a riotous game on the lines of 'Beaver', with the modification that anything artificial in facial adornment was greeted with cries of "Pseudo". Christopher and William smoked contentedly. Of us all, only I was unable to enter into the calm of that evening. At times, though, I fancied that Avice was show-ing traces of anxiety.

At last it was six o'clock, and reluctantly they decided that we must get back to the bungalow. I say 'they', for I so loathed the prospect of the night that I would have been willing to stay there in the garden, for ever. Finbow said quietly:

"I'm rather expecting a parcel, so may I drive the motor-boat back? Ian and Philip and Tonia might come with me."

"We're going to walk," Tonia answered, with her arm through Philip's. "We're fond of you all, but we sometimes like ten minutes by ourselves."

"May I come with you, Mr. Finbow, please?" said Avice quickly, in a strained voice. Her eyes were wide with a sudden fear. Finbow glanced at her attentively, and said:

"Of course, if you want to. William can bring Christopher in the dinghy."

During the three minutes from Potter to the bungalow neither Avice nor I spoke. Finbow remarked that he had not expected to sink to the depths of driving a motor-boat, and Avice smiled bravely. I was too despairing to notice anything but her pale face.

She left us when we drew up at the bank outside the bungalow, and ran up the garden and through the french window. Finbow and I followed at a walk. On the table in the sitting-room there was a parcel addressed to Finbow.

"Good," he said. "This is from Allen. Take it into our room, Ian, will you?"

I put the parcel on his dressing-table, and looked unseeing out of the window. There was nothing to see, now. There would soon be nothing to see again. Avice's face would be a shadow in an old man's memory.

Finbow entered with another parcel, wrapped in brown paper and unaddressed, and laid it beside the one which I had brought in. He straightened himself, and spoke quietly:

"Now we must see what Avice is doing."

"Can't you let it go?" I begged him. "Leave it, for God's sake. Finbow, you can't have that girl——"

"I promised before that I'd do my best," he said curtly.

He went out of the door into the sitting-room, and I was drawn after him by a force which seemed beyond my will. Finbow stood still for a second, murmured "Unless I'm right," rushed across to Avice's door and threw it open.

There was an acrid smell of smoke. On the floor was a mass of charred and blackened paper, the edges of which still flickered with a smoky flame. Avice was watching it burn with her eyes dilated, and a hard smile contorted her mouth. I could never have believed that her face could change from its gentle melancholy to this expression of fierce and scornful victory. My doubts and my last hope vanished: it was the end, I thought.

She smiled at Finbow mockingly:

"Curious manners you have, Mr. Finbow," she said.

Finbow pointed to the floor:

"Something about Roger, I suppose?" he asked evenly.

"Clever of you," she answered. "How *did* you guess? It was my diary, as a matter of fact."

"Dangerous habit, keeping a diary," he said.

Good though her control was, the absolute calm of Finbow's reply shook her. Her voice was shaky as she said:

"Well, you can think what you like."

"That," said Finbow urbanely, "is exactly what I propose to do."

"Oh," she whispered.

"You may be interested to hear that you were doing exactly what I imagined you would do. It fits in with a scheme of mine. It was, in fact, the last missing piece."

"Nice for you," she said, but her eyes looked hunted.

She stood slim and straight in front of him.

"What are you going to do?" she asked.

"You will soon see," he answered softly. "Perhaps you will wait in the sitting-room with Ian and myself until the rest come back."

Avice threw herself on the sofa, lit a cigarette, and lay with a frightened stillness. Finbow stood with an elbow on the piano, completely silent for a moment. I sat wretchedly in an arm-chair. Suddenly Finbow said "So!" quietly, and said to Avice:

"I'm not as clever as I like to think. You and I must go for a walk, Avice."

Avice looked up at him.

"If you say we must, I suppose we must; but I warn you that I don't want to," she replied coldly.

"That is irrelevant, I'm afraid," said Finbow.

He went quickly into our room, and came out with the un-addressed parcel. Asking me to tell the others that he and Avice would not be long away, he led her into the hall and out of the door, which opened on to the footpath over the fields.

Desolately, I stayed in the darkening room. My thoughts whirled a maddening course. Pictures floated before my eyes—Avice crying in my arms, begging me to help her avert suspicion; Avice disconsolate on the deck, saying how she liked Finbow; Avice gazing out over the marshes, with Tonia's hysterical cry "Are you too proud to talk to us?" thrown at her: Finbow in the train, describing how, in the flare of the match, she had looked as though 'she had squashed a beetle'; and now this last scene of Avice burning papers with a twisted smile distorting her charming face.

William and Christopher came in from the garden.

"Sorry we've been so long," said William. "I had to tack most of the way."

"All alone, Ian?" Christopher asked. "Where are Finbow and Avice?"

"Gone for a stroll," I answered. I found time to pity him; poor devil, what a shock it was to be!

"Curious," he said. "It's beginning to rain a bit. I suppose they'll be back soon."

"I suppose so," I replied.

Philip and Tonia entered a minute or two later, and began to talk of the arrangement for their marriage. Tonia was exuberant:

"William," she said provocatively, "you must get married soon."

"Too busy," grunted William. "And also far too careful."

"Nonsense," said Tonia. "The first woman who really wants to will marry you before you have time to get out of the way."

She put a fox-trot on the gramophone, and danced ecstatically with Philip, her body yielding to his. With a strange impersonal compassion, I saw Christopher's brown face furrowed and anxious, as he brooded over a love so much smoother than his own.

William sat down beside me, and started to talk:

"You're very much disturbed, Ian," he said.

"I'm not feeling very fit," I admitted.

"It's probably the effect of all this strain," he suggested. "One usually doesn't feel it till it's over: and then it hits one like a cudgel."

I tried to be polite; but every word that was said to me seemed sillier that the one before it. Meanwhile, Finbow had still to bring Avice in to us, and had still to tell the others the story. The rain tapped against the windows. The fox-trot wailed on. I could feel my heart beat.

At last I saw two figures coming up the garden in the rain. Apparently Finbow and Avice had gone over the fields and come back by the river-bank. William opened the french windows, and they came in, damp and breathless. Avice's hair was dank, and her stockings showed dark, wet splashes. Finbow said, smiling:

"One really oughtn't to go for walks without some sort of protection from the weather."

"Why did you?" Christopher asked.

Avice replied:

"Oh, Mr. Finbow seemed to want to. I thought I might as well humour him."

Tonia burst out:

"Yes, Finbow has to be allowed to amuse himself."

Finbow remarked:

"Fortunately my amusements are mainly harmless."

The banter made me grow cold.

The night had become so dark with rain that the far end of the room was indistinct. Tonia cried:

"Good Lord, we can't live in a gloomy room now that everything's right with the world."

"Of course we can't," said Philip.

"Let's have lights," Tonia demanded.

Mrs. Tufts was called, and Christopher asked for the lamps. She said gruffly that they were out of order, but that she would bring candles. Soon ten candles gave a shadowy yellow light that merged into the grey of the rainy evening. To me, there was a grim resemblance to the watch night round a corpse.

"That's better," said Tonia. "At least it's lighter and more picturseque."

"It's not too cheerful," William remarked.

"Oh, it's good enough," said Philip. "What do we care, now that it's all finished?"

"Yes," Christopher agreed, "nothing matters much now."

"That's right," Tonia drawled, throwing a leg across the

end of the sofa. "It's heavenly to think that it's all finished."

"It *is* all finished," said Finbow smoothly, "or very nearly. I've just received a sort of last word in the shape of the book where Roger entered all the details of his cases."

These words seemed harmless enough to me, but I saw Avice's face go deathly white. I realised that this was in some way the end. Tonia, who had noticed no unusual effect, said:

"Was it interesting?"

"Very," Finbow answered.

William started to tell a tale of a case-book of a friend of his who had just begun to specialise in nervous diseases. Christopher rose and went to his room. William's tale went on, but I looked at Avice, and scarcely listened to a word. Christopher came back into the sitting-room, with a puzzled frown on his lean face.

"Hallo, Christopher," said Finbow casually, "looking for a parcel? I took it by mistake when I went for a walk, and I left it in the dinghy."

"Oh, good," Christopher answered. "I want it for a minute. I think I'll go and fetch it. Whilst I'm out, I'll get some tobacco from the village."

"Yes," said Finbow, and Christopher opened the french window and disappeared into the garden.

The words entered my ears, but I could bring attention to nothing but a pale set face. Fiercely I wished that Finbow would speak. William finished his story, and Tonia began an account of her own adventures with a nerve specialist.

I saw that Finbow was sitting tautly in his chair, as though waiting for some sight or sound. Dully I wondered what he could be expecting.

Suddenly there came a quick snap, like the light crack of a whip. Where it came from, I had no sort of idea, nor did I think it important.

"So," said Finbow, very quietly.

CHAPTER NINETEEN

Finbow Takes a Long Time
to Explain

Finbow went quickly out of the room, and we heard him call for Mrs. Tufts. I listened to his low voice speaking rapid and indistinguishable words, and a submissive: "Yes, sir. Yes, sir" from Mrs. Tufts, which surprised me by its humility. He came back into the room with her: she looked round rapidly, and bustled out. Finbow lay back in his chair and turned to me:

"I'm sorry, Ian, for the time you've had to-day. But it couldn't be helped," he said sympathetically.

"But what——" I was surprised and lost.

"I had to let you think that I suspected Avice," he answered.

Dimly I saw her lean forward, and all round me there seemed the bright excited eyes of the party.

"Well?" said Tonia quickly.

"The answer is simple," Finbow replied. "Christopher killed Roger."

I could hardly speak coherently.

"But—the other night——" I mumbled. "You said he hadn't done it—and there was no reason—why didn't you tell me?"

Philip said: "Christopher! Roger killed himself!"

Tonia and William gave shouts of surprise.

Avice sat very still. In a few sentences Finbow explained

that suicide was impossible. Crisply, he gave them the gist of the argument which I had heard at Horning. Then he looked at me and explained:

"When I told you the other night that Christopher was cleared," Finbow went on, lighting a cigarette, "I believed that to be absolutely true. It was not until the *next* night that I had to consider him again. Up to then I told you every thought I had, Ian: and up to then you observed every fact which I used. That is, the entire medley of facts and thoughts from which I worked the whole thing out—you had in your hands. Since then I've not told you everything that I've been thinking; and you'll see why when I've explained the nature of the murder."

"I've been a fool, I suppose," I murmured. I began to have the first warm pleasure of reassurance. Avice was safe, and nothing could harm her now!

"You have, rather," Finbow agreed. "But I think you could have been excused for not following the whole case. The first real pointer I had you'll probably not guess——"

"What was it?" William asked impatiently.

"Aloysius Birrell," Finbow replied, with a smile.

"Something he said?" Tonia inquired in a husky voice.

"No, something he did. Yesterday afternoon, before you and Philip had absconded"—Finbow laughed at her—"I watched Birrell drive up to the house, when he came to ask some questions. And I could see—and I said so to Ian—that he was an extraordinarily good driver."

"What has that got to do with it?" said Philip. We were all seething with excitement.

Finbow continued casually, as though he were addressing a literary party:

"The trouble is, of course, that we're all far too crude in judging people. We like to give them a label; and when we've given them a label we expect them always to act up to it. In writing, that process is known as keeping up the tradition of the English novel. In practice, it means that we all thought of Birrell as a complete clown, whose only possible purpose in the world was to introduce a certain amount of horse-play. You remember that Christopher, William and Ian were all plunged into the water when Birrell overtook them on his way to the yacht on the first morning. Well, turning the dinghy over as he went by in his motor-boat seemed just like our idea of Birrell. We all thought—after we'd known him for five minutes—that it was magnificently in character."

I confessed to myself that I had thought of the incident in precisely those terms.

"Well, it wasn't," Finbow went on. "Birrell's a clown in lots of ways. He gets utterly unbalanced when he sees Tonia in peculiarly transparent pyjamas; and he's got no conception of carrying two points of view in his head. But he's very quick, both in his thinking and in his reactions. If he were intelligently directed, he'd be useful at his job. Actually, he's just the man to be good at one of those simple quick-reaction things, like driving. If you could only get into the habit of thinking of a man as something a bit more subtle than a character in a nineteenth-century English novel, you'd see that Birrell was far less likely to help to turn a boat over clumsily than—say, Ian or myself."

"We'll grant that," said William.

"On the other hand," Finbow said, "Christopher's a good oarsman. The chance that either of them did it accidentally is very small. As I watched Birrell drive, it struck me as very much more likely that the accident was an accident done on purpose—by Christopher."

"But why?" said William quickly. "The man isn't mad."

"That brought me," Finbow went on, "to five questions which I wrote down on the day of the murder. They appeared to me then the main features of the affair. Here they are:" and he produced the slip of paper on which he had written that first morning as we sat in the garden.

"Number Five* I had already answered," he said. "I'll tell you about that one day, William; I can just say now that if I'd been you, I should not have had any particular use for Roger. Number Four,† on the whole, didn't seem very difficult. Philip, I knew, couldn't have done it; and it was almost certain, I thought, that Tonia's behaviour was dictated by some amorous complication." He looked up, and smiled at them. "You mustn't mind me talking about you all as though you were specimens laid on the table." He continued: "There was a possibility that the amorous complication wasn't enough to account for all of Tonia's worry, but I satisfied myself about that, when Ian and I overheard some of your conversation with Philip on Hickling Broad."

Tonia's eyes glowed fiercely.

"You heard that," she said. "What did you hear?"

"I heard enough to be reasonably certain that you'd prefer Roger to remain alive," he answered. "If you want my complete description of your attitude to Roger, I'll tell you some time—privately."

William looked baffled.

"But you didn't know Roger," he said to Tonia. She ignored him, and threw a question at Finbow:

"How much do you know?" she asked excitedly.

"Quite a lot," he smiled at her. "Enough to make me keep quiet—and to like you all the more."

I had by now attained a reasonableness which had deserted me whilst I had thought that Avice was in danger. Some of my interest in the others was creeping back: I noticed how

* What emotion is William concealing?
† Why did Philip and Tonia seek each other's company so demonstratively after the murder?

Tonia's concern for herself and Philip completely swamped any feelings that she might have about the murder. For her, her love-affair was vastly more important than Roger's death: for Philip, who had been following her questions with distress in his eyes, any new light on Tonia was more important than Christopher's guilt. So it is with us all, of course—and so it ought to be.

"By twelve o'clock that night I had got Questions Four and Five answered satisfactorily," Finbow resumed. "They didn't help the solution of the murder, except in a negative way—and except that their answers gave me a fairly complete picture of Roger. But while Ian was sailing me home, I began to understand how Question Three could be answered, now that I'd had my idea about Christopher's intentional accident. Question Three* had worried me a good deal. For some time I tried to explain it on some emotional grounds or other, such as that Avice was really fond of Roger and kept Christopher at arm's length after the murder. But I soon knew that *that* wasn't true."

"As a matter of fact," Avice said in a low voice, "Christopher didn't come near me after the murder, until he'd come back from Horning."

"So!" Finbow replied in a gratified tone. "That's what I thought. I fancied for a time that Avice might be a young woman one didn't talk to in times of stress; but I saw that wasn't true. Roughly, in moments of trouble, the normal young man who was fond of Tonia or Avice, would run at once to either of them. But he'd act differently when he got there. With Tonia, he'd try to forget the trouble in making love: with Avice, he'd go and talk, and try to console her in a soulful sort of way."

Avice blushed. Tonia laughed. Finbow went on:

* Why did Avice and Christopher not seek each other's company after the murder?

"Avice is simply not an exuberant young woman. But the point is that the young man *would* go: and Christopher didn't go. I had to try some other way out, and the overturned boat gave it to me. It was simply a complicated device in order to give an excuse for performing his toilet."

We were all quiet. William lit a cigarette, and the noise of the match on its box sounded like a shriek.

"Before, I had considered it impossible for a man to murder someone and make a pretence at washing and so on, inside three minutes. It is, of course, much simpler if he merely *didn't* wash. All the time you were talking over the position in the cabin, Christopher had not had a serious wash since the day before."

"No one notices that sort of thing, though, on a yacht," William objected. "We were all near him after the murder, and none of us saw anything unusual."

"That is perfectly true," Finbow agreed. "I was puzzled by it myself. Then I remembered one or two incidents which Ian had described to me. First, when you were all sitting in the cabin, Christopher apparently threw a box of matches at Tonia, instead of lighting her cigarette for her. I wondered; he is usually a pleasant-mannered young man, and in any case he had only to reach a distance of a few feet. It might be a casual chance—but I began to wonder if he had a reason for not wanting Tonia to see his hand.

"And then there was the quarrel between William and Christopher over rowing to Horning. Why was Christopher so unwilling to row? And why, if he were unwilling to row *to* Horning, why should he be so keen on rowing back?

"Now it is quite certain that the murderer had to arrange the tiller between the dead man's arm and his body. The order of events was probably—first, murder; second, tie up automatic, pennant and log-book, drop them overboard making a scratch on the gunwale; third, set the tiller so that the wherry would keep as straight a course as possible. By that time there would be blood on Roger's chest. . . .

"*If* Christopher had got a small smear of blood on his hand during these operations—and *noticed it in the first minute after he had got back to the cabin*—then all these queer disjointed actions were explained. He wouldn't want to let Tonia see his hand at close quarters; he wouldn't want to touch an oar, for fear that the warmth and motion of his hand would leave a trace of the blood on the oar; when he'd been forced to row, he would want to be certain that no one else saw the oar until it had been washed. So on the way back from Horning, it was essential that he should wash the oar— and, more important still, his own hand. He wouldn't let William row, for two reasons: no one else must see the oar, and also it was easier to get his wash if he were rowing. For he intended at the first reasonable opportunity to turn the boat over. When Birrell came by, he did so.

"When I had this idea, I was satisfied that a man like Christopher—as clever and painstaking as anyone I've ever seen—would think and act as I imagined. That was my first step. It amounted to saying that *if* Christopher did the murder, his actions after it were very easily explained.

"It was more difficult to see *why* he should kill Roger. After I'd talked to Avice, I'd ruled him out just because he of all people seemed to have no motive. But I had mentioned to Ian the most significant fact of all—that Roger had more motive for killing various members of the party than they had for killing him. Roger, for instance, must have wanted Christopher out of the way, since Christopher was going to marry Avice. From what I knew of Roger, I felt pretty sure that, if he could, he'd damage Christopher as much as lay in his power. If *that* were true, then it would be quite a possible explanation that Christopher was acting in self-preservation. So I began to think *how* that could be true.

"Then I remembered that earlier in the day Christopher had been extraordinarily cheerful about a medical exam. I decided that only a stupid man would see a connection. He was bound to have a medical exam, he was bound to be examined by the company doctor, he was bound to pass. He was passed as an 'A 1' life. I was, though, rather interested in the cheerfulness. He said that he'd *never* had a medical exam. Is an intelligent man absolutely cheerful and confident before his first medical exam? I'd never known of one who didn't have qualms. I began to wonder if he'd been examined before and, if so, why he concealed it? If he had been examined recently he would naturally be confident of another one. That was all right. But why conceal it?

"Now I *did* see a connection with Roger. If there was something being concealed, might not Roger have known it too? If it were a piece of Christopher's medical history . . . then it was quite certain that Roger would use it to hurt Christopher if there were an opportunity. And I saw that this Malaya job might have been an opportunity."

Avice gave a stifled gasp, and looked at Finbow with wide, dark eyes. Finbow continued:

"I was able to make an assumption. *If,* at some time in the past, when Roger and Christopher were friendly and Christopher was not yet attached to Avice, Christopher had gone to Roger about some disease—it would have to be pretty serious to account for the facts—then the whole business would be explained. Christopher gets well in such a way that only the original doctor can guess the truth—I thought of something like diabetes, where a medical examination will show a perfectly normal man so long as he's got it under control. And only his doctor knows about it.

"Now any disease like that, even if cured, would disqualify one for a job like this Malaya one. Probably wrongly, but it would. People would point out that he mightn't be able to keep it under, or the disease might recur, or something like that. Can't you imagine Roger telling himself that it was his duty to inform the Malayan Board that Christopher was unfit to take the job? Can't you imagine him believing that it *was* his duty? Being cheerful and fat and red-faced about it. Gloating over his own moral righteousness."

Avice bit her lip until it was white. She said:

"You're a clever man, Mr. Finbow."

He answered:

"All I've done is to get a definite picture of the people. Well, that assumption fitted very nearly all the facts. Question Two,* for instance, was more intelligible if Christopher were the murderer than anyone else. If he confessed, then he had a fear that he'd lose Avice; he was a clever man, and he knew that he would be lucky if he ever married her. He knew that she didn't need much excuse to break off the engagement. And I can imagine him thinking to himself, with that sort of bitter humour of his, that she'd think a murder was enough excuse.

"Question One† was still unexplained, but of course wasn't a question any longer when Birrell found the automatic next day. Before Ian brought the dinghy up to the house that night I told him that I was getting things straight; and I meant that, *if* Roger had some private medical information about Christopher, then most of the loose ends fitted."

"Why didn't you tell me?" I protested.

"Because I admired Christopher's ingenuity, and wanted you to go about looking miserably at Avice," he answered. "If he had suspected that anyone knew the truth, there would have been another mystery inconveniently soon. This morning I telephoned to Allen—he's a detective friend of mine— from the village, and asked him to look through Roger's

---

* Why did the murderer not take advantage of the conspiracy of silence?
† Why was there no attempt to lay the suspicion on any single person?

case-book and send it to me. He found Christopher's name in April, 1928, but he couldn't make anything of the data. The book came this afternoon. I haven't looked at it yet."

Avice said mournfully:

"I can tell you something about that. It was a queer blood disease. For a bit Roger thought it was going to be fatal. Then they found an extract which he had to eat and which kept the blood normal, so long as he went on eating it."

Finbow looked intently at her:

"I imagined that you know. That explains a good deal. I'm glad I didn't tell Ian what I was thinking," he added.

"Why?" I asked. "How does the kind of disease affect *your* actions?"

"A man who's been told that he's got an incurable disease is never quite the same again. At least for some time," said Finbow. "He tends to lose his respect for the value of human life—not unnaturally. Even if he recovers, as Christopher did, the mental effects linger on.

"It was just that sort of indifference which made Christopher such a capable murderer. And, if he'd seen any danger, I'm certain he wouldn't have stopped at one murder. Well, I got all essentials of Christopher's story clear last night. The news from Allen was a confirmation: it really wasn't very important, because I was certain that there was some fact of that kind. Then I had to think how Avice's behaviour could be explained."

"Mine?" said Avice.

"Yours, Avice. I had a letter from Allen this morning, in which he told me some episodes from Tonia's life which convinced me that I was right about her. He mentioned as well the terms of the will which Avice was to benefit by, and also the size of her income." He lit a cigarette, and said:

"This is the only feature of the affair in which I take any credit. I had to be very careful to be quite sure how much I knew and how much I was guessing. William and Philip and Tonia I could rule out, for various reasons; the discovery of the revolver put Tonia out of it finally, but I didn't need *that* to convince me. Christopher and Avice were still in. Was Avice a possibility?

"I'd just learned that she was living on two hundred and fifty pounds and probably wanted money. I wasn't impressed by that. A good many young women contrive to present a luxurious appearance on very little, mainly because other people buy them all the necessities of life."

Avice smiled wanly, and said:

"I've not paid for a meal of my own, except breakfast, for nearly a year."

Tonia said in an angry voice:

"God, how women like you dare to live, I don't know. Giving nothing and taking everything and looking like saints!"

Finbow continued:

"On the other hand, ninety thousand pounds is a lot of money. But if Avice did the murder, I couldn't fit it into her behaviour since the murder. If she'd killed Roger for his money, she might have acted the tearful girl in distress and she might have been genuinely frightened; but I couldn't see why there should be such a curious conflict of emotion. Real fright, real bitterness, real self-reproach, real triumph.

"I toyed with the idea that she might have killed Roger because of Christopher—knowing that Roger was going to ruin Christopher's career. I rejected that idea."

"Why?" asked Philip.

"Because Avice wasn't in love with Christopher. In fact, it wasn't long before I put Avice out of consideration as the murderer: but I decided that she had a very shrewd idea who did it."

Avice's frightened eyes met Finbow's cold blue ones.

"There was a peculiarity about the actual murder itself." said Finbow. "No one admitted that a shot was heard. That's all right in the cabin near the wireless: but even a little automatic makes a bit of noise, rather like that sound we heard just now." He stopped a moment, and went on:

"If Avice didn't do it, she was in her cabin next to the well where it was done. So, of course, she heard a shot. She came into the middle cabin soon after, and found Christopher had just come back. I suggest, Avice, that you *knew* from that time."

Avice's great eyes stared into his face.

"And you knew *why* it was done. I suspect that you had told Christopher of something which Roger had said: and from what you told him he gathered that Roger was going to use his medical information. But Roger had no idea that Christopher knew. Roger imagined that he would be able to do his duty—in secret. And that Christopher would never realise why the Malayan Board suddenly decided not to use his services. That's why Roger was so cheerful with Christopher: he felt quite safe and friendly. Roger was smiling when he died. He knew he could afford to be jovial with Christopher."

Avice sat still; there seemed no blood in her face.

"When I'd settled that, the rest of Avice's attitude is fairly easy. She was genuinely afraid, for a minute, that she might be suspected: so she asked Ian for help. When she'd done that, she was worried; because, in asking for help for herself, she might easily have been responsible for the discovery of what she suspected to be true. She was glad——"

Avice shrank.

"*Glad* that Roger was killed, but afraid that Christopher had done it. Chiefly, though, she felt guilty, first because she was suppressing the truth in not telling all she knew and, more important, because she might betray Christopher—

whom she really liked—as a result of a moment's cowardice. Which in fact she has. If Ian hadn't brought me down, this case would never have been proved to be anything but a mysterious suicide. Those are the reasons which made Avice give an extremely convincing impersonation of a murderess. Not consciously, of course. She wouldn't have done it so well if it had been conscious."

Avice's face was a blank white misery. She neither moved nor wept, but sat with her eyes dulled in pain.

Philip interrupted:

"I thought she'd killed Roger."

Tonia added:

"I might have done, if I thought she'd got the pluck——"

Finbow said slowly:

"Stop that, Tonia. You'd better pray that you're never in the same position. When I disentangled her actions, it all began to seem very easy—as I expect it does to you. Then I went and watched Aloysius Birrell dive. I was a bit surprised when I saw the sham suicide device, but I was delighted with it. Of course it explained Question One completely. As I told Ian, it is one of the most daring and beautiful plans I've ever heard of. A suicide disguised as a murder was subtle enough for anybody; but the further sublety of a murder disguised as the first combination was far too subtle for anyone to see through—unless one has an absolutely detached mind.

"When I told you about the suicide, I watched Avice, of course. She acted well: but she was still anxious. Then I decided if she were *still* anxious, it could only mean that there was some material existence damaging to Christopher. Of course, I had known that was something she wanted to get rid of all along. She wanted a fire on the first night; and the next night she was prowling about the house in the dark. This afternoon it was no longer a matter of assumption. It was a matter of fact. So I followed her into her room, and found her burning her diary."

"What did you mean when you stood in the sitting-room and said: 'Unless I'm right,' " I asked, "just before you burst into her room?"

He smiled gently.

"I might have been wrong," he said.

He continued:

"The diary explained her continuous feverish anxiety. She'd been dreading that soon the rooms would be searched, and Christopher would be incriminated. But in a party like this, in a cottage, there isn't much chance to dispose of diaries. What did it say, by the way, Avice?"

With her voice quavering, Avice said:

"There were lots of entries. One was about two years ago. It said: 'Christopher is a finished man. Poor devil, it seems a pity, but he can only hope to drag his life out a bit more. He wants to keep it dark, so we are not going to say anything.' Another was quite recent. 'Roger has just written me a typical letter; he says: "Of course you won't marry Christopher. It might be possible if he got the Malaya job, but his having had his disease will prevent that!" ' There were lots more."

"So!" said Finbow. "No wonder you wanted to burn them. Another curious thing: how did Christopher keep his illness secret? No one else seems to have known, except Roger—and you, because Roger was in love with you."

Avice was near to tears. She said, very low:

"Christopher has more self-control than anyone I've ever known. He decided that if he recovered it would be disastrous for the disease to be known, and if he didn't which seemed more likely, it wouldn't do any good for anyone to know. So he said nothing—and got himself burned brown by the sun. He explained it to me lately: 'All these fools think you're well if you're a deep coffee colour.' No one ever thought there could be anything wrong with him."

"That's absolutely characteristic of the man," Finbow answered. "Just in the same way he's behaved almost perfectly since the murder. With the right sort of not too-innocent attitude. He brought a little automatic back from London, and showed it to Birrell. Christopher told him that he might need it for Malaya. Birrell agreed. I don't mind betting that, if Birrell hadn't found the first automatic, Christopher would have been sure that the next time he dived, he'd find one with a weight of some sort on it—and he'd still have concluded that Roger's death was suicide."

"That would have been such a good joke that it ought to have happened," said William.

"The second automatic was in the brown paper parcel that I put in the dinghy," Finbow said casually.

"Well, you've made it very clear, Finbow," I remarked. "It seems an awful shame that Christopher should be hanged for a man like Roger."

"Roger was a cur," said Philip. "I can't imagine a bigger cur."

Avice was crying. As she wept, she murmured:

"I've never loved Christopher. But I should like to be able to."

Finbow said gravely:

"Christopher was an unlucky man."

William burst out quickly:

"What do you say 'was'?"

Tonia asked:

"What was that noise we heard before you told us this?"

Finbow's voice came slow and even:

"I hope that it was Christopher's shot"—we all waited tensely—"at himself."

William and Philip ran to the french window.

"Wait a minute," said Finbow. "I want to avoid any more trouble for you all. That's why I brought Mrs. Tufts in to see that you were all here. That's why I've talked to you all the time. She's fetched Birrell and you're all safe—if what I hope has happened."

"You told Christopher?" William asked.

"When I mentioned the case-book—I meant him to realise that I knew. And he did," said Finbow.

We went out into the garden. Birrell's motor-boat was opposite the bungalow. Someone pointed out the dinghy's mast some way along the bank. We rushed to it, through a cold wet wind that howled and rustled in the reeds. The dinghy's bow was fast in the mud; the sail flapped with a frenzied futility. Lying in the boat was Christopher, with rain streaming down his face. There was a small hole over his heart, and a stream of blood ran down his coat. No automatic was to be seen: as a last grim joke, he had killed himself as he killed Roger, with a weapon that was dragged down to the bed of the river whilst the boat was under sail.

His mouth was twisted and his eyes stern. The reeds waved desolately over his face, and above there was a grey and hopeless sky.